No.1 Suspect

No.1 Suspect

The Mulgray Twins

ROBERT HALE · LONDON

© Helen and Morna Mulgray 2012
First published in Great Britain 2012

ISBN 978-0-7198-0732-9

Robert Hale Limited
Clerkenwell House
Clerkenwell Green
London EC1R 0HT

www.halebooks.com

2 4 6 8 10 9 7 5 3 1

Typeset in 10/13.5pt Sabon
Printed in Great Britain by the MPG Books Group,
Bodmin and King's Lynn

FIFE COASTAL PATH

[Authors' Research]

Anchored at intervals to the cliff-face
a rusty chain offers hand-holds, robust
enough to tether the *Titanic*. Carved
in the dark age by some frail anchorite
wielding an adze, the rough hews steps climb up
from the bladder-wrack and shingle to the top
where maram grass and machair rim the path
and gulls cavort in the winnowing wind.

Two septuagenarians confront
the rimy chain, the hand-holds, wailing gulls
and wind, the gouged-out upward-leading steps.
Thrift beckons, encouraging their ascent.
In anoraks and bobble hats, stiff-kneed,
they designate the climb, required research.

Norman Bissett
from his collection of poems, *Painting The Bridge,* 2010

Acknowledgements

Our grateful thanks to all who have helped us in the research for this novel and in particular to:

Jack Brown, member of Musselburgh Links, The Old Golf Course, for showing us round the Old Course and pointing out the perfect spot for the solution of a plot difficulty.

Kenny Armstrong, Golf Starter at Musselburgh Links, The Old Golf Course, who was a fount of knowledge on the World Hickory Golf Championship and who patiently answered our questions about the course.

Jimmy Dingwall, whose fascinating guided tour of the Old Course at St Andrews enabled us to walk the course with DJ Smith.

Virginia Fowler of Historic Scotland, guide at St Andrews Cathedral, who allowed us to talk over our ideas for the plot.

Harry Cummings, retired Chief Superintendent, Lothian and Borders Police, for police procedure at different points of the plot.

Maurice and Jennifer Pettigrew, who introduced us to the preview evening of the Pittenweem Festival and its delights over the years.

And, of course, to our agent Bill Hanna, Acacia House Publishing Services Ltd, 82 Chestnut Avenue, Brantford, Ontario, for his hard work on our behalf, and to our editor Gill Jackson and all at Robert Hale Ltd, whose efforts have put us into print.

The poem kindly supplied by Norman Bissett is from *Painting the Bridge*, published by Indigo Dreams Publishing of Stoney Stanton, Leicestershire.

Books

If you are inspired to follow in the footsteps of DJ Smith, consult the admirable *Along the Fife Coastal Path* by Hamish Brown, published by Mercat Press.

But for those who may be tempted to follow DJ Smith's route along the Elie Chain Walk, we draw attention to this notice at the Earlsferry end:

WARNING

Hazardous coastal terrain. Beware of becoming trapped by the tide, being struck by falling stones or rock and falling from steep rock. If you decide to proceed, please do so with great care and wear suitable clothing and footwear.

And for those readers interested in the phenomenon of cats that paint (or find the idea totally incredible), we refer you to the amazing works of art in *Why Cats Paint – a theory of feline aesthetics* by Burton Silver and Heather Busch, published by Ten Speed Press, Toronto.

CHAPTER ONE

The pamphlet showed two cute orange-beaked puffins, a gold-lichened rock, and a cloudless blue sky. *With our high quality cameras you can be close enough to read the rings on the birds' legs! Seabirds nesting, gannets diving, seal pups snoozing.... You'll see them all at the Scottish Seabird Centre.*

It didn't say I'd see a murder.

My name is DJ Smith, Deborah Jane Smith if you're being more formal, undercover investigator for Her Majesty's Revenue & Customs, but even an undercover investigator gets time off between operations. After my last case, I'd stayed on in Edinburgh in my Portobello B&B, determined to enjoy the city and its surrounding area, and today I'd headed off down the coast to the small East Lothian town of North Berwick.

The Seabird Centre there is a pointed-roofed building jutting out from a small beach fringed along the high tide mark with clumps of black seaweed. No pamphlet-blue sky today, just white-caps on a grey sea, an ominously dark cloud threatening rain, and a cold wind blowing sand along pavements and gutters. In the air, the smell of salt and a faint whiff of fish. The volcanic plug of the Bass Rock rose dramatically out of a choppy sea, its vertical brown cliffs topped with a white icing of nesting seabirds. Farther out still, I could just make out the misty outline of the Isle of May, a long flat slab in sharp contrast to the muffin-shaped Bass Rock.

At this time of the morning only a handful of visitors were wandering round the interactive screens in the Seabird Centre's viewing room. *You are controlling pictures shown live around the world.* One camera was showing a clear view of the Bass Rock's sheer cliffs. At sea level, water foamed and swirled over the top of green-brown reefs. I operated the control stick to zoom in on the small stony beach. Perched

on seabird-splattered rocks, long-necked cormorants were hanging out their wings to dry in the strong breeze.

But it was the Isle of May camera that held a particular interest for me. As soon as the family clustered round the controls moved away, I hurried over. I'd very nearly lost my life there on a previous mission and this was the chance to see Pilgrims Haven free from fear and tension. One screen was showing a boulder-strewn grassy slope pockmarked with puffin burrows. I panned round ... a grey drystone wall ... grey-lichened rocks ... a clump of white campion, the fragile stems bending in the stiff breeze.

The other camera was focused on the bay. White breakers pounded on a grey finger of rock rising from the sea. I zoomed in, quite an expert now, able to pan, tilt and focus with the control stick. The fawn tide-mark round the bottom of the rock stack filled the screen. I zoomed out to view the entire stack ... the beach ... the background of white-spattered cliff, then slowly up ... up ... to the cliff top. A man was standing near the edge, making a panoramic sweep of the sea through binoculars. As I watched, he lowered them.

I zoomed in on him. Eyes shielded by heavy horn-rimmed glasses stared straight into mine, the razor nick on the side of his chin as clear as if he was standing only two feet away. Long strands of hair, brushed across to camouflage the balding patch on the top of his head, fluttered in the wind. His lips moved as he put the binoculars to his eyes again.

I zoomed the camera out a fraction. A tall, thin man was striding along the cliff edge towards him. The foreshortened camera angle gave the impression that he was approaching at a run, faster, faster, as in the speeded-up action of an old movie film. All at once I realized that he was indeed running, running as if his life depended on it.

Amusement turned to alarm. He was about to collide with the balding man with the binoculars who was still staring out to sea. The running man's shoulder smashed squarely into the other man's back, hurling him violently forward. I caught a glimpse of the victim's mouth, wide open in surprise. Now on the screen, only empty cliff top and grey sky. And the assailant, *smiling*, looking down over the edge as if to satisfy himself that all had gone according to plan. A sudden flurry of raindrops spattered the camera lens, distorting the image, but in the split second before he turned away and ran out of camera shot, I recognized him.

Hands shaking, I jiggled the control stick, trying to catch the man on camera again. I *must* be mistaken. I was allowing terrifying memories associated with Pilgrims Haven to cloud my judgement – seeing in the features of a stranger the face of the man who had so very nearly succeeded in killing me on that previous mission. My heart hammered in my chest. No, I wasn't mistaken. His was a face I'd never forget.

I pushed the control stick too forcibly to the right, sending cliff and sky whirling by in an indistinct grey blur, then took a deep breath, steadied my hand, and slowly ... very slowly ... inched the lens back till I caught him again on camera as he made his way along the cliff top, the attention-attracting run replaced by a brisk walk. Any lingering doubt about his identity vanished: few can disguise the way they move or the distinctive set of their shoulders. The man I'd just witnessed committing cold-blooded murder was undoubtedly the ruthless drug baron, Hiram J Spinks, a specialist in making murders look like accidents.

In my undercover work for HMRC I'm all too familiar with death. A dead body doesn't frighten me. I began to tilt the camera down, intending to zoom in on the murder victim, then stopped. On the far side of the room a member of staff was helping children manipulate the controls to focus in on the gannets crowding the ledges of the Bass Rock. It would be inexcusable for me to subject visitors, especially children, to the sight of a bloodied body on the giant screen. I left the camera pointing at the sky.

'Excuse me,' I called out. 'I need a bit of help. The camera controls aren't responding.' When the assistant came over, I said quietly, 'There's actually nothing wrong with the controls, but I've just seen a terrible accident on the Isle of May. A man has fallen to his death off the cliff and I didn't want to upset the other visitors, especially the children....'

Her reaction was a sharp intake of breath. 'Are you sure? You couldn't be mistaken?' A quick glance at my face, then, 'No, I can see you're upset.'

'Is there a way of showing you the ... er ... without others seeing the screen?'

With another glance at me she hurried over to a colleague, a tall young man with ginger hair and freckles. They held a whispered conversation.

Then the assistant clapped her hands to gain the party's attention. 'Can I ask everybody to go into the cinema to watch an amazing film of gannets diving into the sea at sixty miles an hour and swimming under-water in the hunt for fish.'

While we waited for the cinema doors to close, I gave the assistant an edited version of what I'd seen. 'He was standing near the edge of the cliff with his binoculars when suddenly he toppled forward. Nobody could possibly survive that fall.'

Hesitantly, she pulled the control stick towards her, slowly tilting the camera. Sheer grey rock slid slowly past ... down ... down to the scatter of rocks at the foot of the cliff. A dark shape lay just clear of the waves surging over the smooth rounded stones of Pilgrims Haven beach.

'That must be the man,' I said. 'But it's a bit difficult to make out with raindrops blurring the lens.'

She peered at the screen. 'The cams are fitted with wipers, but a gull must have ripped them off. We'll get a better view on the other cam positioned near beach level.'

Seconds later the stranger's body filled the screen, a grim addition to the flotsam of fishermen's floats and plastic bottles washed up on the beach. He was sprawled face-down. By his head, pink-stained water slapped the boulders at the foot of the cliff. The backwash of waves lifted and stirred the long hairs plastered across his head, cruelly exposing the bald spot so carefully concealed from view in life.

CHAPTER TWO

Since there was no proof at all that what I'd witnessed had been murder rather than an unfortunate accident, HMRC ordered me to silence, deeming that if I drew the media's attention to myself with unfounded allegations of murder, my undercover status would be blown to no purpose, wasting years of expensive training. Convinced as I was that I had seen Hiram J Spinks, this was hard to accept, but there was nothing I could do about it.

A couple of days later I was called into Edinburgh HMRC. I always look forward to a new assignment: it's a time of excitement and anticipation. But my heart sank when I pushed open the office door to see facing me across the desk the man who was to be my controller, A. Tyler, unaffectionately known to his subordinates as Attila the Hun. He hadn't been given that nickname without reason. Domineering and arrogant, he didn't suffer fools gladly – and anyone who disagreed with him was a fool. On my last assignment we'd crossed swords at a crucial stage. I'd emerged with flying colours; he with humiliating egg on his face. I could tell it still rankled. And always would. So now he'd be coldly professional in the way he directed me, but any mistakes or failures would be mine, not his. I'd be expected to obey his instructions to the letter, never be allowed to follow a hunch. Allowing agents to think for themselves was something utterly foreign to Attila. He swept aside opinions that clashed with his own.

Therefore I wasn't surprised when he dismissed out of hand my belief that the murderer on the Isle of May was the drug baron Hiram J Spinks.

'This *so-called* sighting of Spinks is merely a delusion, Smith. You've become obsessed with the man after your failure to bring about his arrest two years ago.' He looked pointedly at his watch. 'Now let's move on. Cannabis farming's a multi-million pound business in Scotland. Fifteen million pounds worth of the drug was seized last year alone. The man who fell from the cliff on the Isle of May was someone we've had our eye on in this connection for some considerable time. In cooperation with the Scottish Crime and Drug Enforcement Agency we've been building up quite a dossier on Drew Selkirk and his activities.' He lifted a heavy folder and thumped it back down on the desk. 'As well as setting up cannabis farms all over Fife, Selkirk controlled the cocaine and heroin shipments into the fishing ports of the East Neuk. Whoever has eliminated him in order to muscle in on his cannabis farming organiza-tion will also be involved in these other drugs. What we want to find out is this. Who is behind the killing? Your role will be to investigate Selkirk's on-the-surface legitimate business connections and find the answer.'

Before I could stop myself, I blurted out, 'But I *know* who killed him.'

Attila's lips pressed together in the thinnest of thin lines. 'You mean this Spinks character you *thought* you saw. I told you to forget it!' His hard eyes stared into mine, challenging me to protest.

I wasn't going to give him the satisfaction of seeing my anger. I nodded, seemingly compliant, but the order to forget about Hiram J Spinks was one that I was definitely going to ignore.

'What role have you set up for me?'

'That will be revealed in due course.' His hand rested protectively on the briefing file as if suspecting I might lean over the desk and snatch it. 'I've decided that you'll be working as part of a team. You can discuss tactics.'

What could he mean? I always work as a team, but it's with Gorgonzola, my drug-detecting 'sniffer' cat. And though I have the highest opinion of her talents, these certainly do not run to reading and discussing the printed word. The use of a cat to detect drugs may seem a strange concept, but a cat's nose is furnished with many more scent receptors than a dog's. I'd discovered this for myself when I was training sniffer dogs for HMRC. The kitten had been the first to home in on the piece of cheese I'd hidden as a test. Though she is a pedigree red Persian, her coat is scruffy and moth-eaten so that her undercover role as stray alley cat is perfect. Few notice either of us as we go quietly about HMRC business. And that's exactly how we like it.

Attila took my puzzled frown for insubordination. He was staring at me, fingers drumming impatiently on the desk. '*If* I could have the courtesy of your attention, Smith? Thank you. Either you accept that you'll be working as part of a team, in a supporting role, that is, or I give you another assignment, one perhaps you'll find more suited to your abilities.'

And he would just love to do that. Something boring, run-of-the-mill, the sort of case allocated to the rawest of raw recruits. I could envisage all too well the kind of assignment he would have in mind.

I hastened to kill stone-dead his notion that he could get rid of me. 'Whatever you say, Mr Tyler. I've worked with others nearly as often as I've worked alone. It's just that I thought the other team members would be here for the briefing.'

I could sense his disappointment at my failure to play into his hands. 'The other team *member*. You'll be working with Greg Findlay. I've a high opinion of his abilities.' Did I detect a stress on the 'his'? Yes, I definitely did.

He extracted a couple of pieces of paper from the folder. 'It's all here. As I said, we know that Selkirk was running a chain of cannabis factories. Findlay has located one factory. We want to know about the rest and for that reason we've not made a move yet. Selkirk's death, of course, adds a new dimension and urgency.' He pushed the papers across the desk. 'All you need to know is here. Take a few minutes to read it through.'

I scanned the two sheets of paper. Selkirk's business interests were many and varied: all were suspected of being fronts for money-laundering or drug running – they included holiday lets, boat hire, lobster fishing. Some months ago, HMRC had set up Greg Findlay, cover name Charlie Forrest, in a rented cottage in the village of Pittenweem. Posing as a street drug dealer, he'd managed to make contact with Selkirk's organization. No further details were given.

'So what exactly is my *supporting* role to be, Mr Tyler?'

He shot me a look that told me my hostile attitude hadn't gone unnoticed.

'You, Smith, will tackle the money-laundering side of Selkirk's activities.'

I brightened. Investigation of money-laundering was more than a mere supporting role. It seemed my dislike of Attila had caused me to be a trifle hasty in my reactions.

He continued, 'I've submitted, on your behalf, an application for a vacant post at Selkirk's latest venture, the King James Hunting Lodge. It's a sixteenth-century fortified tower house with Victorian extensions that has been converted into luxury five-star apartments for the ultra-rich willing to pay through the nose for privacy and seclusion.'

'And the post is?' I said, envisaging something in the office that would give me access to files and papers. 'I'm not sure I'll have the necessary qualifications.'

'Oh yes, I think you *will*, Smith.' He smiled the smile of a cardsharp producing an ace from up his sleeve. 'It's as cleaner. Charwoman. Mrs Mop,' he added helpfully so there would be no mistake. 'At considerable taxpayers' expense the current cleaner has been – how shall I put it – headhunted to a five-star establishment in Edinburgh. Her sudden departure has left the King James Hunting Lodge bereft of a cleaner, but we've arranged for an immediate replacement – you.' He handed me a large envelope. 'Here are all the necessary papers: national insurance number, references from previous employers etc. etc. This will give you access three times a week to all the wastepaper baskets, and with a little enterprise, the private papers of the residents. Covert investigation, of course.'

Curious to learn my new identity, I slipped the papers out of the envelope. From tomorrow it was goodbye Deborah Smith, hello Agatha Sweeney. I glanced up to see Attila's thin smile. He knew I'd hate the job – and the name.

'Find yourself accommodation somewhere nearby in the East Neuk. I suggest you call in at Selkirk's Holiday Properties agency in Anstruther and see what's available. Just remember that the Department has a budget. Any questions?' His tone made it clear that he didn't expect there to be any.

I wasn't going to let him see that I was upset. 'Fine,' I said. 'But there's just one thing. A 'sniffer' animal is one of the easiest ways to investigate a suspect property for drugs. You know I work with my cat, Gorgonzola. It'll be difficult to find a way to smuggle a cat into the Lodge.'

He stared at me. 'Cat? You won't need that moth-eaten creature of yours on *this* assignment.'

'But Gorgonzola is—'

'Old technology, Smith. In drug detection, the future lies with the superior scent-detecting powers of the giant African pouched rat, a rodent already employed successfully in Mozambique to detect antipersonnel mines. The pouched rat is capable of eight sniffs a second and can differentiate two separate smells in one sniff, so it is *much* more efficient, and eats less, so cost effective too in these credit-crunch days. I've brought the creature to HMRC's attention and they're quite interested. The sniffer rat will undoubtedly supersede the sniffer dog and, *of course*, your sniffer cat.'

It was my turn to stare. 'But ... but ... I don't think.... How will—'

An impatient silencing gesture. 'I've made it *quite* clear that there will be no need of a sniffer dog – or cat – on this assignment. Put your cat into HMRC's kennels tomorrow. Now if there's nothing else....'

There wasn't. I was stunned.

When I got back to my room at the B&B, Gorgonzola was stretched out on the windowsill in a patch of late evening sunshine. Her furry side rose and fell rhythmically in post-prandial snooze. I paced back and forth trying to come to terms with Attila's bombshell. I could have turned down the assignment, could still do so, but then I would be throwing away the only chance I'd probably ever have to track down Spinks.

I was determined Gorgonzola would be part of this operation: we were a team, experienced and successful. No way was I going to obey his order to put her into kennels. On the one occasion that I'd been forced to do so, she had pined, refused to eat, and caused such veterinary concern that she had to be sent to join me. The problem was how not to be found out. Attila would be sure to check with the kennels that I'd delivered a cat, might even demand to see the receipt.

After a moment's thought, I came up with the solution: all I had to do was turn up at the kennels with a cat. Not *any* cat, of course. It would have to be a Persian cat, and it would have to be a red female. I stopped pacing and slumped into a chair as I faced the fact that I hadn't the faintest idea where to find a Persian cat, let alone a red female. I had to accept the unacceptable. I'd just have to put G into the kennels and hope to get her out before she pined.

I leapt up from the chair as the answer came to me. I'd have to put her in, but I could take her *out* again the next day!

And that's exactly what I did.

CHAPTER THREE

When I arrived at the kennels to rescue Gorgonzola, she was only too relieved to see me. She jumped into the hated cat carrier as if she was being offered five-star accommodation. But now that we'd been on the road to Anstruther for an hour, she felt it safe to make clear her displeasure at being treacherously abandoned in the kennels. A low but persistent *yo-o-w-ow-owl* rose above the noise of the engine, a yowl pitched at a level that she knew would irritate.

I cast a quick glance in the driving mirror. 'Stop sulking, G. You're actually a very lucky cat. You spent only *one* night in the kennels.'

Yo-o-w-ow-owl. Louder, signifying that even one night was one night too many.

'I was only acting under orders, G,' I said plaintively. 'If it hadn't been for me, you'd still be in there.'

The yowl increased in volume, making her opinion clear: if it hadn't been for *me* she wouldn't have been behind bars in the first place.

It was my turn to feel aggrieved. '*Blow, blow, thou winter wind.*' I raised my voice in unsuccessful competition with yowls from the cat carrier. '*Thou art not so unkind as* CAT's *ingratitude.*'

Yo-o-w-ow-oooowl. A long drawn-out cry expressed her mental anguish at my betrayal. The fact that she had been rescued didn't compensate her adequately.

Overwhelmed by remorse, contrition, self-reproach, I pulled into the next lay-by and opened the cat carrier. Immediately the yowling stopped. Purring, Gorgonzola leapt out onto my knee, aim accomplished, goal achieved. Her rough tongue licked my hand, magnanimously forgiving. Five minutes of cuddling and stroking later, trust restored, she consented to re-enter the cat carrier and in harmony we continued the journey to Anstruther.

*

In the pale sunshine, the water in Anstruther harbour sparkled a dark greenish-blue, reflecting the clouds drifting across the sky towards the long, low silhouette of the Isle of May which lay six miles away across the Firth of Forth. Yachts and dinghies moored to pontoons bobbed lazily in a slow swell, but I was more interested in the cabined fishing boats linked in a cluster to the encircling wall of the quay by ropes decoratively draped with emerald seaweed. One of these boats could very well have a role in the shadowy underworld I'd come to investigate.

A row of shops and pastel-washed houses with traditional Scottish crow-stepped gables formed a backdrop to the harbour. I parked on the quay and opened the cat carrier door.

'Freedom to roam, G. Stretch your legs,' I said rashly. Taking me at my word, she tried to wriggle past me. '*Inside* the car.' I deposited her firmly on the back seat.

Leaving the car well-ventilated, I crossed the road to Selkirk's Holiday Properties. The window featured a large A4 photograph of a crow-stepped and turreted tower house overlooking a bay. An impossibly blue sea lapped on a white sand foreshore, in the background the smooth emerald-green turf of a private golf course. An accompanying placard exhorted: *Live as royalty in the Kingdom of Fife at the King James Hunting Lodge! Invest in a luxury apartment on a five-hundred-acre private estate – when you're not there, others pay to stay! A once in a lifetime opportunity!*

My reflection in the glass nodded and smiled back at me. I was on the right track, this was an ideal way to launder drug money. Of course, some owners and renters of the apartments would be genuine, but others would be merely names on paper. A shady individual like Selkirk would have seen the possibilities – and have acted on them. My intention had been to enquire about a cheap and cheerful studio-let for myself, as Attila had suggested, but that could wait. Now I had a much more interesting line of enquiry in mind.

I pushed open the door. A small plastic sign identified the elegant creature behind the desk as *Carla Windsor, Senior Sales Consultant.* There was no sign of a desk for anyone less senior. She looked up and hastily slid a magazine into a drawer. Business was obviously slow.

I mentally ran through my repertoire and selected a suitably aristocratic accent, one guaranteed to impress. 'I'm *so-o* intrigued by your window display, Carla,' I fluted. ' I just *had* to come in and enqui-ah.'

Beneath a long ash-blonde fringe and lashes heavy with mascara, her eyes brightened. 'Do take a seat, madam.' She plucked a glossy prospectus from a pile and slid it across the desk. 'The King James Hunting Lodge is a mere fifteen minutes from the historic city of St Andrews and its famous golf courses. It is an *exclusive* residential development, a pied-à-terre with a difference.'

To encourage her to elaborate, I raised my eyebrows in well-bred scepticism.

'Oh yes, madam. Mr Selkirk has tapped into a *niche* market for those whose lifestyles keep them on the move. Stay and enjoy, or earn fees in your absence! Madam understands the concept?'

I understood very well indeed. To conceal money laundering, Selkirk had hit on the idea of a constantly changing list of names of short-term renters, people who would move on and be impossible to trace.

'And as you can see,' a long fuchsia-pink fingernail flicked over a couple of pages, 'the apartments are *superb* in every way....'

It was my cue to be suitably impressed, but I disappointed her. 'Aah yes, just what is to be expected. But what I want to know is ... if I buy one of your lovely ap-aht-ments, just how much...?' I raised eyebrows conveying the distaste of the well-bred at having to allude to sordid monetary transactions.

Fuchsia-pink lips parted in a well-rehearsed smile. 'Each apartment sells for upwards of a million pounds.' Her eyes probed my face seeking for an adverse reaction, then reassured, she continued. 'What you are buying into, madam, is a guaranteed income. Yes, for the first two years, we can confidently *guarantee*' – the hushed tone heralded a breathtaking revelation – 'that you will receive, not five, but *ten* per cent of the purchase price back in rentals.' She held up ten fingers in pink-nailed emphasis.

'And that would be?' I said.

'So that *will* be ... a moment, madam....' Her fingers performed an anticipatory dance over the keys of a calculator. '... that will be ... a hundred thousand pounds.'

'I'm impressed,' I breathed. And I was. I'd been doing a quick calculation of my own. Millions of pounds of cannabis money could be laundered in this way. An operation on this scale was exactly what would interest Hiram J Spinks. I was now more certain than ever that he was indeed the man I'd seen on the screen at the Seabird Centre.

Sensing a sale, Carla fished in a drawer and whipped out a blank application-to-purchase form.

I made no move to reach for it. 'Impressed, yes ... but...' I frowned. 'I think there must be a snag.'

She leaned forward earnestly. Her eyes fastened me to my chair like a notice pinned to a corkboard. '*Not at all,* madam. After the first two years, you will still receive an income of fifty per cent of the apartment's achieved rental. Fifty-two weeks,' again the fuchsia nails danced over the calculator, 'minus those when you will be enjoying your apartment at no charge – let's say six weeks' annual stay.... That's forty-six times one thousand and that means....' The calculator finger-dance came up with the answer. 'The rental you receive will be forty-six thousand pounds! So what does madam think of that?' Shining eyes and a wide smile said it all: sale clinched.

As a scheme for an investor, madam didn't think much of it at all. The key words 'achieved rental' had been so under-stressed that they had almost disappeared. How many weeks would, in fact, be rented out? A more realistic assessment would be anything from nil to ten, and unlikely to be more than twenty-four. But as a cover for money-laundering, madam rated it highly, very highly indeed.

'*Most* interesting. I really *am* impressed.' There could be no mistaking my sincerity.

'This is a once in a lifetime opportunity.' She swivelled the form invitingly towards me. When I made no move to pick it up, she leaned forward. 'Confidentially, madam, very few apartments remain.'

'I'll have to think about it.' I made as if to rise to my feet.

Fearful that the fish nibbling at the bait was about to escape, she said quickly, 'So that you can purchase with complete confidence, we can offer you a six month rental before the whole amount is due. That way you can be sure you will be *entirely* satisfied with your chosen apartment, madam.'

To give me time to decide on my next move, I said slowly, 'That *could* be the deciding factor. I'll have to make a phone call. Excuse me a moment.'

I stepped outside and walked up and down in front of the shop, ostensibly speaking into my mobile, but in fact trying to convince myself that the idea that had just sprung into my mind was a complete non-starter. Surely it was crazy to think I could make an on-the-spot investigation of the King James Hunting Lodge by renting one of its luxury apartments? Gathering evidence could take weeks, even months. How could I conjure up a payment of a thousand pounds a week for an unknown number of weeks? It would be no use asking Attila for such a large amount of money. He would have to justify it to HMRC Accounts and he'd never put himself in the firing line for what was after all only a hunch, the hunch, moreover, of someone he disliked. What is more, to prevent Attila finding out that I'd defied his orders to turn up at the Lodge as cleaner Agatha Sweeney, I'd have to lie to my colleague Greg Findlay – something I wasn't at all happy about.

I couldn't deny that these were very good arguments for playing safe and following orders. And yet the temptation was great … if Gorgonzola and I were residents at the Lodge, I would be able to investigate my fellow residents and the Selkirk set-up there much faster and more thoroughly than by looking in the waste bins three times a week. It was the conviction that the King James Hunting Lodge was the major outlet for concealing the monetary profits from Selkirk's drug empire that decided me. Those private grounds, that secluded sandy bay, would be ideally suited for slipping drugs ashore. Yes, there'd be so much to lose by playing safe and not renting.

I walked up and down trying to work out a way to make my plan work…. What if I could persuade Carla to agree to a much shorter trial rental with an appropriately low deposit? The three months' funding I had at my disposal from HMRC for accommodation in a house or flat in Anstruther should be enough for three weeks at the King James Lodge. It was worth a try. Through the glass door I could see her sitting at her desk nibbling nervously at a strand of her long ash-blonde hair, anxiously following my every movement. Selkirk would have been careful to employ someone of limited intelligence, someone incapable of working out what was really going on. If business was as slow as it appeared to be, what I was about to suggest might just work. I would soon find out.

I breezed into the shop, mobile in hand. 'I've been having a word with my partner and I'm afraid….' I let the pause fester while I settled myself comfortably in the chair. 'Yes, I'm afraid that he is opposed to me going ahead with a purchase….'

Carla's face fell.

I sighed. 'I'm *so* disappointed. If only there had been a way of arranging a trial, for … say, three weeks.' Another sigh of regret. 'Oh well, that's that.'

I made as if to rise, but there's only so long that you can hover your bottom above your seat. Would my gamble come off? In the next few moments I'd know.

As I stood up, she came to a decision. 'A most unusual request, madam. But if we had a credit card and proof of identity, perhaps….'

Just what I'd been hoping. 'Of course,' I said. 'My passport's in the car. I'll just pop out and get it.'

HMRC's forward planning sees to it that an agent can switch identity if required. A fake passport, driving licence and credit card in the name of Vanessa Dewar-Smythe was concealed under the carpet in the boot. Back in Carla's domain I sank onto the chair, extracted the fake passport from my bag and handed it over. She flipped it open.

'And here's my credit card,' I said.

Half an hour later I emerged from Selkirk's Holiday Properties, in my hand the glossy prospectus of the King James Hunting Lodge. For the next three weeks Vanessa Dewar-Smythe, alias DJ Smith, was the prospective owner of flat 4 on the ground floor.

Triumphantly, I made my way back to the car. When I opened the door, Gorgonzola leapt gracefully down from the rear window ledge where she'd been keeping surveillance on the local gulls. She jumped down onto the pavement, a *miaow* and a wave of her tail indicating that the expected reward for her patience was freedom to investigate the fascinating smells of fish, creels and nets.

I slid behind the wheel and watched her slow progress along the quay in search of a discarded fish scrap. It wasn't hunger, but the *possibility* of a find that drove her, the keen anticipation of a bargain-hunter at a car boot sale or a seeker in a bookshop for that rare first edition. I left her to it and began flicking through the expensive King James Hunting Lodge prospectus. When I glanced up, it was to see G in drug-detecting crouch beside a neat stack of lobster creels. Locking the car, I walked along the quay towards her as quickly as I could without attracting attention. That low distinctive croon of hers signified a find.

I gathered her into my arms making a fuss of her, and took the opportunity to study the boat moored closest to the creels. In shabby contrast to the smart white superstructure of the other fishing boats, its wheelhouse was painted a drab dark-blue, the roughly daubed star-shaped patch on the weathered black hull testimony to a past collision with some harbour wall. The name on the bow was *Selkirk Harvester*. Andrew Selkirk's boat.

CHAPTER FOUR

The exhilaration of outwitting Carla had seeped away by the time I drew up in front of the King James Hunting Lodge. If this was indeed the centre of a money-laundering scheme, I'd be putting myself in constant danger of discovery by Selkirk's gang. And if Spinks had taken over from Selkirk, I could very well become the target of one of his little 'accidents'. There'd be no immediate back-up as I intended to keep Attila in the dark about my new role as a resident of the Lodge.

Of more pressing concern, I had only a few days' grace before it reached Attila's ears that the expected cleaner hadn't turned up. If I hadn't produced enough in the way of results by then, I'd be heading for a disciplinary hearing.

'Deliberate insubordination, Smith,' he'd snap. 'Running up a bill of one thousand pounds a *week* at the King James Hunting Lodge when I expressly ordered you to find cheap accommodation through Selkirk's agency.'

Too late for regrets now, burnt bridges and all that. I stared up at the crow-stepped gables of the sixteenth-century fortified tower house. Later centuries had seen the addition of wings further enhanced in the nineteenth by those little turrets so beloved of the Victorians. Were suspicious eyes at this very moment vetting me from the multi-paned windows? Any one of the residents could be in Selkirk's pay, staying here as the fleshly embodiment of non-existent owners, or perhaps running one of Selkirk's other illegal businesses. I'd have to be very careful, not take anybody on trust. I lifted G out of the car and snapped on her collar and lead.

'Come along, Smootchikins,' I cooed in the bell-like tones of an ultra-rich woman with more money than sense.

Stunned, Gorgonzola looked up at me. To her, collar and lead signified Duty and the expected command was a firm, 'Search.' While she was puzzling out my strange behaviour, I led her round to the boot and lugged out a designer suitcase, in reality a cheap imitation purchased after a swift detour to nearby St Andrews. Inside lurked my somewhat shabby holdall and a few of G's favourite food tins. The suitcase wasn't the only expense footed by HMRC. My car, a long-in-the-tooth Ford Focus from the Department's fleet, had been left in rented garage space, in its place a hired, sleek, black Mercedes more in keeping with my identity as upper-class Vanessa Dewar-Smythe. I trailed cat and suitcase across the forecourt, past a low-walled lily pond and up the front steps.

The Victorian reconstruction of a sixteenth-century entrance hall was certainly striking – flagstone floor, minstrels' gallery and crackling logs in a wide carved fireplace. The walls were hung with expensive tapestries on a Scottish theme: a golfer at the height of his swing; a fisherman in waders, knee-deep in a peaty Highland river hooking a salmon; a hunter in deerstalker sprawled on a heather-clad hillside with a stag in his gun sight.

'Good, aren't they? Specially commissioned from the Dovecot Studios in Edinburgh.' The voice came from a doorway on my right. Advancing towards me was a man wearing a red tartan waistcoat over a white shirt. 'You'll be Vanessa Dewar-Smythe? Carla phoned me to expect you.' Smiling, he held out his hand. 'Steve Collins, Lodge Manager. I'm here to ensure everything runs smoothly at the King James. Anything you need to know, just phone extension zero or call in at the office. There's someone on duty from eight till eight.'

I stored away that piece of information. If I wanted to leave the Lodge between these hours without being observed, it would have to be via the French doors of my own apartment.

His gaze transferred to Gorgonzola. 'Pets must be under control at all times.'

'Have no fear, Mr Collins. Smootchikins has lived all her life in five-star establishments.'

We both studied Gorgonzola. She'd pulled the lead taut and was sniffing curiously at a carved oak chest. With her scruffy coat and moth-eaten tail, anything looking less like a five-star cat would be hard to find.

'I'm afraid she's not looking her best just now,' I sighed. 'Alopecia from stress when I had to put the poor darling into kennels while I flew abroad on business. It's so *awfully* distressing to see her beautiful coat in such a terrible state.' A skilful blend of fact and fiction. G's coat was in its usual patchy condition and the only stress she'd suffered was that one night in HMRC kennels.

Collins gave a non-committal grunt. 'As I said,' he continued, 'I'm here to sort out any problems. Anything you need to ask, you just have to.... ' With a wave of his hand he indicated the door through which he'd come.

I smiled my thanks. 'Apartment 4 is...?'

'On the left past the restaurant and the bar-lounge.'

Aware of his eyes still on me, I steered suitcase and cat through the archway under the minstrel gallery. The doors of apartments 3 and 4 faced each other across the carpeted corridor.

'*Prepare to live as royalty in the Kingdom of Fife at the King James Hunting Lodge*,' I quoted, inserting my key in the lock of apartment 4.

I unclipped the lead and ushering G ahead, wheeled my case into the bedroom. No expense had been spared with the furnishings. Afternoon sunlight streamed through the windows onto a curtained and canopied four-poster bed, at its foot a day-bed in coordinating green and cream fabric. As we advanced into the room, paws, feet and wheels sank into the deep pile of the sand-coloured carpet. G took possession of the day-bed while I unpacked the suitcase and stowed my clothes in the imposing green and gold wardrobe. I did a quick calculation. Presumably there were another eleven apartments furnished like this, which showed just how much in drug profits Selkirk must have had at his disposal.

'You're going to help me find these drugs, aren't you, G?'

She wasn't listening, her thoughts elsewhere. She'd abandoned the day-bed to circle the open suitcase and investigate the carrier bag of tins. Neither of us had eaten since our breakfast, mine of muesli, G's of decidedly non-gourmet HMRC cat food. My pangs of hunger were joined by pangs of guilt – in G's opinion, non-gourmet food didn't count as food at all. In the state-of-the-art kitchen I spooned a generous helping of salmon into her bowl, and pausing only to change into a smart black ensemble, went off on a food reconnaissance of my own. It was three o'clock, too late for lunch, too early for dinner, but according to the information folder, the lounge supplied snacks and hot and cold drinks till midnight.

A few steps along the corridor took me back to the entrance hall. A brass plate identified the lounge. It was furnished with comfortable settees and armchairs in loose floral covers and elegant little tables with lamps. Oil paintings in ornate frames hung from the picture rail. A three-tiered crystal chandelier reflected in a huge gold-framed mantel mirror gave the impression I was stepping into the drawing-room of a nineteenth-century stately home.

On one of the settees near the fire a man with rimless glasses was reading *The Antique Dealer*. Judging by the strands of grey in his black curly hair and his neatly trimmed beard and moustache, he was in his forties. This was my chance to make contact on a one-to-one basis.

'Hello, I'm Vanessa Dewar-Smythe. I've just moved into apartment 4. How does one order a snack here?'

He looked up. 'Clive Baxter, apartment 3. Just press the button on the table. The barman'll appear like a genie from a bottle.' With a brief smile he went back to the perusal of his magazine.

I sat down on the settee opposite him and pressed the indicated button. The genie having duly appeared, I ordered from the menu. I left Baxter to make the first move, mustn't let him think I was being in the least inquisitive. If he had been planted there by Selkirk to legitimize the Lodge in the eyes of the tax authorities, any probing questions would set alarm bells ringing.

I took the Pittenweem Festival brochure out of my bag, holding it in such a way as to make it easy for him to see what I was looking at, and started scribbling down some notes.

I didn't have long to wait before he gave a little cough. 'Will this be your first visit to the Festival?'

'I've never been to it, but I'm hoping to exhibit there for the first time.' Keep it simple as far as possible, it's too easy to be tripped up by over-embroidering a lie. 'I'd arranged a venue for my exhibition but the owner of the garage has just died and that's why I'm here – in a desperate attempt to arrange a new venue to showcase my work. It will be difficult – more than eighty artists and craftspeople are taking part this August. I'm hoping one of the other exhibitors will have enough space to let me share a garage, a courtyard, or a room in a house.' The perfect excuse to wander the narrow streets of Pittenweem, knocking on doors and poking my nose in where it wasn't wanted.

He turned back to his magazine. 'Damned difficult to find anywhere at this late date.'

'Ah, Clive' – a sigh and an expressive shrug – 'that's what I think. There's a fearful amount of competition.'

He marked his place in the magazine with a finger. 'So what's *your* angle – pots, plates, unusual glazes?'

'Actually I dabble in clay sculpture. I'm quite good at it, others say.'

I make sure there's at least a grain of truth in my cover stories, though perhaps 'dabble' was a bit of an exaggeration. During a long wait to get operationally fit while recovering from an injury, I had indeed attended a pottery class, but had in reality attempted only one sculpture. One day, after weeks of working on my creation, I'd whipped off the plastic bag and damp cloth essential to keep the clay soft and pliant. Disaster! Excess moisture had caused prominent parts of my reclining woman to slump. Voluptuous bosom had drifted southwards, hips ballooned, head elongated into a smooth featureless oval. But when the instructor had jokingly called it a modern Work of Art, I'd looked at it with fresh eyes, seeing in the distorted shape a distinct touch of the Henry Moore, Barbara Hepworth, or indeed of Pablo Picasso.

I handed him a photograph of the sculpture. 'This is the sort of thing I do. How do you think something like this would sell at the Art Festival?'

He studied the photograph for a moment, then handed it back. 'I'm afraid you're asking the wrong person, Vanessa. My field of expertise is antiques. I come to Fife twice a year to wander round the farms and small villages sourcing items. I jumped at the chance of an apartment at the Lodge because the fishing villages of the East Neuk are an especially fruitful hunting ground.'

Was he spinning me a line? How could his finds be of such value that he could afford an apartment here? I raised a sceptical eyebrow, something I've found guarantees a response.

Smiling, he leaned back in his chair. 'Wemyss Ware, now, that can fetch quite a sum. The Queen and Prince Charles are collectors, you know. You'd be surprised what people here have in their attics, at the back of cupboards, or sitting unrecognized on their mantelpieces. I always give them a fair price and that way they're keen to do business with me again.'

The arrival of my mozzarella and bacon baguette brought our conversation to an end. I took a sip of lager. Was Clive Baxter's story as fabricated as mine? I reserved judgement on the man on the opposite settee.

Fortified by my snack, I went back to my apartment. I stood at the window looking out at a golf course and beach, just as depicted in the Selkirk Properties' display. My attention was attracted by a man on the sand occasionally stopping then moving on as if searching for something. Anything out of the ordinary is always worth investigating. Gorgonzola was curled up on the day-bed snoring gently. I gave her a gentle poke.

'We're going for a stroll. Cats without exercise get *fat*. You don't want to be a fat cat, do you?'

She made no move to rise. Ignoring her mew of protest, I lifted her up and carried her out through the French doors. Realizing that resistance was useless, she wriggled out of my arms and together we set off towards the shore. The path led across the landscaped golf course, its bushes and trees artfully placed, its bunkers irregular pale shapes in the bright green turf.

'Bunkers are out of bounds, G!' I called as she darted towards the ultimate in cat litter-trays.

She recognized the tone of command, and obeyed, but like a child denied a wished-for treat, trailed beside me in a sulk. I stood at the edge of the fairway looking down with a professional eye at the gently shelving beach and the sheltering arms of the bay, an ideal place to bring in a small boat with a cargo of drugs transferred from a larger vessel out at sea.

There was no sign now of the figure I'd seen from my window, only a couple of red-legged oystercatchers stabbing at the wet sand with their orange beaks, and half a dozen gulls shrieking and squabbling over something found on the sand. Sulks abandoned, Gorgonzola stiffened, targeting a prey. Before I could grab her, she leapt out of reach and slunk forward in a slow-motion stalk towards a gull preening its feathers in the gentle wash of the waves. As I rushed forward, G tensed, tail twitching, then sprang, forelegs outstretched to strike.

The gull, quicker than both of us, flew off with a throaty mocking *sqwaaaahahah*. Though there was no wind, the silvery leaves of a nearby clump of sea buckthorn shivered and shook as if they too were quivering with laughter. I froze as brown boots followed by cord trousers and a dark green anorak wriggled out from the prickly depths.

'Fantastic action shot, that!' A young man scrambled to his feet clutching a camera with a telephoto lens. 'Your cat, is it?'

Recovering from my surprise, I said, 'Yes, the cat's mine. I'm Vanessa. I've just moved into the Lodge, apartment 4, renting with a view to buying. Are you a resident too?'

He ran a hand through tousled fair hair. 'Yup. Terry Warburton's the name, Terence when I'm presenting my portfolio to a gallery. I didn't expect to get as good a shot when I came out this evening.' He flicked on the camera and showed me the screen. There was G, frozen in tigerish spring with claws extended, and the gull taking off, flight feathers spread like fans.

This was another chance to do a little digging into the background of the residents. 'What kind of photography do you specialize in?' I asked casually.

'Anything that sells. Photography's all about the *light*: fishing boat on moonlit sea, dawn sunrise over the bay, that sort of thing. There's real atmosphere at dusk and dawn and I can see it all from the windows of apartment 6 on the upper floor.' He waved an arm in the direction of the Lodge.

Sometime I'd ask to see those pictures. I handed back the camera. 'I don't suppose I could have a print of my cat and the bird?' He looked at me from under lowered brows. 'I'll pay, of course,' I added quickly.

After a moment he said, 'I wouldn't have captured an image like that without your cat. So, OK.' He looked over my shoulder and raised the camera. 'Perhaps the moggy will give me a repeat performance.'

I turned to follow his gaze. G, ever the optimist, was crouched on the sand, motionless, in the hope that a bird would mistake her for a harmless piece of flotsam and stray within pounce range.

'Well, she's certainly willing, ' I said, 'so if you can be bothered to wait around, by all means try. I'll just take a stroll along the beach....'

As I scuffed my feet through the powdery white sand, I analyzed my first impression of Terry Warburton – likeable, and on the surface, above board. He was what he said he was, an expert photographer, there was no doubt about that. He was unlikely, therefore, to be one of Selkirk's men put in place to lend authenticity to the set-up at the Lodge. None of the residents, however, could be ruled out at this stage, they would all *appear* to be above board.

The Lodge as a front for money-laundering was only an unsubstantiated hunch, so at the meeting Attila had set up between Greg

Findlay and myself for tonight I wouldn't feel guilty about keeping quiet about Lodge resident Vanessa Dewar-Smythe, stand-in for cleaner Agatha Sweeney. I picked up a flat pebble and sent it skimming over the calm water. One bounce ... two ... three ... then, like my little secret, it sank below the surface.

CHAPTER FIVE

Like many picturesque fishing villages in the East Neuk of Fife, Pittenweem is a tangle of red-pantiled houses, tiny courtyards and narrow alleyways or wynds. I'd come via St Andrews where I'd picked up the Ford Focus, the Mercedes being a trifle too distinctive for my undercover meeting with Greg Findlay. With the aid of a streetlight I studied the map provided by the tourist board. School Wynd was the most direct route to our rendezvous point near the Fish Market.

I descended a flight of worn steps to an ill-lit narrow lane sloping steeply down to the harbour between high walls overhung with trees. The High Street was still busy with cars and people, but here the *pad pad* of my trainers sounded unnaturally loud, and the distant shouts of children playing down at the harbour only served to emphasize just how alone I was. The height of the walls on either side shut off all views apart from pantiled roofs and an occasional glimpse of dark sea intermittently punctuated by a pinpoint beam stabbing out from the lighthouse on the Isle of May.

The wynd made a sharp turn to the left, blocking off sight of the way I'd come. Was that a stealthy footstep behind me? I held my breath, straining to hear....

Overactive imagination. It was only the leaves of the overhanging trees brushing against the wall.

I shrugged deeper into my jacket. I'd done nothing to rouse anyone's suspicions. Nevertheless, I cast a glance over my shoulder and quickened my pace, relieved when a couple of minutes later I stepped out from the wynd onto the well-lit harbour front. Though it was not as busy as the High Street, the number of people still wandering about at 10.30 at night was reassuring. A group of smokers puffed at cigarettes in the light spilling onto the pavement from the open doorway of a pub; a boisterous gang of youths headed noisily uphill towards the High Street; and a few pedestrians were making their way along the waterfront beside the harbour.

I consulted the map again. That two-storey stone building with a decorative line of seagulls slumbering along the roof ridge must be the Harbour Office. A couple of hundred yards off to the right was the part of the waterfront known as Mid Shore where Greg had said he would be sitting on one of the seats that faced the harbour and the open sea.

Only he wasn't. Nobody was sitting there, perhaps not surprising, given the cold wind blowing off the sea and the spatter of raindrops now stinging my face. Rather than draw attention to himself, he'd be standing in the doorway of one of the small shops, watching for me to arrive.

Keeping a lookout for Greg, I strolled casually past the inner harbour with its forest of antennae and tangle of masts sprouting from the fishing boats moored three abreast. Unlike the pleasure craft at Anstruther with their gleaming paintwork, these were working vessels – grimy, rust-streaked, their decks strewn with ropes, empty plastic fish boxes, nets and stained rubber matting.

To give him the chance to spot me and come forward, I stood beside one of the seats watching a ghostly ship loom out of the darkness and slip in through the harbour mouth, the faint hum of its engine barely audible.

I sat down, head bowed and for some time made a pretence of texting on my mobile. But the seat beside me remained empty. I looked at my watch. I'd worked with Greg before and never known him to be late for a rendezvous without a good reason. Perhaps he was at a crucial stage of surveillance, staking out a house he'd identified as being a cannabis factory. In that case, he'd have sent me a text on the lines of, 'Working late tonight. Party without me.' I'd give him another ten minutes....

I was cold, and now that there was more than a hint of rain in the wind, I'd draw attention to myself by sitting here. An undercover agent must merge into the background, pass unnoticed on the street. That's what I aim to do. It's what makes me successful at my job. Time to go.

A long cold wait for Greg followed by the walk in driving rain to the car hadn't put me in the best of moods, so it was the last straw when there was no sign of Gorgonzola in the apartment. I'd left her curled up on my bed sleeping off her meal, but a circular dent in the duvet was the only evidence that she'd ever been there. Unsettled by the new surroundings and the night in the kennels, she'd be hiding somewhere, probably under the bed.

After a few encouraging calls of, 'I'm back, G,' I lost patience. I hung up my sodden jacket in the bathroom, tugged closed the curtains in bedroom and lounge, stomped off to the kitchen to make myself a warming cup of coffee and open a packet of digestive biscuits, vowing that tomorrow I'd stock up the freezer with ready meals. I carried a tray into the lounge, sank into one of the comfortably padded armchairs and switched on the wide-screen plasma TV. I listened with half an ear to the Scottish news as I nibbled my way through the biscuits, my thoughts on the missed rendezvous. There could be many reasons why Greg had not turned up....

I stopped mid-nibble, full attention now on the television news. Selkirk's face filled the screen.

'The funeral of Andrew Selkirk, well-known Anstruther businessman, took place today in St Monans Parish Church, four days after a tragic accident on the Isle of May.' The camera shot showed a tiny stone church with a square tower topped by a pointed spire. 'Friends and business associates filled the small church, and the service was relayed to the mourners outside.' The camera zoomed in to focus on the line of men in dark clothing filing into the church behind the coffin, then panned slowly along the sombre faces of those standing outside. I leaned forward, studying each face. Friends or associates of the departed Selkirk were likely to be shady characters themselves. If I came across any of them again, I'd be on my guard.

Above the murmur of the television commentary I heard a *tp tp tp tp* coming from behind the curtain drawn over the French doors. Somebody was tapping on the glass. I sat very still, the hairs on the back of my neck prickling. *Tp tp. Tp tp tp tp.* I jumped up from the armchair and flung open the curtains. There was nobody there, only my reflection staring back at me through the rain-streaked glass. *Tp tp* Outside in the inky darkness, a darker shape low down near the ground gave a faint plaintive *mew*.

I turned the key and opened the door. Fur plastered to body, Gorgonzola darted in, pausing only to deposit a scrap of soggy brown wrapping paper at my feet before slumping down in front of the living-flame fire.

'Just look at the mess you've made of Mr Selkirk's expensive carpet, G!' I shrieked, staring at the muddy trail that dripping paws had trekked across the cream carpet. 'HMRC won't be *at all* pleased if they have to pay for professional carpet cleaning, especially as neither of us have permission to be here at all.' Muttering to myself, I scrubbed at the marks with a damp cloth and washing-up liquid.

Oblivious of my frantic efforts, she lay as one dead, her fur steaming gently in the heat of the fire. Usually, I would have fussed over her, sat her on my knee and dried her off with a towel. But I'm sorry to say I lost my temper. It was the snore that did it, the snore of a self-satisfied cat at peace with the world.

'And not content with dirtying the carpet, you've brought in litter, a *filthy* bit of paper. Goodness knows *where* it's been!' I snarled.

I scrambled to my feet, snatched up the offending item, strode to the kitchen and stamped down on the pedal of the bin. *Clang.* The lid banged back against the wall. I flung the paper in and let the lid slam shut. 'There!' I snapped. 'That's the place for it.'

As I'd hoped, these histrionics had the effect of rousing G from her slumbers. She rolled over and stood up, but instead of a gratifying show of remorse and due penitence, her response was what could only be described as airy insolence: a long-drawn-out ya-a-wn, a slow, slow stretch of her front legs, a sharp digging of claws into the pile of the expensive carpet. A final touch was an arch of the body and a protracted extension of first one back leg, then the other.

'Right, that's it!' I seethed. ' No supper for *you* tonight.' I threw myself back on the armchair, reached for the newspaper I'd bought in St Andrews and held it up in front of me, ostentatiously excluding her from my company.

Miaow. She brushed against my legs. *Miaow.*

Aha! She was sorry now. 'Shoo!' I pushed the newspaper forward to prevent her jumping up on my knees. That should get the message through. And it did. There was no rubbing up against my legs, no atten-tion-seeking pat of paw or even a gentle dig-in of the claws, no plaintive mews. No response at all. For a couple of minutes, nothing. What *was* she up to? I sneaked a furtive peep round the edge of the newspaper. She'd gone.

Clang. Clang. I flung aside the paper and ran through to the kitchen to find her standing on her hind legs sniffing at the lid of the metal bin.

'Oscar-winning performance of a starving cat reduced to raking for scraps in the rubbish bin,' I jeered. 'You won't find anything in there. Look, it's empty.' I lifted the lid. 'Except for *this*.' Wrinkling my nose to show disgust, I held up the soggy wrapping paper between finger and thumb.

G leapt in the air, forepaws outstretched like a rugby player leaping for the ball in a line-out. One moment the piece of litter was dangling from my fingers, the next it was snatched from my grasp. As if playing with a mouse, she crouched over it, then picked it up and deposited it at my feet. From her throat rose a triumphant croon. She was telling me that the wrapping paper I'd dismissed as litter bore traces of drugs.

Mortified, I scooped her up, burying my face in her damp fur. 'Clever girl, G. *Clever* girl,' I whispered.

G had done what she'd been trained to do. As a token of affection, she'd brought her find to me as a *present*, as cats do with mice, birds and frogs, expecting their owner to be delighted. And how had I reacted? I'd been angry and scolded her for muddying the carpet. I seized her towel from the cupboard, laid her on my lap and dried her with long strokes till rumbling purrs told me I'd been forgiven.

How had she managed to get out of the apartment to make the discovery? Cradling her swaddled in the towel, I toured the apartment, tweaking aside the curtains over lounge and bedroom windows as I came to them. As expected, all were firmly closed. I found the answer in the bathroom where swaying curtains revealed that the sash window was open at the bottom. G had jumped onto the small chair and from there to the windowsill, squeezed through and dropped to the lawn outside. On the return journey she'd obviously miscalculated the difficulty of balancing on the narrow ledge to position herself for the necessary limbo through the gap and had resorted to tapping on the French doors.

But where had she found that piece of wrapping paper? In one of the other ground floor apartments? As she wandered across the lawn? Or had it been lying on the golf course? Wrapping paper indicated a large packet of drugs. Somebody in this building was a dealer.

I returned to the armchair and my biscuits. That find of G's vindicated my decision to rent here at the Lodge. With her curled up on my lap, I stared into the leaping flames of the fire.

'If only cats could speak, you could tell me where you found that bit of paper, G,' I murmured.

CHAPTER SIX

I was uneasy. By 10 a.m. the next morning there'd been no word from Greg Findlay. The arrangement had been that a missed rendezvous would generate another one by text. I drove to St Andrews, left the Mercedes in the rented garage once more, and in the more inconspicuous Ford Focus headed back to Pittenweem. It's an HMRC rule that the address of another undercover agent is a no-go area except in an emergency, so I suppose I was stepping out of line once again. But the instinct that has never let me down told me that something was wrong. Follow that instinct, or comply with the rules? The choice wasn't difficult. I'm a bit of a rebel at the best of times with no qualms about sidestepping rules when occasion demands, but it's never on impulse, I always act after careful weighing up of the pros and cons.

I left my car near the High Street and made my way to a printer's shop I'd passed the previous night. In the window I'd seen a notice that would serve my purpose admirably by giving me an excuse to go house to house without arousing suspicion.

WANTED
Persons to deliver advertising material in the area
Payment per 1000 leaflets

I went in and emerged five minutes later with a satchel bulging with leaflets advertising a business offering attic conversion and joinery services. I walked from the harbour to the West Shore's picturesque row of fishermen's cottages colour-washed in attractive pastel shades and worked my way towards the house Greg had rented, ringing bells and knocking on doors, ready to enquire if the householder was interested in taking a leaflet. That way, if his house was under surveillance, I'd have the chance to speak to him without rousing suspicion. Few people came to their door, and those who did, looked at the leaflet briefly and retreated indoors with it. In one case, it was dropped at my feet and the door rudely slammed in my face.

It didn't take me long to arrive at Greg's house. Blood-red geraniums in plant pots made a bright splash of colour on either side of the door. To make it clear to any watching eyes that I was merely delivering leaflets, I held one up as I put my finger on the bell.

Brinng. I waited, listening for footsteps on the other side of the door. After a moment or two I rang again, this time loud enough and long enough to waken the dead. *BRINNG*. Still no movement from behind the door or a twitch of the net curtain at his window. Conscious that as a deliverer of leaflets, I'd stood here long enough, I stuffed the leaflet through the letterbox and walked leisurely on. There was nothing more I could do. I'd already bent the rules by calling at his house.

I visited the remaining houses in the row, trying to convince myself that I was over-reacting in feeling something was wrong. In all probability, Greg wasn't at home because something important had called him away. He'd get in touch as soon as he could. By tomorrow I'd have heard from him.

In the meantime all these damn leaflets would have to be delivered. Tempted as I was to dump them behind a wall, this undercover role had to be maintained, and what is more, what better way to locate properties where an attic or house showed telltale signs of conversion into a cannabis factory? I spent the next couple of hours trudging the streets shoving leaflets through letterboxes, speeding up the process by not wasting time ringing doorbells.

It was on the outskirts of Pittenweem that I identified a two-storey house betraying some promising signs of being used as a cannabis factory: it was detached from its neighbours, all the windows were heavily obscured by net curtains, and there was a neglected garden of knee-high grass and a fine display of dandelions. This was a house that would certainly merit closer investigation. The owner could, of course, merely be a harmless old lady now in hospital or living in a care home.

This time I didn't just slide a leaflet through the letterbox, I rang the bell. When there was no answer, I lifted the flap and with some difficulty pushed the thin paper through the draught excluder. My hopes rose. Its thick brush might be designed to prevent the escape of the sweet pungent smell given off by cannabis plants. Inserting a thin paper through the bristles was quite a struggle, involving sticking my fingers through the flap to poke a gap in the obstruction. I bent down to peer in, pretending to check progress. This gave the ideal opportunity to put my nose close to the opening and give a few sniffs. No doubt about it. The smell of cannabis was faint, but unmistakable.

I'd return later armed with holiday-let enquiry forms and deliver them to all the houses in the street. And, of course, there was the visit I'd make with Gorgonzola by night.

Before I'd left for Pittenweem, I'd checked that there was no escape route from the apartment for G. Confined indoors for hours, she would be eager to get out and, I hoped, go back to where she had found that scrap of paper. With this in mind, on my return I engineered an action replay of yesterday's escape. She'd sneaked out via the bathroom window, so I pushed it up and left it invitingly open, then sat on the settee and kept watch from behind the pages of the newspaper till I saw her slink out of the room. She could, of course, have asked to go out by the French doors, but I knew she would find it much more exciting to exit unobtrusively by a route Disapproved of by Authority.

As soon as the tip of her tail disappeared through the door, I rushed through to the kitchen. By leaning over the sink and craning sideways I could see the bathroom window. A moment later, paws hooked themselves over the edge of the sill, then head and body slithered through the narrow gap. She gathered herself on the ledge and jumped down onto the grass. I craned further forward to see which direction she would go. Keeping close to the wall, she strolled under the kitchen window, reappeared, then vanished from sight round the corner of the building.

I hurried back to the lounge and was in time to see her pass the French doors, not aimlessly strolling, but heading purposefully across the grass, a definite destination in mind. Soon it became all too awfully evident what was in her mind; she crouched on the edge of a bunker and leapt down onto the sand. I sucked in a breath. If anybody saw her, the Lodge manager would soon be hammering on my door, penalty notice in hand.

Ablutions completed to her satisfaction, G emerged from the bunker and headed back towards the Lodge, making this time for the door of apartment 2. This was promising. I stepped outside to watch. She didn't hesitate on the step, but went straight in through the open French doors.

A shrill voice screeched, 'Shoo! *Shoo*, you nasty beast! Get out, damn you, get *out!*'

My cue for action. I hurried across on a rescue mission. G was engaged in a favourite game – the persecution of a cat-phobic.

'Hello there?' I paused in the doorway. 'Would you by any chance have seen my cat?' I ducked as a heavy book hurled from within narrowly missed my head. 'Oh, I see you have.'

G was peering smugly out from the shelter of a table piled high with books and papers, calculating how much more she could get away with. Her victim was a tall angular woman, oval face accentuated by a pointed chin. Her iron-grey hair was scraped severely back to expose ear lobes elongated by heavy silver earrings set with a dark red garnet. She was at bay against a bookcase, hands clutching the shelves, fingers feeling for another missile to hurl at her tormentor.

I pounced on G before she could dart away. 'Naughty, *naughty* cat.'

I deposited her outside, and came back in, pulling the French doors closed behind me, pleased that Gorgonzola's mischief-making had given me the chance to meet another of the residents.

'Hello, I'm Vanessa Dewar-Smythe, apartment 4, just moved in yesterday.' I smiled and held out my hand. She made no attempt to take it. I switched to apologetic overdrive. 'I'm *so* sorry about Smootchikins. She just *loves* people.' And that was partly true. G just loved people who cowered in fear and loathing when she came near them.

The woman with the earrings let go of the bookcase and glowered at me. 'I expect you to keep that brute under control in future. Otherwise I'll definitely be making a formal complaint to Mr Collins.'

Now it was my turn to be at bay, my back, as it were, against a metaphorical bookcase. Given half the chance, G was more than likely to give way to temptation. With a confidence I didn't feel, I said, 'I'll *certainly* make sure that she won't bother you again, Ms ... er ...?'

This was met with a grudging, 'Nicola Beaton, writer and historian.' She had a disconcerting way of looking past me, as if something I ought to know about was happening behind me. Could it be that G was peering in, face provocatively pressed against the glass of the French doors?

'Not *the* Nicola Beaton?' I breathed, tone suitably awestruck, a useful technique to flatter and disarm.

It worked. An expression I couldn't quite decipher flitted across her face. After a pause, she said stiffly, 'The very same.'

'Gosh, I've never met a *real* author. Are you working on anything at the moment?' This approach should produce information without betraying my total ignorance of the woman and her works.

'Naturally. We writers have to put pen to paper every day.'

'*Every* day?' I feigned surprise, hoping to elicit when she was likely to be in her apartment; important to know, as G and I would certainly be paying it a visit in her absence.

Again a pause. 'Of course. Discipline is a must. I sit at the laptop each morning from eight till twelve, and the historic ambience of the Lodge helps me get in the mood. Some mornings or afternoons I take time off from writing to devote to research. For example, on Saturday morning I'm catching the ten o'clock bus to St Andrews to make notes on the castle.'

During this exchange I'd been scanning the room. The layout was a mirror image of my own apartment. I noted the corner of a laptop case just visible under the books and papers piled on the table. On my clandestine visit with G, I'd see if I could get access to the laptop files. White A4 paper was piled up on the table, but of brown wrapping paper there was no sign at all.

I turned to go. Too many questions can put a suspect on guard. 'I'm a great fan of yours, love your books. It's been wonderful meeting you,' I gushed.

I had the distinct impression that this last sentiment was not reciprocated by Ms Beaton. I'd do some internet research of my own on Nicola Beaton, historian and writer.

As I left by the French doors, I tried once again to smooth relations. 'I'm *so* sorry that Smootchikins upset you. Perhaps we could have tea or a drink together in the lounge some time?'

My words hung unanswered in the air. Judging from her pursed lips, a friendly tête-à-tête didn't seem at all likely.

G was sitting on the step outside in the hope that another opportunity to harass Nicola Beaton might present itself. I pounced on her and carried her back to my apartment.

'That's certainly messed up future relations with Ms Beaton, writer and historian. You're a very naughty cat, G,' I hissed. 'Sometimes I *despair*.'

CHAPTER SEVEN

The next morning I sat at the breakfast table gazing out across the golf course to a sea as smooth as grey silk. Sky and sea merged seamlessly at the horizon in the pearly morning light. Beyond the arm of the bay a white yacht, green sail furled tightly round the mast, floated ethereally as in a Whistler watercolour. Two swans flew low over the water, one behind the other, long necks outstretched and, far out at sea, reduced by distance to tiny black dots, a cluster of seabirds speckled the silver-grey surface like dust on a glossy photograph.

But this was not a time to sit and stare. I'd still not heard anything from Greg. Yesterday I'd been merely uneasy, but overnight I'd become convinced that something was distinctly wrong. Now I had to decide what to do. One option was to contact Attila, but it's a cardinal rule of HMRC that undercover agents remain out of contact except in direst emergency. It *was* just possible that Greg thought I was under surveillance and didn't want to blow his cover. There *might* be a perfectly reasonable explanation for Greg's failure to get in touch, and if so, Attila wouldn't hesitate to carpet me, might even take me off the case. And that way I'd lose any chance of tracking down Spinks.

An urgent *miaow* from the kitchen doorway indicated that Gorgonzola had decided to spurn the litter tray in favour of performing her ablutions in the great outdoors.

'OK, but it's collar and lead for you, my girl,' I warned.

That would keep G away from a bunker and demonstrate that I had my cat under control in compliance with Nicola Beaton's wishes if she happened to be watching. More importantly, the collar was a sign to G that after ablutions she was in work mode. I was hoping that she might head for the spot where she'd found the drug-contaminated piece of paper.

When she made straight for the forbidden bunker, those hopes were raised. Could the scrap of paper have come from drugs buried there, the packet wrapping having disintegrated in the damp sand? Keeping her on a tight lead, I stood for a moment looking down into the bunker. There was no sign of disturbance from G's ablution-visit the previous evening since a conscientious groundsman had taken the trouble to rake the sand into neat ridges. Or could this be an attempt by someone to cover up evidence that a package had been hidden there? A drug packet buried deep in the sand would remain undetected even by a golfer's wildest chip shot.

'Search, G!' I encouraged.

Confident that she was in work mode, I unclipped the lead. She jumped down into the bunker and began a systematic search of the raked sand. When she scraped a small investigative hole, I held my breath.

'Atta girl.'

A moment later it was clear that she was searching, not for drugs, but for the perfect spot to dig a hole for her ablutions. She squatted. Oh, *no!* As she scratched away at the sand to cover up the hole, I gazed back guiltily towards the windows of apartment 2. Was the formidable Nicola Beaton even now reaching for the telephone to report this misdemeanour to Steve Collins, Lodge Manager?

'*Bad* girl!' I snapped. 'A bunker's *not* a catty loo.' I jumped down into the bunker.

She turned her head to stare at me with a look that said plainly, 'A girl's got to do what a girl's got to do.'

I flicked the lead at her. A mistake. She made a playful pounce, regarding this as a new game, a game designed to make amends for my behaviour last night. I made a lunge. She swerved easily out of reach. Another grab, another swerve. I lunged again, tripped over the lead trailing from my hand and stumbled forward onto my knees. Panting, I glared at G, sitting just out of reach, scratching an ear.

'Thought it was you!' a voice barked.

I looked up. With the bright light of the early morning sun in my eyes, I couldn't make out the face of the man standing, hands on hips, on the edge of the bunker. For a heart-stopping moment I saw before me Hiram J Spinks in his golfing plus fours, yellow sweater and checked cap. My throat constricted, my mouth opened. What came out was a strangulated squeak.

Recovering from the initial shock, I could see that the only resemblance to Spinks was in his clothing. This man was not tall and thin, but middle-aged and portly. The relief was short-lived.

'May I ask what the devil you're doing, madam? You've only just moved in and already I've caught you wantonly spoiling the surface of the bunker. Sheer vandalism, in my opinion! A ball landing in there will be the devil to play. Collins will be hearing about this.'

Still on my knees, I shaded my eyes to peer up at him.

The stranger's clipped military moustache bristled, his florid complexion darkening to apoplectic purple. 'Get out of there *at once*, or—'

'Oh, thank God you've come along!' I cried. 'I fell into the bunker trying to stop my cat catching a seagull and I seem to have hurt my ankle.' The unexpected response halted him in mid-rant. 'And when I tried to stand, my leg gave way under me. *Ow*!' I winced as I made a show of putting my weight gingerly on my right leg and attempted to stand up.

Had I convinced him? Gorgonzola came to my aid in support of my story by leaping gracefully out of the bunker to stalk a seagull pecking viciously at something in the grass.

I hopped to the side of the bunker and made a half-hearted attempt to clamber over the edge. 'Oh, dear, I'm awfully sorry but I'll need a bit of help to get out of here, Mr ... er....'

'It's *Major*, Major Spencer St Clair,' he said stiffly. Somewhat reluctantly he held out a hand to assist me.

With much *ow*-ing and *ouch*-ing I scrambled up onto the fairway where he transferred his grip to my arm as if placing me under arrest. I'd obviously not convinced him with my story. Together we stood looking down at the churned-up sand of the bunker.

'Oh dear, what a mess I've made.' I gave a shaky laugh. 'I *do* hope it won't be held against me.'

His hold on my arm loosened fractionally, but tightened again as I made to move away. Was he going to march me off to the office, a vandal caught in the act, to face a court-martial?

Keeaarg keeaarg keeaarg keeaarg. We whirled round at the gull's raucous alarm call. Gorgonzola was holding grimly onto a flight feather of a very large gull, heedless of the powerful wings battering at her and the beak aiming for her eyes. Her ambush had misfired. She'd miscalculated the pecking power of that cruel yellow bill and was in danger of losing an eye.

I wrenched myself free from the Major's grip. Hurling myself forward and down, like a rugby player stretching out for a try, I brought the cat-versus-gull skirmish to an abrupt end. Distracted, G released her grip. The startled gull rose into the air with a flurry of wings.

From Gorgonzola a frustrated, long-drawn-out *waaagh*.

From the Major, an irate, 'Damned disgrace! That cat should be shot! Put up against a wall and *shot*, I say!'

From me, winded by the force of my landing, not a word.

By the time I'd picked myself up, the Major had stomped off, having made it quite clear that in his opinion, cats *and* their owners should be lined up for the firing squad. I snatched G up and made a big show of limping back to my apartment in case the Major might be watching from afar.

'You should be ashamed of yourself, G,' I scolded. 'That's the second resident you've upset. It's going to make it harder, a *lot* harder, to chat them up and find out more about them.' I fixed her with a stern gaze that she pretended not to notice.

But every cloud has a silver lining. The incident had given me the idea that a bunker in close proximity to the beach would make a very convenient place to store packages of drugs. Raked sand had obliterated all traces of G's visitation last night; in the same way, all trace that drug packages had been buried in a bunker could be conveniently raked away.

At first light, before the groundsman started work, G and I would pay visits to the bunkers to check if the sand had been disturbed overnight.

Half an hour later, G having been confined to barracks, as the Major would put it, I returned to Pittenweem in search of Greg Findlay, this time by bus. I sat in the bus pondering how best to disguise my visit to his house, not paying much attention to the two women gossiping in the seats behind me until I heard the words 'West Shore'. Pretending an interest in the passing hedgerows and fields, I gazed out of the window and tuned in to their conversation.

'Aye, you don't know when it's going to be your last day, do you? One moment that man was working on his car, the next moment there he was, dead.'

'Some men think they know it all.' Reflected in the window, a head nodded slowly. 'Just like what happened to Jimmy Cuthbertson. He was working under his car, propped it up with the jack, and the whole thing collapsed on top of him.'

'His widow's a strange woman. Told me she saw the postman at my door with a parcel yesterday, but did she go out and offer to take it in? No, just let him drive away....'

I tuned them out, busy with my own thoughts. That talk of a parcel had given me an idea. I'd go straight to Greg's door with a parcel and if he was in, pretend I had the wrong address and let him direct me elsewhere, then wait for him to get in contact. If there was no reply when I knocked, his neighbours might be able to give me some information. I'd pretend to be a friend of his trying to deliver a birthday present.

I came out of a gift shop on the High Street with a small gift-wrapped picture under my arm, made my way down to the harbour, and in a couple of minutes was ringing Greg's bell. Again there was no answer.

I lifted the flap of the letterbox and called loudly. 'Hello, anyone at home?' My voice rang out emptily in the small square space that served as a hall.

I peered through the slit. The door to the front room was ajar. On the left, the bottom of a flight of worn stone steps spiralled upwards out of sight. A dark blue reefer jacket hung from the coat-hook on the wall. Of Greg Findlay himself there was no sign.

'You'll no get any answer there, missus. He's deid.'

I whirled round. A yard away, a scruffy teenage youth in a grey hoodie top and baggy tracksuit trousers was standing on the pavement astride a mountain bike.

'*Dead?*' I stared at him in disbelief, then leapt forward to confront him. 'What do you mean?'

He gave me a surly look. 'What d'you think I mean? Deid as in stone deid.'

He put his foot on the pedal to ride away, but I grabbed the handlebars, forcing him to an abrupt halt.

'Hey, missus, what you doing? Bugger off.'

This wasn't getting me anywhere. 'I'm sorry,' I said, releasing the handlebars and stepping away from the bike. 'It's just that you gave me an awful shock just now. This here's his birthday present.' I held up the wrapped picture. 'I can't believe it. What happened? When?'

His eyes narrowed as he calculated how much he could wring out of me. 'What's in it for me if I tell you?'

'Well ... nothing,' I said and turned away. 'I'll just ask a neighbour.'

And that's what I had to do, for he rode off. In his wake drifted a stream of insults, 'effing old cow' being one of the more complimentary.

Greg's neighbour, an old man wearing a fisherman's jersey came to the door smoking a battered, evil-smelling pipe.

'I called next door,' I said, 'with Charlie Forrest's birthday present. And he doesn't appear to be in. I wonder if you could give it to him.' I held out the parcel.

'I'm afraid that'll no be possible, lass. An awfu' thing's happened, you see....' Seeking how best to break the news, he puffed hard at his pipe, the haze of smoke a protective screen veiling him from my pain. 'I'm sorry to have to tell you that Mr Forrest died in a terrible accident two days ago.'

The reply destroyed any faint hope that the youth had been a malicious liar out to shock. 'Died? Accident?' My heart pounded in my chest.

'Aye, fixing something under his car, he was, and—'

I stared at him, recalling the conversation behind me in the bus. 'And the car fell off the jack and crushed him?'

He took the pipe from his mouth. 'No, it wisna' that.... They say he was half under the car with the engine running and there was a hole in the exhaust.' He shook his head. 'By the time someone noticed that he'd been there for some hours, it was too late. Carbon monoxide.' He reached out a hand and awkwardly patted my shoulder. 'He wouldn't have suffered.'

I nodded and turned away. 'Thanks,' I called, my voice shaky. Behind me, the door closed softly.

I sat on one of the benches looking out over the small beach and the sea, seeing nothing, mourning the loss of a colleague, shocked not just by the news of Greg's death, but because I was sure that it had been no accident. He had never as much as changed a tyre, let alone tried to fix an exhaust, had been quite open about the fact that the workings of cars were a complete mystery to him. 'If anything goes wrong, leave it to the guys who know,' had been his attitude to all things technical. Yes ... this was not an accident, but murder.

After a time, I got up and walked slowly away. As I turned into Calman's Wynd to make my way back to the High Street, I glanced back at the picture in its cheerful wrapping propped against the back of the bench. Shock had given way to anger. Greg's death had been murder. Of that I was quite certain. And murder made to look like accident was the speciality of one man, Hiram J Spinks.

Sometime later I took out my mobile and sent Attila an encrypted message informing him of Greg's death and my reasons for thinking it was murder. That I was convinced his death had been engineered on the orders of Spinks, I kept to myself. Attila didn't believe in hunches, only hard evidence.

CHAPTER EIGHT

At 2 a.m. the next morning I turned the handle of the wooden door set in the wall of Greg's backyard. He must have stumbled on information that threatened to put a stop to one of Selkirk's lucrative activities. A search of the house might very well uncover what he had found out. The yard door opened a few inches and stuck, its lower edge obstructed by a slightly raised flagstone. A push and a heave and it scraped open enough for me to slip through. I set down the rucksack and unzipped it enough to allow G's head to poke out. A street lamp in the wynd faintly illumined the curved stones at the top of the high wall, but left the yard itself in darkness. No lights showed in the houses on either side, but two back yards away, warm light spilled through the open curtains of an upstairs window.

I took a black balaclava out of my pocket and pulled it over my head. For five minutes I stood motionless, a shadow among the shadows, peering into the dark of the yard and listening to the mysterious rustlings of the night. At length, satisfied, I picked up the rucksack and flitted across to the house, narrowly avoiding tripping over lobster creels arranged in artistic formation a short distance from the back door.

I went to work with my pick-lock. *Click.* I pushed open the back door and let G out of the rucksack. She darted into the house and I followed, locking the door behind me. I drew the curtains closed and flicked on my pencil torch. In the faint hope that Greg might have stowed away a sample of a drug find, I gave her the order, 'Search!' If there was a package, there might also be a note as to where he'd found it.

The narrow beam of the torch moved over the wooden floor … the worn rug … table … the dresser with its neat rows of plates and mugs … sink … a couple of saucepans on the stove. Nothing there of interest. The beam moved on, catching the glint of G's eyes as she prowled past.

Facing me was the doorway to the front room. A street lamp on West

Shore cast a yellow rectangle of light onto its floor through the open curtains, a warning to take care that my pencil torch didn't attract the attention of a passer-by. I certainly didn't want a police car screeching up to the door, the resulting explanations, and Attila having to be contacted to get me out of the mess.

I moved cautiously into the front room. What I saw in the light cast by the street lamp told me I was too late. A small bookcase stood against the wall, most of the books it had contained scattered on the floor, some spines-upwards. Cushions had been dragged from the sofa, the doors of a small cupboard forced open, the drawers inside pulled out, the contents of the wastepaper basket upended on the floor. Somebody had come looking for something, but had they found it? I knelt down to run my hand under the bottom shelf of the bookcase, feeling for anything that might be taped there.

Scratch. The faint sound came from the kitchen. *Scratch. Scratch.* Louder this time. G had found something, but I'd heard no triumphant croon. *Scratch Scratch.* This wasn't her normal behaviour when she made a find. As sounds came from the kitchen, more metallic this time, fur and whiskers brushed against my hand. Someone was using pick-locks on the back door. In one, two, three swift paces, I moved into the kitchen and pressed myself against the wall beside the back door with G at my feet.

Click. The lock turned. Whoever it was wouldn't risk switching on the light, so perhaps ... just perhaps, I could slip out unnoticed. The back door opened. Unconcerned that passers-by in the street might see the light of the torch, the intruder swept the bright beam round the room and played it on the dresser. The silhouette of a burly man moved slowly forward into the kitchen. Self-preservation urged me to make a dash for it *now* while his back was turned. I resisted the urge. He was too close to the back door. I'd have to wait....

Now was my chance. Too swift a movement would attract his attention. Slowly ... slowly ... I inched my way round the edge of the door, careful not to make a sound. Just one more step and G and I would be out into the yard. I glanced down. She wasn't there. A moment ago she'd been right beside me, now she was across the room, sniffing at the legs of the intruder. *Rrrooooo.* Her sensitive nose had detected clothing contaminated by contact with drugs. He spun round. As the beam of the torch swept towards me, I flung myself through the doorway.

How many vital seconds to cross the yard, turn the handle of the yard door and haul it open? My shadow stretched ahead as his torch beam settled on me. The smell of stale sweat. A cry of triumph. A rough hand on my shoulder halted my flight, spinning me round. A yowl from Gorgonzola. A shout. The *crack* of wooden creels splintering was followed closely by the thud of a heavy body falling to the ground. The torch clattered on the stone paving, plunging the yard into darkness.

'Bloody cat! I've done in my sodding ankle!' The groan of pain too agonized to be other than genuine.

I didn't wait to play Florence Nightingale. I lurched forward, wrestled with the handle, pulled the door open and half-fell out into the wynd. I was quick, Gorgonzola was quicker, streaking ahead of me. I pulled the door closed behind me. Which way to run? Down to West Shore and the lighted promenade? But there he'd have a good view of me, possibly recognize me by my rucksack and my clothing and attempt to follow. Up in the direction of the High Street? That way might lead to a cul-de-sac, a dead-end in both senses. Noises from the yard gave warning that my assailant was stumbling towards the yard door. I'd only seconds to decide.

I ran downhill and crouched in deep shadow between the lamp on Greg's wall and the next lamp fifty yards away, feeling around for one of the small pieces of mortar shed by old walls. The yard door scraped open. For an instant he stood in the wynd, listening...

I hurled one piece of mortar, then another high over his head to land some distance to the right of the gate with a soft *pit pit*, the sound of pebbles shifting under an incautious foot. His head turned towards the sound, then he hobbled away, uphill in the direction of the High Street. I waited for a few moments, then slipped back into the yard and stood pressed to the wall behind the open door. He'd retrace his steps when there was no sign of me ahead of him and head off down the wynd to West Shore. All G and I would have to do was make our way as far up the wynd as we could. Even if that way was a dead-end, he wouldn't search in that direction again. Yes, brownie points to you, DJ, I thought.

Loud curses and laboured breathing drifted down the wynd as he retraced his steps. What if he decided pursuit was pointless and resumed his search of the house? I unzipped the rucksack and held it open.

'Get in, G!' I whispered.

There was no mew of acknowledgement, no brush of fur against my legs. It was then that I realized I had no idea where Gorgonzola was. I held my breath, hoping that my assailant would pass by on his way down to West Shore. He didn't. He stopped in the doorway. The lamp in the wynd cast his shadow onto the flagstones of the yard as he stood, one hand leaning on the doorjamb for support. I'd made a big mistake in assuming that he would continue the chase with a painful ankle. As he stood there, Gorgonzola's shadow appeared alongside his in the wynd. The next moment she darted past him through the doorway.

'That bloody cat again!' The roar of rage echoed off the high walls of the narrow wynd.

Any movement I made would attract his attention, giving me no chance to edge away. My only hope was to take him by surprise. The shadow on the courtyard flagstones straightened as he prepared to hurl himself in pursuit of G. I tensed, ready to launch an attack against a man twice my weight and strength.

A light flicked on above the back door of the neighbouring house with the lighted window, a key rattled in the lock, the door opened and a truculent voice bellowed, 'What the hell's going on out there? Piss off, you drunken bum, or I'll call the police!'

The assailant's shadow on the flagstones turned, narrowed and was gone. Limping footsteps retreated down the wynd. After a long moment, the neighbour's door slammed shut, the key rattled in the lock and the light snapped off. Silence settled once more over wynd and backyards.

I held open the rucksack at cat level and whispered, 'Here, G!'

This time she responded quickly. A rough tongue licked my hand and she leapt lightly into the rucksack. I glanced longingly at the dark oblong marking Greg's wide-open back door, a tempting invitation to re-enter the cottage. Reluctantly I decided the risk of the Unknown's return was too high. I pulled off the balaclava, shrugged the rucksack onto my back and made my way up the wynd – which, to my relief, led not to a cul-de-sac, but to the High Street and my parked car.

Who was the intruder? What was he looking for? Had he ransacked Greg's room, and if so, why had he returned? What *was* the mistake that had blown Greg's cover? More to the point, by making that mistake, had Greg also blown *my* cover? I'd soon find out.

CHAPTER NINE

I was not up bright and early after my night's adventure. In fact I was still sleeping soundly at 8 a.m. when my slumbers were rudely interrupted by a jarring *TRRINNGG*. Jolted awake, it took me a moment or two to realize that someone had their finger glued to the doorbell. *TRRRINNNGG*. I pulled the duvet over my head. *TRRRRINNNNGG*. *TRRRRINNNNGG*. Whoever it was, wasn't going to go away.

Eyes half-open, I stumbled over to the videophone and peered blearily at the urgent caller's image, a woman with long, swirling chestnut brown tresses hanging down like spaniel's ears on either side of an oval face. Relieved that it wasn't my assailant of the night before, I pressed the intercom button.

'Yes?' I croaked.

She leaned towards the camera lens. Dark glasses, goggle-sized, and full lips surgically enhanced with collagen zoomed in to fill the screen.

'I must speak with you urgently, *most* urgently,' the lips insisted.

'Can't it wait? I've had a bit of a late night,' I snapped crossly. 'Who are you, anyway?'

'Maxine St Clair. And no, it can't wait, it definitely *cannot*.' She emphasized the point with another fierce *TRRRRINNNNGG*.

Fuddled with sleep and jangled by the loud peal on the bell, it took me a few seconds to conclude that the virago on my doorstep must be the mate of the formidable Major St Clair, Defender of the Bunker.

'Are you going to open the bloody door, or not?' the lips demanded.

'Not' didn't appear to be an option.

I looked down at my crumpled cheap-and-cheerful pyjamas. 'Just one moment till I put on my robe.' From a charity shop in St Andrews I had purchased a faux silk, faux designer robe under which my cheap-and-cheerfuls could modestly lurk if called from bed to door.

TRRRRRINNNNNGG. One moment was obviously one moment too long. I opened the door, cheap-and-cheerfuls on display.

'Ms Dewar-Smythe—' She stopped, lips pursing in disapproval at the sight of my shabby attire and dishevelled hair. Her expression hardened. 'Look here, Dewar-*Smith*, this has got to stop!' The deliberate mispronunciation of my name underlined that my social rating had plummeted.

I stared blankly at her. 'This?'

'*This!*' With a dramatic gesture she held up a plastic carrier bag.

I stared at it uncomprehendingly, then transferred my gaze back to the impenetrable dark glasses.

She heaved an impatient sigh. 'On your arrival here you will have noticed the lily pond?'

I nodded.

'Stocked with prize koi by Spencer at his own expense. And this, *this*, is all that remains of one of them.' She brandished the bag and thrust it at me. 'That disgraceful creature, your cat, devoured it. Look!'

It did indeed contain the head and bones of a large fish, whether koi or not, it was difficult to say, as only shreds of the flesh remained.

'I'm afraid you must be mistaken, Mrs St Clair. 'The culprit can't have been *my* cat. She's been with me all night.' Sure of my ground, I called back into the apartment. 'Here, Smootchikins!'

Maxine St Clair stood with folded arms and waited. G did not appear.

'Give me a moment. She'll be sitting in her favourite spot beside the radiator in the lounge.'

I hurried from room to room, but she wasn't in the lounge, or the kitchen. Her previous escape route, the bathroom window, was firmly closed. The bedroom window, unfortunately, wasn't. While I'd been lying dead to the world, G obviously had not. A quick catnap in the early hours and she'd been ready to get up and go. And it was my fault. I'd forgotten to feed her when we got in last night. Now, with the killing of the koi, the fat *was* in the fire.

The virago was standing where I'd left her. One expensively shod foot had inched forward over the threshold to ensure the interview could be terminated only on her terms.

Grovelling and contrition might pacify her. 'Oh dear, oh dear! It seems Smootchikins must have managed to squeeze out of the window while I was sleeping. What can I say, Mrs Sinclair?'

'The name is *St* Clair,' she said coldly. 'I suggest you say that you will pay to restock the pond.'

'Of course, of course,' I babbled.

A grim nod acknowledged my capitulation, but ungracious in victory, she gave no quarter. 'The Deeds of Condition, Miss Smith, state – and I recommend that you commit them to memory – that pets may be kept *only* with the agreement and approval of the other residents. Rest assured, the Major and I will be keeping a very close eye on you and your animal.' Her foot removed itself from the threshold. Shoulders stiff with outrage, she marched off along the corridor.

I shut the door and leant against the wall, eyes closed, shaken by the encounter. Thanks to Gorgonzola's misdemeanours, I and my activities were going to be subjected to the most unwelcome scrutiny. Another unfortunate incident featuring fish, fowl, or sandy bunker, and I had no doubt at all that I would be asked to leave. With that disaster looming, the future explanation to HMRC Accounts of the entry on my expenses sheet, *purchase of prize carp*, paled into complete insignificance.

My eyes flew open. Where *was* G and what was she doing? The heinous offence that would send us packing could be happening *right now*. Gone would be the chance of further contact with the residents of the Lodge; gone the chance of investigating the bunkers on the golf course as a temporary stash for drugs brought in from the bay.

I rushed off to the bedroom to fling on some clothes. The picture of innocence, Gorgonzola was lying curled up on the bed simulating deep unbroken sleep, her sides rising and falling rhythmically. But the fresh muddy smears on the previously pristine duvet cover told an altogether different story.

I would normally have greeted this flagrant attempt at a cover-up with amused tolerance, but in my heightened state of anxiety I metamorphosed into an enraged Maxine St Clair.

'Look here, Gorgonzola, this has got to stop!' I snarled.

Her eyes slowly opened.

'Explain *this*!' With a dramatic gesture I whipped the fishy skeleton out of the carrier bag and dangled it in front of her.

A blank stare signified, 'What *is* that? I've never seen such a thing in my life!' Her eyes closed to indicate that the object – indeed the whole subject – was of no interest, no interest at all.

It was useless to remonstrate. It was plain that preventive measures against any recurrence would be up to me.

The skirmish with Maxine St Clair was a reminder that time was of the essence. If I was going to probe the secrets of the Lodge, only eighteen days remained of my three weeks' stay.

So far, the only resident I'd researched in depth was Nicola Beaton, historical novelist. On the internet I'd found a number of her press and radio interviews. Her website displayed a list of published novels alongside a publicity picture that was either flatteringly air-brushed or had been taken some years previously, for her hair was a soft framework to a much younger face, not scraped back in Victorian schoolmarm fashion as it was now. Perhaps her current severe hairstyle was an attempt to immerse herself in the ambience of the historical novel she was in the process of writing.

Was she in Selkirk's pay? Perhaps the files on that laptop semi-hidden under the pile of papers on her table would provide an answer and confirm her apartment as the source of the drug-tainted wrapping paper. She'd stressed that she took a disciplined approach to research, so there was a good chance she'd keep to her plan to go to St Andrews today, making this an ideal opportunity for G and me to pay her apartment a visit.

In preparation for the break-in, I stationed myself at 9.30 in the medieval entrance hall on one of the settees by the wide carved fireplace, warming myself at the crackling log fire and leisurely turning the pages of one of the newspapers thoughtfully laid out on a side-table for residents to browse through. I might, of course, be wasting my time sitting here. She might have taken an earlier bus, or indeed, have decided not to make the journey at all. If she didn't appear by 10.15, I'd ring her bell on the pretext of apologizing once again for G's intrusion into her apartment.

There was no need for that, for ten minutes later she strode purposefully by, satchel on shoulder. I glanced up casually and ventured a smile, but her lips remained pressed in an uncompromisingly hostile line and her eyes studiously avoided mine. I watched her head off down the drive towards the bus stop. Her budget obviously didn't extend to travel by taxi.

She might very well get halfway down the drive, remember she had forgotten something and return to collect it, so I sat there reading the newspaper for another fifteen minutes. Now was the time to make my move. I replaced the newspaper on the side-table. It was only then that I noticed the name *St Clair* scrawled on the top right hand corner. I'd been reading the Major's personal copy. I, not G, had committed another heinous offence, the last straw that might get us thrown out. Hastily I smoothed and refolded the pages, but in spite of my efforts the newspaper showed distinct signs of having been opened and read. Feeling eyes upon me, I looked up. Steve Collins was watching me through the open door of his office, and when the Major complained about the state of the paper....

'I thought the newspapers were complimentary.' I smiled weakly and beat a hasty retreat.

Beaton's apartment was in the opposite arm to mine in the T leading from the entrance hall, and, unfortunately for my intended use of the picklock, the front door was directly opposite the St Clairs' apartment. With Maxine and the Major on red alert for any misdemeanours on my part, I couldn't risk their catching me in the act of lock-picking. Illegal entry would have to be via her French doors, only a short distance away from mine at the rear of the building. Having studied my own locks, I'd calculated that sixty seconds were all I needed. Anyone seeing me standing there for that short time would assume that Nicola Beaton was at home and was about to let me in. As a precaution, I didn't go directly to the scene of my crime. With Gorgonzola on the lead I strolled towards the golf course, then wandered back on a route that would take me past the Beaton apartment. All went according to plan.

Confident that there had been no witnesses, I closed Beaton's French doors behind me, let G loose and watched her begin a methodical search of the room. The piles of books and papers covering the table were bigger than on our previous visit, but there was no sign of the laptop in this room – or elsewhere in the apartment. I turned my attention to the papers on the table and read quickly through them, replacing each one face down and at the same angle as she'd left them. Disappointingly, they turned out merely to be research material for a novel, descriptive notes of Fife fishing villages headed *Crail, St Monans, Lower Largo, Pittenweem.*

A loud *miaow* from at my feet signalled that G had finished her search of the premises and had also found nothing.

'That makes two disappointed HMRC agents, eh, G?'

As I stooped to pat her head, my elbow jolted the table. A stack of paper slid off, fell to the floor and lay scattered over the carpet. It only needed one of them to be out of place, and she'd know for certain that someone had been snooping. Hand outstretched to gather them up, I stopped. She might, just *might*, think nothing of it, put it down to the vibration of the door shutting, or a gust of air as she left. Even if she *was* suspicious, she wouldn't be sure that there'd been an intruder. After all, would not an intruder have tidied up in an effort to conceal that someone had been there? Decision made: I left book and papers just as they were.

'OK, G, we've finished here.'

As I clipped on her lead I noticed a memory stick peeping out from among the papers scattered on the floor. Perhaps my visit hadn't been wasted after all. I pocketed it and having ascertained that the coast was clear, relocked the French doors and we hurried back to my apartment.

I prepared to open the files on my laptop, my heart beating a little faster. Would the files on the memory stick be the manuscript of her novel, or the breakthrough I needed?

The screen showed three folders. I opened *Life*. Under the heading *NICOLA BEATON, HISTORICAL NOVELIST* were very detailed autobiographical notes for publicity purposes: date of birth, education, titles of press and magazine articles featuring herself, likes and dislikes, and opinions expressed on various topics from fashion to politics. The folder *Books* listed fifteen published novels, while *Characters* was just that, character descriptions. Disappointed that this was all the memory stick contained, I nevertheless copied the folders.

Leaving G tucking in to the remains of her breakfast, I returned to Beaton's apartment, entering once again by the French doors. I positioned her memory stick so that once again it was half-hidden by a sheet of paper and stood back surveying the room. Apart from the items that had fallen from the table, everything appeared to be as Beaton had left it. I nodded, satisfied.

I should have left then, but I couldn't resist the golden opportunity to do a more thorough search of the apartment. Though G had given it the all-clear for drugs, eyes might discover something a nose had not. I'd left the lounge and was making my way along the hall to the bedroom when I heard a man and a woman arguing outside in the corridor. The woman was Nicola Beaton.

The exit route via the French doors would be in full view of Beaton as she came in the front door of the apartment. I darted into the bedroom, feet making only a whisper of sound on the thick pile of the carpet. The layout and furnishings were the same as my own. I'd hoped to roll under the bed, but Nicola Beaton, like myself, had dispensed with the heavy tapestry-effect king-sized bedcover as being too much bother to take off and put on each day. Consequently, most of the under-bed area was clearly visible from the hallway. I discounted the elaborate armoire wardrobe as a possible hiding place: half of it was given over to drawers and shelves, and even if there were enough clothes hanging in the remaining space to conceal me, she might decide to hang up her coat there. I was trapped.

I heard the sound of the key being inserted in the lock.

'I told you not to come here.' Beaton's tone was sharply critical.

'Quit nagging. You might as well make the best of it, Nikky. There's something important we've got to sort out.'

For a vital moment the front door remained closed. Then I remembered the walk-in broom cupboard in the hall. The squeak as I turned the door handle seemed alarmingly loud, but the sound was covered by the voices of Beaton and her companion raised in argument.

The inside of the broom cupboard door was completely smooth with no handle or anything to grip on. I hooked my fingers round the edge of the door and pulled it to as far as I dared without shutting myself in. Now only a slit of a gap remained between door and jamb.

The front door opened and closed. They were standing in the hall, only feet from the cupboard. I could smell sweat overlaid with cheap aftershave. Beaton's visitor, it seemed, wore nylon shirts but didn't believe in deodorant.

'He was quite clear about it, Bert: no face-to-face contact.'

'Well, if you hadn't turned your phone off, I wouldn't be here. So if it's anyone's fault, it's bloody well yours.'

The handle of the vacuum cleaner was pressing uncomfortably into the small of my back, and I was seized by an overwhelming urge to move my leg which was awkwardly positioned between a bucket and the vacuum cleaner, but any attempt to ease my position might shift mop, brush, or other cleaning equipment. The slightest sound from the cupboard and.... Unfortunately, Beaton and her visitor seemed in no hurry to move away into the lounge.

'Whatever your reason for coming, Bert, it had better be good. I was all set to catch the bus for my visit to St Andrews. The new man has made it clear he won't stand for anyone stepping out of line, and if I—'

'Get a grip, woman. Missing the bus isn't stepping out of line. If you don't think that's a good enough excuse, do some creative thinking. You're supposed to be the writer – tell him the bus broke down, lost a wheel, ran over a pensioner, anything you like, for Christ's sake. Now, instead of standing arguing the toss, get that kettle on and I'll tell you why I had to come here.'

The rush of water from the kitchen tap gave me the chance to ease my leg slowly into a more comfortable position. My relief was short-lived, for I became aware that the tiny gap I'd left between door and jamb had widened to a finger's width. If I hooked the tips of my fingers round the edge to close it, they'd be all too visible to Beaton or her companion if they happened to look in that direction. The opening faced away from the lounge. Would Beaton notice the door was ajar when she showed her visitor out? She might, and push it shut, locking me inside.

I heard the *chink* of cups and saucers being put out, and, above the rumble of a kettle coming to the boil, Beaton call out, 'Don't you be meddling with any of my papers, Bert. I'll be with you in a minute.'

Any moment now she'd go into the lounge and see the papers scattered on the carpet. How would she react?

When she did, it turned out even better than I'd dared to hope. The tea tray clattered down violently on the table.

'I bloody well *told* you not to mess with my papers, you nosy bugger!'

'Shut it, Beaton! It's not my fault, nothing to do with me. The rest of the bloody pile's ready to go the same way. Look, only got to touch it and—' The thump of books hitting the floor.

A wail of rage from Beaton. 'Look what you've done!'

'Sort it out later, you silly bitch. Do you think I've got bugger all to do but stand here while you shuffle through some papers? I'm not a fool, you know. I wouldn't have come here if it wasn't bloody important. Sit down, woman, and listen, damn you! I'm trying to tell you that the package we nicked wasn't in his house.'

'Wasn't in his house? Don't say you didn't *find* it?'

'Worse. When I went there last night, some other bastard was there before me.' The sound of tea being poured, the clink of spoon on saucer, the slurp of tea noisily sucked from a cup.

'Don't keep me in suspense, Bert. What *happened*?'

'He scarpered before I could get my hands on him. You know what that means? Looks like someone else knew about the package.'

A dismissive laugh from Beaton. 'You had me worried for a moment there, but you've got it all wrong. Charlie Forrest's death was in Thursday's paper and Pittenweem's a small place so everyone would know where he lived. Some thief's taken the opportunity to break into the empty house, lift anything of value and go off with our package. You said he ran away, it's what burglars *do* when they're caught in the act. That's all it was. You know yourself when....'

I didn't hear what was said next. I was trying to come to grips with the realization that my burly attacker of last night was sitting yards away from me, drinking tea and telling Beaton of his encounter with me in Greg's house.

'... now that bloody Forrest's got himself killed...' snapped my attention back to the conversation going on in Nicola Beaton's lounge.

A moment of silence, another noisy slurp of tea. 'We'll just have to find ourselves another dealer.'

'I don't know if that's wise, Bert.' The rattle of crockery being collected. 'Perhaps we should lay off for a bit now that the new man's taken over.'

A snort. 'No way! We've lost a hell of a lot of money. Whoever's got that package, we're not going to get it back. That silly bugger Forrest should have waited to have his accident until *after* he'd paid us. Leave it to me. I'll trawl around the pubs of Anstruther and Pittenweem. It won't take me long to net a replacement for him. Just you see that the next package is ready for the boat to collect with the rest on Monday as usual. Don't let me down, Nikky, I bloody well need the cash.'

'Well, Bert Mackay, I hope *you* appreciate the time it takes *me* to make up a substitute package from dried leaves, not to mention topping it off with the real thing. If it was left to those banana fingers of yours, a babe in arms would spot the difference. And it'll be no joke to dig for the drug package in the bunker and replace it with ours now the sand's been fouled by the ghastly cat of that woman in the next apartment.'

'Best place for a cat's under the ground. I tripped over one of the brutes last night and did in my bloody ankle. The answer's simple,

63

woman. Buy some rat poison, stick it in a bit of fish, and the cat's a goner.'

'I might just do that. Come on, Bert. Next bus'll be along soon. You go now, and I'll follow in five minutes.' The dry rustle of papers being gathered up, the faint thump of books being replaced.

As Bert Mackay lumbered past, I again caught a whiff of sweat not quite masked by cheap aftershave and glimpsed a beefy red-faced man with black moustache and sleeked-back hair, shiny with oil.

It was clear that Beaton and Mackay, minor cogs in Selkirk's organization, were running a neat little drug-dealing scheme of their own, banking that the fake would go undiscovered until it had passed through so many hands that the substitution could not be traced back to them. But they were playing a dangerous game by sneaking off a package from a consignment about to be shipped out and replacing it with a dummy.

A couple of minutes after Beaton had left, I let myself out by her French doors, locking them behind me. I now knew the identity of last night's attacker and what he had been looking for. But what I'd overheard raised other questions: Beaton and Mackay believed that Greg's death was an accident. They were mistaken. Someone had wanted Greg dead and I was convinced it was Spinks. Was it because he had discovered that Charlie Forrest was an HMRC agent? Or was it that he'd realized that his consignments were being tampered with and blamed it on Forrest?

These were questions to which I had as yet no answer.

CHAPTER TEN

By midday I was in Pittenweem outside the detached house with the mass display of seeding dandelions and its windows heavily obscured by net curtains. Holiday let enquiry form and clipboard in hand, I pushed open the gate of the house next door, number 33, *Dun Roaming*. Its closely mown lawn, razor-sharp edging and beds of yellow daisies and purple asters were a conspicuous reproach to its neighbour's knee-high grass and weed-choked path.

My plan was to enquire about the availability of the suspect house as a holiday let. I was optimistic that the owners of *Dun Roaming* would be eager to give all the information they possessed about their neighbour in the hope that it might lead to improvements to the neglected property. The bell rang faintly somewhere in the interior of the house, but no one came to the door. I rang again. Still no answer. Disappointed that I'd made the journey for nothing, I was turning away when a small woman rushed round the corner of the house from the back garden. She was wearing a shapeless cardigan, a cowl-necked jersey, a long black skirt and muddy walking boots without laces.

'I *thought* I heard the bell,' she said breathlessly.

'Excuse me,' I said, indicating the clipboard. 'Can I ask—?'

'You've come to read the meter? I've been waiting in all morning for you, and the minute I go out to deadhead the roses, here you are.'

'Oh, I'm not the meter-reader. I'm doing a survey for the Tourist Board to find properties that could be offered as holiday lets. Now, can I ask about the house next door, Mrs ... er ...?'

'McRoberts, Jeannie McRoberts.' Her white hair, gathered loosely back from forehead and sides, was tied up in an old-fashioned bun from which strands escaped like a spindrift halo round her head.

'When will I be likely to find your neighbour at home? I've called several times without success.'

'The owner's been in a care home for about a year.' She lowered her voice. 'Dementia, you know. I go to see him, but sometimes he doesn't recognize me. Sad, isn't it?'

I nodded. 'Ah, that accounts for the state of the garden, then. So nobody lives next door at present?' A seemingly casual question on which a lot depended.

She shook her head. 'After Mr Brand went into the care home, I saw the notice in Selkirk's window that his house was available for rental. Selkirk's don't seem to have had any interest, though.' She produced secateurs from her cardigan pocket and snipped off the fluffy seeding head of an aster. 'The man from the property company comes twice a week on Tuesdays and Fridays to check everything's all right, but they haven't done *anything* about tidying up that mess of a garden. Dandelions! The seeds get *everywhere*.'

I was on the right track. The indications were good that the house might have been converted into a cannabis factory: the house was up for rental and Selkirk Properties made the frequent visits needed to check on the plants and the live-in cannabis gardener.

The secateurs snipped fiercely at another aster head. 'I was going ask Selkirk's man this week if there was a plan to do something about the garden, but missed him both times. Can't keep looking out of the window all day, can I? I've got other things to do.'

To keep up appearances I scribbled a few notes. 'Well, you've been very helpful, Mrs McRoberts.' I tucked the form under the clip on my board. 'Would you happen to know of any other owners in the area who might be interested in putting their properties up for holiday let?'

She thought for a moment, then shook her head. 'None in this street, anyway, but when I do see Selkirk's man I'll be sure to tell him the Tourist Board was making enquiries.'

I managed a smile. 'That's very good of you, but it won't be necessary. I've finished the survey now, so I'm off to Anstruther and I'll call in at Selkirk Properties while I'm there.' With a wave of my hand from the garden gate, I walked briskly off down the road.

If the Spinks organisation got wind of someone asking questions about number 32, they'd instantly abandon the property. It was essential to pay a visit before Tuesday.

*

The first indication that there was something amiss at the Lodge was the sight of the police car drawn up in the forecourt. My first thought was that I had been careless, left signs that an intruder had been in Nicola Beaton's apartment, thus putting her on her guard.

Apprehensively I mounted the shallow steps to the front door, but there was no police officer in the entrance hall, only the Major in full rant again, holding Steve Collins at bay outside the office. I tried to sneak past, but St Clair caught sight of my reflection in the office window and swung round.

'Ah, Miss Dewar-Smythe. The police are here. They would like a word with you.'

I *must* have been seen tampering with Beaton's French doors.

'Yes?' I said, lips dry, hoping my expression was one of mild enquiry rather than alarm.

Steve Collins stepped forward. 'I'm afraid there's been a break-in and theft from—'

'My apartment!' I cried, shock and alarm feigned, until it suddenly struck me that my apartment was vulnerable to anyone who possessed picklocks and it could indeed have been broken into because the photocopy of my passport in Selkirk Properties' office files had been a time-bomb waiting to explode. If Spinks had recognized the photo, he'd have searched my apartment for notes, papers, and laptop files. My laptop was encrypted and in the safe, but Gorgonzola, trapped in the apartment, would have been at his mercy. At the thought, I felt the colour drain from my face. He would have killed her as a warning that I was next, before arranging a little 'accident' for me.

'My cat—!' I whispered and sank onto one of the settees.

'No, no, it's nothing to do with your cat,' Collins said hastily.

From the Major, a muttered, 'Unfortunately.'

'No, no,' Collins repeated, embarrassed. 'I'm sorry if I gave you the wrong impression, Ms Dewar-Smythe. The theft was from apartment 6. Mr Warburton's camera and a portfolio of photographs have been stolen. Worth a considerable sum, I believe. The police want to ask if you saw anything suspicious.'

'Or anyone acting suspiciously,' the Major snapped. 'As Warburton's apartment is on the first floor, the felon must have walked straight past your office, Collins. Theft from one of our apartments is an indefensible breach of security, that's crystal clear! An *indefensible* breach of security, in my opinion a court-martialling offence that—'

'I don't know if I can be of any help,' I cut in, feeling sorry for Collins. 'You see, I've been out since about half past eleven this morning.'

'The ... er ... incident,' Collins cast a quick sideways glance at the Major, 'was discovered when Mr Warburton returned from Anstruther in the early afternoon. In a terrible state, he was. I called the police immediately—'

'Closing the stable door, man!' St Clair barked. 'The point I'm making is that the lock of the apartment wasn't forced. And how, therefore, did the felon gain entry?' He looked from one to the other of us, and when we both looked blankly back, delivered the answer with the triumph of a conjurer producing a rabbit out of a hat. 'Your master key, Collins! And *that* is kept in your office.' His eyes narrowed as if sighting down the barrel of a gun. 'The question being, is it there *now?*'

Steve Collins reeled back as if he'd taken a bullet in the chest. 'Well ... er ... of course, er ... naturally.' Then as the Major's eyes bored into him, he stuttered, flustered, 'I ... I ... assume so, I ... I ... haven't looked....' His voice trailed away.

He rushed into the office with the Major in close attendance, eager to find proof of negligence. I lingered in the doorway, keen for my own reason to find out if the master key was in its rightful place. We watched as Collins fished round desperately in a drawer.

The Major pounced. 'Missing, eh?'

'Not at all. Here it is!' Collins held up a key.

'Harrumph!' Far from being put out by his theory having been shot to pieces, the Major opened an offensive on another front. 'Can you assure me that the office was not left unattended at *any* time this morning, even for a few minutes?'

Collins flinched. 'Well ... er....'

'*Exactly*. A lamentable lapse in security. This will have to be reported to the police.' He marched off in the direction of apartment 6.

All too conscious of the picklocks nestling in my pocket, I said, 'I think the Major's got it wrong. It's not *likely* that a thief would know that a master key was in that drawer.' I moved away. 'Tell the police I'll be in my apartment if they think it's necessary to interview me, but, as I said, I've been out from mid-morning till now, and before that I didn't see anyone suspicious.'

That was true, if I didn't take into account the malodorous Bert Mackay. But at that point there didn't seem to be any connection between him and the break-in to Terry Warburton's apartment and the theft of his camera and photos.

Having ascertained to my relief that all was well with my own apartment, I fed and watered G and went off to the residents' lounge in search of some sustenance for myself. Though none of the other residents had yet put in an appearance, the table lamps were lit and flames were licking at the logs in the fire basket with a lively spit and crackle. I took my time over my snack in the hope that I'd encounter Clive Baxter. Was he a bona fide antique dealer with an interest in Wemyss Ware? After my meeting with him, I'd looked up that Fife pottery on the internet. The most highly prized Wemyss Ware items seemed to be pre-1930 cats and pigs painted with cabbage roses. If he came into the lounge, I would feign an interest in that type of pottery, make some notes and check out his answers. I was finishing my snack when I heard the door open and glanced up to see, not Baxter, but burglary victim Terry Warburton. I waved him over.

'I heard about the theft, Terry. You look as if you need a drink.' I pressed the button to summon the barman. 'It's on me.' As he sank down onto the settee beside me and put his head in his hands, I studied him. 'That bad, eh? What exactly was taken?'

'Everything! The whole bloody lot! My new camera, the portfolio of fifty photographs I'd got ready for an exhibition in Edinburgh, even the images I took last week of boats in Anstruther and Pittenweem.'

I watched him toss the drink back in one. I said slowly, 'Don't you think it a bit odd that a casual thief would steal photographs? A camera, yes, but photographs? To *you* they're valuable, but an exhibition-size picture is not the sort of thing you slip to somebody in a public bar for cash.'

'Who bloody cares! They've gone.' He passed a hand wearily over his face.

'I was just thinking that if we could work out *why* they'd been taken, we might get a line on *who* had taken them.'

'I appreciate your concern, Vanessa, but—'

'Just *listen*, Terry. It has just occurred to me' (well, five minutes previously it had, as I was munching on my snack) 'that a casual thief takes advantage of open doors and windows. Agreed?' He nodded reluctantly. 'But this was no casual thief because he obviously used a master key. Or a picklock if he was a professional,' I added – speaking as one myself – 'so every one of us who was out could have been burgled, including me, but he targeted you and you alone. Has anyone else reported anything missing? No. And the point I'm making is,' I said, echoing the Major's words to Collins, 'that you must have had in your possession something *in particular* that he wanted. And I don't mean that he broke in just to get the camera. If so, he wouldn't have taken the photographs. Yes ... it was those he was after, and he took the camera because he wanted a picture that might be on the card and didn't know how to remove it from the camera.'

He stared at me. 'I'm impressed, Van. You really know how to figure things out. Well, the bugger will be disappointed.' For the first time since he'd come into the lounge, he smiled. 'You see, there *wasn't* a card in the camera. I have it here.' From the top pocket in his shirt he produced a small plastic case. 'There was space left on it for only half a dozen more shots, so I put a new card in.' He brightened. 'Wait a mo, the computer was too big for him to carry away, and the portfolio images are on the hard drive. All I've got to do is print 'em out again. Expensive, but–' He leapt to his feet, hoisted me up and whirled me round in a little dance. 'Should have thought of that, shouldn't I?' He pressed the service button. 'Drink's on me, this time.'

As we waited for the barman to come and take our order, we sat in silence for a few moments, lost in our own thoughts. Bert's appearance at the Lodge and the disappearance of Terry's photographs was too much of a coincidence. After his departure from Beaton's apartment, I'd assumed he'd left the building, but what could have been easier than for him to slip upstairs to apartment 6? If he *had* come with the express purpose of stealing the photographs, his encounter with Nicola Beaton at the bus stop had to have been pre-planned so that he could pass Collins's office in the company of a resident, and thus receive no more than a passing glance. It all fitted, but how could Bert have been sure that Terry would be out?

The next moment Terry supplied the answer. 'There's one thing bothering me,' he said suddenly. 'And that is, how did the swine know I'd be away in Anstruther delivering the photos that Selkirk Properties had asked me to bring in for their window display?'

'He probably just took a chance.' I shrugged, resisting the impulse to shout, *That's it*! 'But coming back to the reason for him stealing the photographs ... there must be something there that someone doesn't want anybody to see. When we've finished our drinks, do you fancy doing a little detective work?'

'To see if we can spot anything, you mean? Sure thing! Anything that might help me nail the bastard!'

'Two eyes good, four eyes better,' I grinned.

Terry opened up the photo folder on his laptop and the screen filled with thumbnail-sized pictures.

'Let's narrow it down,' I said, 'to photos that include people, even if they're just in the background.'

An hour later, Terry had printed out twenty that fell into this category. I kept up the pretence and slipped them into an envelope. 'I'll pass these to a detective friend in the local force and tell him our theory, perhaps he might see a connection that's not obvious to us.'

The 'detective friend' I had in mind was Attila. My first 'cleaner's report' would voice my suspicions that Selkirk's gang was behind the break-in and give my reasons. The snag was that if I also sent him the photos, Attila would ask awkward questions about how, as a mere cleaner, I'd obtained them. So, as none of the photographs appeared to be of any interest to HMRC or myself, there'd be nothing lost if I didn't actually send them but kept them safe.

I wandered over to the windows. When I'd first met Terry, he'd told me about the wonderful view from up here, and he was right. In the fading light, a V of geese were arrowing their way across a pewter and silver sky tinged peach on the horizon by the afterglow of the sunset. The curve of the beach itself was obscured by a low sea mist that had rolled in over the edge of the golf course swallowing up Gorgonzola's bunker.

'Just look at this sky, Terry. If I was a photographer, I'd be snapping away till the memory card was full.'

Terry joined me at the window. 'I got a *sensational* shot a couple of weeks ago – a fishing boat silhouetted against a huge full moon rising above the horizon. It's still on the card.' He pulled it out from his shirt pocket and inserted it in the printer. 'It was one of the last shots I took, so we'll work backwards.' As the thumbnail images began to appear on the screen, he clicked on one to increase its size. 'Here's the pic I took of your cat and the seagull. I'm rather proud of it. Doesn't matter how experienced you are, wildlife photos need so much luck. You've got to be in the right place at the right time.' He pressed a button. 'Here's the print of her I promised you.'

A *whirr whirr* from the printer and in my hands was Gorgonzola's leap, immortalized on photo paper.

He enlarged another image. 'And this is the photo I was telling you about.'

The pale globe of the moon filled the screen, the grey patches of its 'seas' a striking piebald pattern on the cream disk. Just off centre of the pale circle was a fishing boat, the outline as sharp as a Victorian black-ink silhouette. No riding lights, no cabin lights. In the bottom right hand corner, on the edge of the shimmering path thrown by the moon across the water, and only visible because I was looking for it, was the tiny black dot of a rowing boat.

'*Wow*! That's a prize-winner.' And it was – not only for its breath-taking beauty, but also because I was in no doubt that this was the activity that Bert's boss, Spinks, wanted kept under wraps.

When Terry had first hovered the cursor on the thumbnail image, the time the picture had been taken flashed up on the screen: 02:35. And according to Mackay, the next consignment was due on Monday morning, two days from now.

Well before 02:35 I'd be down on the shore.

CHAPTER ELEVEN

That night I should have slept the sleep of the well content, knowing that I'd made considerable progress, but as the hours ticked by I stared at the patterns cast on the ceiling by the moon, watching the elongated rectangles of the multi-paned window moving infinitesimally slowly across it.

I tried counting up the successes of the day: I'd identified the neglected house as a cannabis factory; I'd justified the expensive gamble of taking up residence at the Lodge – as a Mrs Mop I'd never have got wind of Beaton and Mackay's little scheme; I'd established that Mackay and the intruder in Greg's house were one and the same; and I'd proved to my own satisfaction a connection between the ship in the bay and Selkirk Properties.

But satisfaction didn't bring the reward of sleep. The green display on the alarm clock crept relentlessly on: 00.00 ... 01.00 ... 02.00.... Still I tossed and turned. Several times I was on the point of drifting off, only for Gorgonzola to plod restlessly up and down the bed, finishing off the parade by clambering over the barrier of my legs and casting around, it seemed forever, for the perfect spot to settle down. At 02.16 I lost patience.

'For goodness sake, G!' I snapped. 'Keep *still*. Do that *once* more and....'

And what? I was trying to think of an effective threat, or any threat at all, when the whole diabolical ritual started up again.

'Hell and *damnation*!' I shrieked. 'That's it! I'm putting you *out*.' I flung back the duvet, picked her up none too gently, flung open the bedroom window and chucked her outside. 'There! That'll teach you!' I slammed the window shut.

It was only as I watched her strolling nonchalantly off in the moonlight, tail erect, tip twitching, that I realized that I'd been duped. Fed up with being cooped up all day, G's tactics had been directed to achieving this very end – a fancy-free, on the loose, nocturnal outing. So that I could retrieve her before the other residents would be up and about, I sighed, reset the alarm for 5.15 a.m. and fell into an uneasy slumber disturbed by disagreeable dreams only half-remembered when I awoke.

An unrelenting *beep beep beep* jolted me awake. I silenced the alarm and sank back against the pillow. Brain dulled by lack of sleep, it took me a few moments to register that G wasn't in her usual position curled up at the end of the bed, and a bit longer to recall what had happened during the night. When the realization hit me that she could be up to *anything* – hunting for koi, creeping into Nicola Beaton's apartment via a left-open window, using a bunker as a catty loo – I sat bolt upright, swung my legs over the edge of the bed and staggered over to pull the curtains aside and look out.

It was barely light: bands of cloud smudged a pale grey sky over a gunmetal grey sea. Bleached of colour, the grass of the golf course sparkled with dew in the first rays of a weak sun peeping over the horizon. I'd hoped to be the first to get out there and catch her before anyone was about, but already a small tractor was busy on the fairway, a cone of light fanning out ahead of it.

I opened the window as an invitation to G. The air blowing in was damp and distinctly cool, an indication that warmer clothes than yesterday would be necessary. Gorgonzola had still not returned by the time I'd pulled on jeans, jersey and light jacket. I went through to the lounge and stood at the French doors, staring out. The sky in the east was now a fiery red, the gunmetal sea a slate grey. The tractor had drawn up beside a bunker at the far end of the course.

I opened the French doors and stepped outside. It was then that I noticed the paw prints in the dew. Ten minutes ago when I'd first staggered up from bed to look out of the window for G, those paw prints had not been there. They curved across the grass straight to the wall below my bedroom window before angling off at an angle of forty-five degrees in the direction of the forbidden bunker. She'd returned, seen the open window, the invitation to come in, and spurned it.

Muttering to myself, I eyed the line of cat prints. The greenkeeper would have been put on alert by the Major to report any sign of feline mess, but the tractor was still at the far end of the course. Armed with a plastic carrier bag to scoop up any evidence of bunker pollution, I set off across the fairway.

She'd walked round the edge of the bunker and then.... I stared down into its depths, expecting to see signs that G had visited. But there was no scratched-up sand or even paw prints, just freshly raked lines in a neat pattern. I was too late. My heart sank. Earlier, when the tractor had passed this way, the greenkeeper must have seen the disturbance and tidied it up. He'd be sure to report the defiling of the bunker to the Major.

I glanced down the course towards the distant tractor. For a moment its light flashed bright as it performed a U-turn. It paused at a bunker, engine idling while the driver got down from his cab and jumped down into the bunker to rake the sand.

Gorgonzola must have been here no more than ten minutes ahead of me, but there was no sign of her. She was proving harder to track down than I'd envisaged. As the sun warmed the air, the paw prints in the dew were fading, barely visible as they headed for the next bunker. Was she crouched down in there hiding from me? I strode forward, ready to pounce. Not there.

I looked down the course at the tractor. It was nearer, and had once again paused at a bunker, its light switched off now that it was fully daylight. I turned away from the bunker, then turned back to study it with renewed interest. Why had the sand in *this* bunker not been groomed despite it being only a few feet from the raked one? But finding Gorgonzola was more important than speculating on the reason why this one had been left unraked. From time to time casting an anxious glance at the windows of the Lodge, I trotted on up the fairway following the ever-fainter line of prints towards a small pavilion with a veranda and a bench seat.

I didn't spot her at first. It was only when I got nearer that I saw Gorgonzola, lazily *couchant* on the veranda rail. When she was sure that I'd seen her, she yawned an unrepentant yawn, exposing sharp eye-teeth, expressive of, 'About time too. What's taken you so long? While *you* were snoring in your bed, what do you think *I've* been doing?'

A red mist of fury rose before my eyes. 'I know *exactly* what you've been doing. You've been using the bunkers as catty loos, probably visited each and every one of them. Come here *at once.*'

I lunged forward, but she was too quick for me. My hands closed on empty air. One moment she was on the rail, the next, her hindquarters were disappearing round the corner of the pavilion. Grinding my teeth,

I darted after her in time to see her nudging wider the open door of a small windowless hut. She disappeared inside.

'Gotcha now!' I cried, rushing forward.

At the hut door I stopped. From the darkness came the unmistakable croon of drugs detected. I put out a hand and pushed gently at the door. Daylight spilling through the widening gap revealed the usual tools and bags of fertiliser found in any greenkeeper's hut. And G prowling the interior crooning gently. Without pausing at any one spot to indicate the presence of drugs, she came back to sit at my feet. This told me that drugs had been here recently, but that they had been moved elsewhere. Could it be to that so carefully raked bunker?

The noise of the engine, once distant, was now much louder, *very* much louder. The tractor must be very close to the pavilion. The open hut door should have been a warning that the greenkeeper intended to return. An experienced agent like myself shouldn't have made such an elementary mistake.

I made a grab for G. Misunderstanding my intention, she gave a squeak of outrage and retreated back into the hut, leaving me no choice but to abandon her. I'd only seconds to get away. Five strides took me round the side of the pavilion. I saw the nose of the tractor coming into sight on the far side just as I reached cover, but there was no shout to indicate I'd been seen. I bent down, pretending to examine my shoe in case suspicious eyes were watching from the direction of the Lodge. I heard the engine note slow to an idle.

'Bloody cat! Gerrout of there!' The sharp sound of a thrown stone striking wood.

The hut door slammed. A few moments later, the tractor's engine note picked up and by the time it came into sight heading back down the course, I was sitting on the veranda bench shading my eyes against the sun and staring out across the bay, outwardly relaxed, mind busy.

I'd been so exhilarated about finding out *where* the cannabis packages were being stored until they were uplifted by the boat, that I hadn't given much thought about how they had got from the cannabis factory to the bunker. Now, thanks to G, it was clear. Transport was by tractor to the hut and then to the bunker. No one would have thought it strange to see the tractor grooming the course in the half-light of dawn.

Unsure of her reception, a tentative mew announced G's arrival. Guiltily I held out my arms, then patted my knee.

'Come up here, you clever girl.'

She twined herself round my leg, then leapt onto my lap and curled up. I stroked her soft fur.

'A good night's work there, G,' I murmured in her ear. 'All is forgiven. But not forgotten,' I added, stifling a yawn.

When I got back to the apartment, Gorgonzola retired to bed – my bed, that is – and settled down to make up for lost sleep. I fought off the temptation to join her. I couldn't afford that luxury. Today being a Sunday, there was an opportunity for the public to walk round the famous Old Course at St Andrews. I'd go there: Spinks's obsession with the sport could mean that there was the slimmest of slim chances I might spot his lanky figure on one of the courses. Even at a distance I'd be able to identify that distinctive swing seared on my memory since that mission when he'd attempted to kill me with a lethal drive of a golf ball. Even if I didn't spot him, it wouldn't be a wasted journey: on the tour of the Old Course I'd hear stories about famous golfers that I could bring into conversation with caddies. When I sounded them out about their American golfing clients, I'd have to have some knowledge of golf at St Andrews.

As I carried my breakfast tray from the lounge back to the kitchen, I saw that a communication from Collins had been slipped under my front door. It concerned the weekly cleaning of the apartments or, more accurately, the non-cleaning of the apartments.

Dear Residents,
I regret there was no cleaning service yesterday. This was due to circumstances beyond my control. Rest assured that the matter is receiving my most urgent attention. Steve Collins, Manager

Agatha Sweeney had messed up, if that was the appropriate term, and I, DJ Smith, didn't care a damn – till it dawned on me that the words 'urgent attention' meant that Collins had been on the phone complaining to the supply agency. The non-appearance of cleaner Agatha Sweeney would eventually come to Attila's ears. Well, sufficient unto the day the evil thereof. Perhaps by then I'd have nailed Spinks and identified Selkirk's cannabis factories.

But it was only half an hour later that the subject of the missing cleaner came up again. As I left the apartment I heard a raised voice in the entrance hall. Maxine St Clair was on the warpath.

'... no cleaner yesterday and no prospect of one, it seems. It just won't do, Collins, it won't do at all! The Major is furious that despite paying a service charge, he had to do the cleaning himself.'

A soothing murmur from Collins.

Maxine was not pacified. 'You've got it in hand, you say. That's all very well, but when can we expect *results*, that's what I want to know?'

Though there was little chance of sneaking by unnoticed, I made a beeline for the front door, trying to look as if I had some urgent business in hand.

An imperious, 'Ah, Vanessa, a moment if you please!'

It was Maxine's unexpected use of my first name, an indication that she wanted some kind of favour, that brought my headlong rush to a halt. I crossed the hall toward them.

She waved Collins's letter like a rallying banner on the battlefield. 'Cat hairs on the carpet and the soft furnishings must be a *big* problem for you, Vanessa, so I'm sure you'll support me in demanding—'

Collins raised his eyes heavenwards in exasperation. 'As I've been *telling* you, Mrs St Clair, I had *firm* assurances from the supply agency that the new cleaner would start yesterday. Unfortunately, she let us down.'

'Tut, tut. One can't rely on staff, nowadays, can one?' I said, successfully suppressing the slightest trace of guilt. 'But I expect that Mr Collins got onto the agency straight away when he realized that the cleaner wasn't going to turn up.'

I flashed him a supportive smile, hoping that his reply would give me an indication of how much time I had left before I could expect an urgent encrypted text message from Attila on the lines of, 'What the *hell* do you think you are playing at, Smith? Report *at once*.'

'Well ... certainly ... I phoned as soon as I was aware of the situation.' Collins sounded decidedly shifty.

Maxine thought so too, for she pounced. 'And *when* exactly was that, Collins?'

Stung by her tone, Collins snapped, 'Look here, Mrs St Clair, I'd more important things on my mind yesterday than the arrival of a cleaner.' The words, 'a paltry matter like that' hung unspoken in the air. 'In the morning I had my hands full with an emergency, and in the afternoon there was—'

Her eyes narrowed. 'Emergency? What emergency? '

'If I hadn't dealt with the threatened leak in the apartment above you, Mrs St Clair, you would have had water through your ceiling.' This time he made no attempt to hide his irritation. 'I had to make a temporary repair and then phone around to get a plumber. *Naturally* I assumed the cleaner had arrived at the usual time and started work.'

'She would have arrived while you were upstairs, Mr Collins?' I put in.

He nodded.

Maxine was silent for a moment, then her collagen-enhanced lips pursed. 'You can't deny that at two o'clock I came to the office to inform you that the cleaner hadn't come to us—'

'You did indeed,' Collins snapped, 'but I'd managed to check with only one apartment as to whether the cleaner had been there, when I was called away to—'

'The burglary,' I supplied helpfully.

'Yes. Mr Warburton came rushing into the office shouting that he'd been burgled. And by the time *that* was all sorted out, it was too late to get in touch with the agency, as they close at five. Rest assured, I'll be on the phone first thing on Monday.' He turned away. 'Now, I have things to attend to, so if you'll excuse me....' He marched into the office and shut the door firmly behind him.

Maxine stared at the closed door. 'And *I'll* be down here, on Monday at nine to make sure you do!' She tossed her head, sending her long hair swirling round her shoulders, and flounced off to report to the Major on this unsatisfactory state of affairs.

Well, that was a bit of luck. The delay in informing the cleaning agency that Agatha Sweeney had not reported for duty had given me an unexpected twenty-four hour reprieve from Attila's summons back to base. His immediate reaction to my flouting of his orders would be to take me off the operation. The fuse had been lit. By tomorrow, I'd have to make a breakthrough that would convince him that I was justified in taking up residence at the Lodge.

As I came over the hill, my first sight of St Andrews was a thin line of grey sea and a distant cluster of steeples and grey roofs. A pale sun was shining on the fields on the far side of the Firth of Tay, but grey clouds hovered over the town itself. The car park on the shore was almost deserted. I put this down to the fact that on a Sunday people lie in bed late, or dally over the breakfast table with newspapers, or go to church.

A signpost pointed to *Old Course, New Course, Jubilee Course, Links Clubhouse*. St Andrews was a town whose very heart was golf: golf museum, golf hotels, golf shops clustered round the Old Course. I bought my ticket from the Old Course Golf Shop and joined the group waiting for the Sunday tour to begin. Red tractors with whippy yellow aerials were zipping around the vast expanse of grass doing whatever it is greenkeepers do; a few people were taking the chance of strolling across fairways usually out of bounds; and seemingly overcome by the magic of the holy ground, a man was kneeling on the billiard-table-smooth grass of the eighteenth hole, his head bowed to the turf in silent prayer. To the man wearing the badge *Tour Guide*, this was a familiar sight.

'He's just taking a photo of the hole.' The guide laughed. 'Americans, they're the most excited about playing on the Old Course. You'll see a lot of that kind of thing here. There's another thing you'll find only on the Old Course.' He pointed to a small grey car being driven straight across the fairway. 'You can't see it from where we're standing, but there's a one-way road there, Grannie Clark's Wynd, it's called. Just another little hazard for the golfer. If you land on it, you've got to play the stroke.'

A bit of a hazard for the driver too, I thought, as we set off with the guide. But as we walked the seventeenth hole, I saw that it wasn't only on Grannie's Wynd that the car driver was at risk. The dented bonnet and cracked windscreen of a car parked on the road nearby bore silent testimony to the imperfect aim of golfers.

For forty minutes, our group followed the guide round part of the Old Course listening to his anecdotes. I stood on the famous Swilcan Bridge where Jack Nicklaus and Arnold Palmer had waved to the crowds on their farewell appearance. At the seventeenth, I peered into the depths of the fearsome Road Hole bunker where a TV camera is set in its wall during championships to catch the failed wedge shots that lose the Open. I walked virtuously through The Valley of Sin, the final hazard before the eighteenth green. But neither then nor later did I see what I most wanted to see, and that was the tall figure of Hiram J Spinks.

What now? Outside the famous red sandstone building, the background to the eighteenth hole in postcards and TV broadcasts, I studied the little booklet I'd picked up in the golf shop. *St Andrews has a kaleidoscope of attractions waiting to be discovered – take time to explore.* I'd do just that, but first a cup of tea and slice of cake would be just the thing.

On the way to Market Street with its choice of cafés, I stopped to read the inscription on a sandstone needle, the memorial to the sixteenth-century Protestant martyrs burnt at the stake for their religion. Fiery-red, clear-yellow, and coppery-orange begonias and spiky red-leaved phormiums unsettlingly mimicked tongues of flame licking at the base. Men inflict such cruel deaths on fellow men and women.

I was about to move on when I paused. There was something familiar about the solitary figure sitting on a seat beside the wrought iron Victorian bandstand in the grassy hollow below. That unbecoming scraped-back hairstyle, those large earlobes elongated by the heavy silver earrings – it could only be Nicola Beaton. She closed a notebook, put it in her bag and stood up. Sensing eyes upon her, she turned round.

Better to appear open rather than shifty. I jumped to my feet and waved. 'Hello-o there, Nicola.' She looked up and for an instant stiffened. I picked my way down the slippery grass of the mound to where she stood. 'Here doing more research for your book, are you?'

She certainly wasn't pleased to see me. 'Er … yes. But what brings *you* here?'

Aware that she suspected that I'd been following her, I hastened to play the innocent. 'I've been on the Sunday tour of the Old Course walking round the last few holes. It's been the most *interesting* forty minutes.' I produced the souvenir scorecard with a flourish and sensed her relax. 'Have you done the tour yourself? I can thoroughly recommend it, if you can take time off from your research, that is,' I continued smoothly.

She shook her head, indicating either that she hadn't done the tour or couldn't spare the time.

I put the scorecard back in my bag. 'Now I'm ready for a cup of tea and a slice of cake. Would you like to join me?'

As I'd expected, she made an excuse – then her eyes flickered, shifty and calculating. 'Perhaps, after all, that's a good idea, Vanessa. We'll go for a cup of tea and you can tell me all about your plans for showcasing your sculpture at the Pittenweem Festival.'

I had mentioned that to only one person, Clive Baxter. So she had not only been researching the background of the Stewart kings, she had been investigating the background of a certain Vanessa Dewar-Smythe.

In case my face betrayed my thoughts, I rummaged in my bag for the tourist booklet with its map. 'Just show me on the map where we're going, and I'll know where to go for a cup of tea next time I come.'

Nicola neatly bisected her piece of carrot cake. 'And so, Vanessa, how far have you got with finding a venue for exhibiting your sculpture at the Pittenweem Festival this year?'

This was the latest of seemingly casual questions, each one testing my cover story as assiduously as ski patrols probe the piled-up snow looking for victims after an avalanche.

I had my answer ready. 'Well, I've been a couple of times to Pittenweem to get the feel of the place and trekked round venues on last year's and this year's programme looking for a suitable location,' I said, sipping my tea and absentmindedly chasing a crumb round my plate. 'But I must admit it was more difficult than I thought to find anywhere suitable.'

'Any success?' In another attempt to make her question appear merely conversational and my answer of merely passing interest, she let her gaze wander to a smudgy watercolour of the Old Course, one of a set of golf-related pictures on the far wall.

It would be easy for me to say something that would confirm her suspicions. Safest to assume that I'd been under surveillance while I took the leaflets round, while I spoke to Greg's neighbour and when I called on Jeannie McRoberts to reconnoitre the cannabis factory.

I looked round as if I didn't want anyone at the neighbouring tables to hear what I was about to say, then leaned towards her and lowered my voice. 'Can I let you into a secret?

She nodded, speculation in her eyes.

'I saw a notice in a shop window advertising for people to deliver leaflets round the town. I don't like to admit it, but I'm a little short of cash. I thought to myself, why not be paid while I do my research? So there I was, going round Pittenweem with a bag of leaflets to push through letterboxes and at the same time looking out for likely venues.'

This was greeted with a polite smile and evident disappointment. She probed again. 'Did you look at the places down by the harbour? The

Shores are where I'd choose, if I were you. There were half a dozen venues there last August and that's where the crowds are.' She made a show of concentrating on pouring tea into our cups, my reply seemingly of secondary importance.

So Greg's place had been under surveillance and I had been seen.

Again I had my reply ready. 'Yes, I did. I was thinking that near the harbour would be the best place to be. There are some really attractive fishermen's cottages on West Shore. I really fancied the one with geraniums in plant pots either side of the door. I tried to speak to the owners.' How would she react?

'More milk, Vanessa? She was outwardly calm, but the hand that passed me my cup trembled slightly.

I said with a sigh, 'But there was nobody at home, so I couldn't ask if they'd let out a room for the festival. There's probably a waiting list anyway, so I'll just have to keep looking.'

I expected to have to field another question, but she put down her cup, leaving her tea untouched, and checked her watch. 'We must do this again. But I must *rush*! I've just time to get to the bus station.'

I studied the bill to calculate her share. 'That'll be four pounds ea—' The last word died in my throat. She'd already gathered up her bag and pushed back her chair. Leaving me to look at the steam rising gently from her cup, she was gone.

From my seat at the café window I watched her hurry off along Market Street till she was lost to view.

I poured myself the last half-cup of tea from the pot and went over our conversation again. It seemed I was in the clear as regards being seen near the cannabis factory, for she hadn't asked a leading question about *that* location. No, that could be a dangerous assumption. Perhaps she couldn't think of a way of doing so without making it too obvious. I'd have to be very careful. I sipped my tea and stared into space.

'Excuse me, but if you've finished, can I ask you to vacate your table? Now that lunches are being served, we're getting very busy.' With an apologetic look, the waitress began clearing away the cups and plates.

I stood in the doorway of the teashop and consulted my guidebook. *Eleven golf courses are within ten minutes' drive of the town.* I had as much chance of finding Spinks as of scoring a hole-in-one. I might as well resign myself to failure. What a foolish idea it had been to think that I'd be able to track him down here in St Andrews. He could be playing on any one of the eleven courses.

But perhaps tracking him down was not as impossible as it seemed. Spinks would only consider pitting himself against the very best, the most difficult, of the golf courses. Since there was no golf on the Old Course on a Sunday.... With renewed hope I scanned the guidebook and ticked the three most likely courses to attract a man like him. According to the guidebook, the Jubilee was one of the toughest golfing tests in St Andrews, the Duke's was ranked as one of the top hundred courses in Britain and Ireland, and Kingsbarns had been voted seventeenth out of the hundred best courses outside America.

The nearest was the Jubilee, next to the beach. In fact I'd seen part of it on my walking tour of the Old Course. From the roof garden terrace of the clubhouse I'd be able to see who was playing the nearest holes. Perhaps my luck would be in. If not, I'd console myself with something from the bar.

It was while I was tracing my route on the map from the café in Market Street to the Links Clubhouse, that I made an interesting discovery. Nicola Beaton had rushed off without so much as a farewell nod, leaving me under the impression that she would have barely enough time to get to the bus station. So why had she set off in entirely the wrong direction for the bus station? Where had she *really* been going?

CHAPTER TWELVE

Not unexpectedly, there was no sighting of Spinks from the roof terrace of the Links Clubhouse and I was back at the Lodge by three o'clock, feeling more than a little dispirited. I'd been counting on having some success to counteract the effect of Collins's phone call to the cleaner supply agency. And I had only eighteen hours left to pull something out of the hat.

As it turned out, I had even less time than I thought, for just as I flung myself onto the sofa, I received a 'new message' alert. The sender was Attila. I selected 'View'.

Am arranging replacement....

He must somehow have got wind of the fact that I'd failed to turn up at the Lodge in my role as Mrs Mop. I was being taken off the case. But ... Collins wasn't due to phone the cleaning agency until *tomorrow*, so this message must be in response to the one I'd sent on Friday informing him of Greg's death. With a sigh of relief I brought up the rest of the message.

Carry on as instructed until advised. T.

That I wasn't 'carrying on as instructed' would be all too evident when the cleaning agency passed on the message from Collins. With a sigh, this time of resignation, I got up from the sofa and began to prepare G's next meal. If only I'd seen Spinks in St Andrews, that might have gone some way to make up for flouting Attila's orders. I stared unseeingly at the tin of salmon on the worktop, absentmindedly adding an extra chunk of salmon to G's bowl. On second thoughts, being the kind of man he was, Attila wouldn't have believed me even if I *had* seen Spinks. 'Delusion,' and 'obsessed after your failure to bring about Spinks's arrest two years ago' were the words he'd used when I'd told him I'd seen Spinks push Selkirk off the cliff on the Isle of May. Until I could deliver *proof* that Spinks was in Fife and that he'd taken control of Selkirk's cannabis factories, I was in deep trouble.

Thump. Goaded beyond reasonable self-restraint by my dilatory delivery of her very late lunch, Gorgonzola made an impatient four-paw landing on the worktop.

'*Off!*' I shrieked. 'Out of bounds.' I whipped her bowl down onto the floor. Which, of course, was just what she'd wanted me to do. While I watched her nuzzling daintily at the chunks of salmon, I planned a last-ditch attempt to redeem myself with Attila before that irate text message, due any time after 9 a.m. tomorrow.

My last chance to make a breakthrough and stay on the case would be during the early hours of tomorrow morning when the boat came into the bay to collect the packages, including Beaton's fake one. If I didn't get that evidence tomorrow, my only option would be to delay my confession as long as possible, perhaps by pleading that I had mislaid my phone. After all, something like that would be typical of a low-level operative assigned to looking for evidence in wastepaper baskets, wouldn't it?

At 1 a.m. on a night when the moon didn't rise, a shadow slipped out of the French doors of apartment 4. Me. With blackened face, in black neoprene wetsuit, black surfboard boots, black neoprene balaclava revealing only eyes and nose, I moved slowly, feeling my way. The light of a torch would signal my presence to the Lodge and to any boat out in the bay. I set off at an angle from the corner of the building, keeping out of sight of the many windows overlooking the golf course and the sea.

When I reached the cover of bushes, I stopped to glance back at the Lodge. All the windows on this side were dark. Except one. Light rimmed the bedroom curtains of Clive Baxter, the Wemyss pottery man, undoubtedly the source of Nicola Beaton's knowledge of my sculpting talents and efforts to get a venue at the Pittenweem Festival. Nothing necessarily suspicious in him passing on that information, of course. Naturally they could have discussed the newcomer when they met in the lounge, but it would definitely be worth investigating him in more depth.

Overhead the stars were bright pinpricks in the blue-black canopy of the sky. The *shushshsh* of waves washing up the beach to my right was loud as I crossed the far end of the golf course. My original plan had been to conceal myself on the edge of the beach, in the bushes where Terry Warburton had lurked to photograph the gulls and Gorgonzola, but that might be too far away to overhear anything that was said. Any surveillance had to be from the sea, hence the neoprene suit and the waterproof night-vision camera.

That jagged line of rocks, half-submerged at high tide, would provide excellent cover and be close enough to hear conversations and take photos. I'd slip into the sea and take advantage of the shallow Vs in the ridge to get a good view of the cannabis packages being loaded onto the boat sent from the *Selkirk Harvester*. In the dark water there was little chance of anyone spotting my head in its close-fitting black neoprene hood, and if they did, I was confident I'd be mistaken for a seal.

I pressed the backlight button on my watch. I'd taken twenty minutes to cover the four hundred yards to my present position on the edge of the beach. I hunkered down on the sand in the shelter of the ridge of rock and stared out to sea. Terry's photo had timed the entry of the boat into the bay at around 2.30 a.m. I settled back against the rock for a long wait....

... I stared out at the dark sea. On the horizon only the faintest differentiation of shade distinguished sky from sea. To the south-east, broken strings of twinkling lights marked the Lothian coastline. If it kept to schedule, the boat would be here in five minutes. I closed my eyes, concentrating on listening ... listening.... Long before a dark shape slipped into the bay, the first indication I'd have of the approach of the boat would be the muted beat of its engine. That would be the signal for me to take to the water.

Listening ... then I heard, not the expected murmur of a ship's engine, but alarmingly close, a short distance away on the other side of the ridge of rock, a cough followed by the whisper of feet on sand. I cursed my stupidity. I'd assumed that the *crew* would unearth the cannabis packages from the bunker and load them onto the boat, and that Bert, or the greenkeeper, or someone else from the Lodge, would keep well clear. In my line of work, assumptions can be fatal.

Berating myself for my stupidity and careful not to make a splash, I slithered into the sea, suppressing a gasp as the cold penetrated the neoprene suit, and swam out twenty yards to one of the V gaps where the ridge came down to within a few inches of the surface of the water. Gripping the rock, I angled myself to look towards the shore. A figure was making its way across the sand towards the water's edge. I waited, camera ready, toes supported on an underwater ledge.

From out at sea, faint but unmistakable, came the beat of a diesel engine. The beam of a torch flashed once, twice, marking the position where the figure on the sand stood waiting. The beat slowed as the engine was throttled back, a dark shape glided shorewards and seconds later came the rattle of the anchor chain. A hundred yards from shore the ship slowed and stopped. A small boat was lowered over the side and with a light splash of oars two men rowed towards the figure on the beach. I raised the camera and took a picture, and another as they pulled the rowing boat up on the sand.

As soon as the three men had disappeared over the rise of land between the golf course and the beach, I slipped round the rock. If the boat was the *Selkirk Harvester* and I managed to get a picture of the name on the bow, that should be enough to demonstrate to Attila that my residence at the Lodge had paid off.

I calculated that I had less than ten minutes, perhaps only five, before they came back to the beach with the cannabis packets. Swimming breaststroke – slow, but it avoided the betraying splash of the crawl – I started on the two hundred yards to the fishing boat. At fifty yards I still couldn't make out the name in the dark, but darkness would be no obstacle to the night-vision camera. Treading water, I peered through the viewfinder: dark superstructure, star-shaped patch on the hull, name on the bow *Selkirk Harvester*. Exultantly I composed the shot. Gotcha!

But I hadn't. Just as I pressed the shutter, a wave passed under the ship and the bow swung away. I didn't waste time cursing my luck. I turned in the direction of the bow to bring the painted lettering back into camera shot.

Something splashed into the sea beside me and a sudden painful blow on the back of my head pushed my face below the surface. The shock loosened my grip on the camera. I clutched at it but it was gone, spiralling down into the depths. Heart thumping, I lifted my head clear of the water. Bobbing on the waves in front of me was an empty beer can.

'Bloody seal!' The shout came from the *Harvester*.

Fishermen take illegal potshots at seals suspected of stealing fish from their nets, but I could assume that the *Harvester* wouldn't want to advertise its presence that way in the bay. Missiles hurled from the deck, however, could injure or kill just as effectively. I wasn't going to wait around to be a target. I dived down and swam back in the direction of the ridge of rock till forced to the surface, gulping in air. I blinked water from my eyes to check my progress. *Hell.* Underwater, I'd veered off to the left and was now between the boat and the shore.

Thump. A sharp pain shot through my shoulder. No empty can this time, a heavy blow. The missile sank without trace. Taking another gulp of air, I dived again. When my head next broke the surface, the ridge of rock was appreciably closer. I swam steadily on, hoping that at this distance the black dot of my head in the water would be invisible from the deck of the *Harvester*.

Hwhoooo Hwhoooo. A bird-like whistle from the beach was followed by a double flash of the torch. While I'd been concentrating on getting evidence on camera, they'd been wheeling packages down to the edge of the sea on some kind of trolley and were now in the process of loading them into the rowing boat. I was in an ideal position to witness it all, but without the camera I had no evidence to convince Attila.

The engine of the *Harvester* throbbed into life. Frustrated, I trod water and watched one of the figures hold the bobbing boat in position at the end of a rope while the others waded through the line of waves with the packages. The boat was low in the water, an indication of the weight of cannabis on board.

Five minutes later, as the rowing boat started back towards the Harvester, the lone figure on the beach called softly, 'Next pickup, Shell Bay.'

Something had been salvaged from tonight's setback. I had gained advance notice of the rendezvous. And since sound is amplified over water and carries over a great distance at night, I recognized the voice. The shadowy figure standing on the beach was Clive Baxter.

CHAPTER THIRTEEN

TRRRRRRINNNNNNGG. The bell rang for the second round of the boxing match.

'Seconds out! Box!' The referee, the Major in full military regalia, medals glinting under the strong lights, signalled for us to begin.

Attila bounded out of the red corner, gloves punching the air. In the blue corner I heaved myself reluctantly off my stool, my shoulder stiff and sore from the covert jab in the back during round one when we were in a clinch and the referee was engaged in polishing his medals.

We met in the middle of the ring. 'Take *this* for putting Gorgonzola into the kennels.' My unexpected southpaw jab followed by a left cross knocked his spiked brass helmet askew. 'Sting like a butterfly, float like a bee!' I cried triumphantly, dancing round him in my lightweight neoprene suit.

TRRRRRRINNNNNNGG. 'End of round.' The Major motioned us to our corners.

Attila grinned and punched me hard below the belt.

'*Oof,*' I gasped.

The Major thrust his face close to mine. 'Foul, you bounder!' To emphasize the point, he poked me several times on the chest with his finger, then raised Attila's gloved arm aloft in victory.

'Objection!' I whimpered.

'Overruled. A clean-cut case, clean—'

'Cleaner! Hullo, anybody there!' The voice from my hallway punctured the nightmarish dream as suddenly as a pin stuck in a balloon.

Jolted awake, my eyes flew open to see Gorgonzola standing on the duvet, paw raised to tap my stomach.

'Cleaner.' The voice called again. 'Anyone at home?'

I sat bolt upright. 'Just a moment.' I pushed G away and, groggy with sleep, stumbled across to the wardrobe, groped for my faux-designer robe and shrugged it on.

I went out into the hall. Scrutinizing me through steel-rimmed glasses was a round ball of a woman, muscled arms holding a bucket, squeezable foam mop and a plastic sack. Her mousy-brown hair was gathered back with an elastic band into a pert embryo ponytail, 'scarce a stump', like the mare's tail in Burns's poem *Tam o' Shanter* after the witches had torn off most of it. The cleaner's sallow complexion and the yellow of her tabard-style uniform were an unfortunate combination. Embroidered over her left breast in pale blue was the logo Spick 'n Span Kleening Services.

Still half-asleep, I said slowly, 'You're the new cleaner?'

'That's right, ma-dum.' The accent was uneducated, but I wasn't fooled. This was the replacement Agatha Sweeney, sent by Attila.

Having made her assessment of me, she lowered her eyes, but not quickly enough to hide the intelligence behind them.

'I didn't expect you *quite* so early.' I frowned, trying to judge what time it was from the sliver of daylight visible through a gap in the curtains. How could the agency have responded so quickly to a phone call from Collins?

'It's twelve o'clock, ma-dum.' She banged down her bucket, more than a hint of reprimand in her tone. 'Where would you like me to make a start?' My apartment wasn't going to escape her scrutiny.

'The lounge, start on the lounge.' As the cleaner picked up her bucket, Gorgonzola seized the opportunity to slip past me and make a dash for the unguarded front door. 'Don't let the cat out!' I cried.

Reacting with surprising speed for one of her bulk, she thrust out a beefy leg and thumped down her mop to block G's escape. Foiled, G made for the kitchen, pausing only to turn her head and stare balefully in my direction. Well she might. Dead to the world, I'd slept for eight hours. As a result she'd been forced to resort to the cat litter tray and her breakfast was an unforgivable six hours late.

'Thank you, er ...'

'Mandy.' The slight pause before she replied was possibly because she wasn't yet used to her cover name.

In search of the contents of the wastepaper basket, she headed purposefully for the lounge with her bin bag.

'Just do the lounge today, Mandy. You'll find the vacuum in the hall cupboard. Don't bother with the bedroom and the kitchen.' I headed for the shower, confident that she wouldn't find anything to blow my cover. My laptop was in the safe and I'd slipped my phone into the pocket of my robe. I vanished into the bathroom, leaving the substitute Agatha Sweeney to her poking and prying.

I lifted my damp wetsuit out of the shower cabinet, hung it on the back of the bathroom door and turned on the shower. If I were undercover agent Mandy, I knew what I would do. I put my ear to the door and waited. Barely audible above the hiss of the water, stealthy footsteps passed the bathroom door. She was taking advantage of the golden opportunity to search my bedroom, and after that the kitchen. Turning off the shower would give her enough warning to move back to the lounge and whip out a duster. I'd give her plenty of time for snooping. For ten minutes I abandoned myself to the soothing effect of the hot shower until the chilly waters of the Firth of Forth were a distant memory.

As I opened the bathroom door, the rattle of the door handle was her cue to appear in the lounge doorway, duster in hand.

'Since I'm only doing the lounge today, would ma-dum like me to spend the extra time vacuuming up the cat hairs on the sofa?' From the tone and wrinkled lip she might have been offering to wipe up Gorgonzola's sick. Mandy obviously had little affection for cats.

'That'll be fine.' I went into the bedroom and closed the door.

How good an agent was Mandy? Her dopey appearance was no guide. I stood surveying the room. As a practised snooper myself, I was looking for those tell-tale signs of disturbance only visible to the skilled eye. How well had she done on the little test I'd prepared for her? Well, but not quite well enough. The pillow was in the same position on the bed, but no longer bore the indent of my head; the wardrobe door, left some inches ajar after my half-blind groping for the robe, was now open only a crack; and a drawer in the tallboy jutted slightly out of alignment with the others. She had a bit to learn. Somebody on the alert for snooping would notice such inconsistencies. I could only hope that she would be more careful with Baxter and Beaton, both of whom might very well be on the alert.

When I went into the kitchen, G was pawing urgently at her upended bowl, the plaintive guilt-inducing mews artfully designed to pull at my heartstrings. The message was clear. Blighted hopes. Desperation. *Starvation.*

I filled her bowl and then mine, aware of the vacuum cleaner humming away in the lounge. I took my bowl over to the window, sat on the bar chair at the tall glass table and spooned up muesli, looking round the kitchen for signs that Mandy had been poking about here too. The lid of the metal pedal bin was slightly raised, a sign that it had been opened. She'd be looking for crumpled pieces of paper, hoping to come upon telephone numbers, addresses, or memos to myself. I put down my spoon and looked in the bin. The St Andrews café bill was no longer there. I lowered the lid, careful not to let it clang, and went back to finish my breakfast.

Gazing out over the golf course to the sea, the scene of last night's adventure, I took a last spoonful of muesli and leisurely set about spreading butter on a slice of toast. The vacuum's note faltered and picked up again. She was still busy – or was she? She might have left the machine running and slipped off to search the bathroom. Well, she'd not find anything suspicious there.

Halfway through my second slice of toast, the vacuum was switched off. A moment later there was a light tap on the kitchen door and I turned to see that Mandy and the vacuum cleaner had materialized in the doorway.

'That's me done. I'll be back on Wednesday, ma-dum.'

'Thank you, Mandy. Don't bother about the vacuum. I'll put it away.'

She clumped along the hall ahead of me, the heavy tread very different from the soft pad I'd heard passing the bathroom door.

As I was closing the front door, I said apologetically, 'I had a late night. I'll be a bit more organized on Wednesday.'

On my way back to the kitchen, I stopped short. Reflected clearly in the bathroom mirror was my wetsuit hanging behind the door. I shrugged. There was nothing particularly suspicious about that – unless … unless … she'd slipped into the bathroom, found the suit still damp and connected this with my foolishly unnecessary remark about having had a late night.

I pondered this as I sat at the window, a replete Gorgonzola comfortably settled on my lap and my tea cooling in the mug. '"Careless talk costs lives",' I sighed. Never, never, *never* say more than absolutely necessary, it was a cardinal rule in undercover work. And I'd broken it.

I tried to put myself in her place, read her mind. Agents are trained to make connections between seemingly unrelated pieces of information. She'd think, 'Maybe there's no connection with the remark the woman in apartment 4 made about having had a late night … that wetsuit might have been used earlier in the day for sailing … but there *could* be a link.' And that would be enough for her to mention it in her report to Attila. He'd ask for a description of me, that and the presence of the cat would be enough. I'd be recalled.

When things looked bleak, Gerry Burnside, the controller I usually worked with, encouraged his agents with the somewhat clichéd, 'To every black cloud there's a silver lining.' And there usually was, if one looked. So I set about looking … and found it: Mandy was snooping for HMRC. All I'd have to face would be a severe reprimand from Attila rather than a murderous attack by Spinks.

I had to acknowledge, however, that it wasn't much of a silver lining. Being taken off the case was the least I could expect. Not only had I wasted HMRC's valuable time, I'd wasted taxpayers' money by renting expensive accommodation at the Lodge.

It might be better to pre-empt her report and confess – well, not exactly *confess* – to put it somewhat more acceptably, somehow I'd disguise, camouflage, draw a veil over the fact that I'd *deliberately* ignored his orders. Tucking G under my arm, I went to the bedroom to retrieve my mobile from the pocket of the robe.

Too late, I remembered why I'd kept the phone switched off. A text message from Attila pinged into my inbox as if he had a hotline to my thoughts. I ran my tongue over suddenly dry lips.

I selected 'View.' The words leapt out at me from the screen. *Wherever you are, Smith, contact me IMMEDIATELY. T*

He'd sent the message only a minute ago. I sat down on the bed with a thump. Jolted from her semi-snooze, G wriggled out from under my arm and stalked up the bed with the obvious intent of curling up on the pillow. I made a half-hearted attempt to ward her off with my free arm, but sensing I had other things on my mind, she set about trampling herself a hollow and sank down into the forbidden territory.

I steeled myself and started to text. *Investigating factory in P. Will report soonest. S.* Yes, that should do the trick. It was deliberately ambiguous, implying that I was actually *in* the factory and that I didn't have time to say more.

I'd chickened out of telling him I was resident at the Lodge, but by shelving that problem, I'd just presented myself with a much more pressing one: the necessity to report shortly on the result of my investigation into the cannabis factory in Pittenweem. I'd have to go there without delay, tonight in fact.

CHAPTER FOURTEEN

sat in the car, two doors down from number 32. Two o'clock in the morning is a good time, I've found, for illegal explorations of properties: streets silent and empty, honest citizens deeply asleep, bedroom curtains tightly closed. The hazards of a passing patrol car or an insomniac householder cannot be discounted, of course, but on the whole I've encountered few problems. Which perhaps made me a little careless....

No lights were showing in any of the houses up and down the street. I eased open Jeannie McRoberts's gate and in my black outfit walked confidently up the garden path. An open and above-board demeanour is vital on such occasions: to act furtively would bring a squad car along in double-quick time if somebody on the way between loo and bed gazed out at the street. I waited to pull on the black balaclava and gloves till I'd gone round the side of the house. On my two previous visits I'd taken note that the division between the two properties was a somewhat rickety fence that would provide easy access to the back garden of number 32. A last check of Jeannie's curtained windows and I gripped the fence to hoist myself up. *CR-EE-EAK*.

Yap yap yap, yap yap yap. A burst of furious barking spiked the stillness of the night. A light flicked on in Jeannie McRoberts's upstairs bedroom. In one movement I was over the fence, crouching down, and peeping through a gap between the boards. Her bedroom curtains twitched and she peered out, her hair loosed from the confines of that old-fashioned bun. *Yap yap yap, yap yap yap*. A tiny Yorkshire terrier joined her at the window, its long coat shaking like a demented floor mop.

'*M-i-aaaa-oooow*,' I screeched, in the hope that it would take me for an alley cat warning off its rivals.

The sash window squeaked up, and above the frenzied *yap yap yap* I heard a quavered, 'Away with you, or I'll let Dandy loose.'

I dashed a handful of gravel against the side of the fence to simulate the hurried withdrawal of cat. This provoked another loud burst of high-pitched yapping, then with a last, satisfied *yip* the dog jumped down out of sight, triumphant that he'd seen off the hated enemy. The window squeaked down. Silence.

I let fifteen minutes pass before standing up and stealthily making my way through the long grass of the neglected lawn to the back door of number 32. Dandy and his mistress slept on. At first, the rear of the property seemed to be in complete darkness, but a closer inspection of the ground floor windows revealed thick blackout curtaining covering the windows. Threads of moisture on the inside of the glass and the tell-tale whirr of an extractor fan poking out of the wall above my head were signs that high-intensity sodium lamps were burning within.

I inserted my picklock in the first of three locks protecting the kitchen door. *Click*. The other two locks surrendered just as easily. As I pushed at the door I felt a slight resistance from the thick curtain hung behind it to prevent the escape of the pungently sweet smell of cannabis. I eased past the heavy folds of material to be met with blinding light and a blast of heat. A battery of powerful lamps hanging on chains from the ceiling shone down on the tooth-edged palmate leaves that filled the floor space from silver-foil-lined wall to silver-foil-lined wall. Worktops, oven, washing machine and fridge were islands in a sea of green. In the sink stood a five-litre pump sprayer of the kind keen gardeners use to administer insecticides or plant food. Shiny large-diameter aluminium tubing had been punched through the ceiling, and the room was loud with the hum of fans. The kitchen door had been removed to facilitate the movement of air, enabling me to see a river of plants flowing through to the hall and into the room beyond.

I wasn't going to take the chance that someone might come from outside to check that all the equipment was working, so I relocked the back door before stepping carefully through the plants and out into the hall. Each of the adjoining ground floor rooms had their complement of aluminium tubing, blower fans, tangle of electric cables and blazing lights. In the confined space, the heat and near hundred per cent humidity were overpowering. Wearing a black outfit, so essential outside to escape detection in the dark, quickly became a test of endurance as sweat trickled down my face and body. After a quick inspection of the rest of the house, I'd get out.

In place of broom, vacuum cleaner and ironing board, the hall cupboard held a hotplate and microwave on a shelf, and beside them a couple of cooking pots, chopsticks, and some packets of dried food printed with oriental lettering. As was frequently the case, the cannabis gardener must be Vietnamese or Chinese.

The top of the stairs was in darkness, but a rectangle of bright light on the wall of the landing was evidence that the upper rooms had also been converted into cannabis gardens. The younger plants and seedlings in propagating units would be up there, the ground floor being assigned to mature plants, some of which were coming into bud.

Suddenly from upstairs came a hacking cough and the gurgle of catarrh being cleared in the throat. It had been careless of me not to recall that the semi-slave gardeners live in and are not free to come and go. I heard the creak of a floorboard ... the shuffle of feet ... saw the shadow of a man thrown onto the rectangle of light on the wall at the top of the stairs.

Once he moved forward to the top of the stairs I'd be in plain view. Seconds stood between me and discovery. It would take more, much more, than those vital seconds to avoid crushing any plants in my dash for the back door, heave aside the blackout curtain, and fiddle with not one, but three locks. It was not the thought of being attacked that set my heart thumping. I was confident I could defend myself against one man. But once the gang was alerted to the presence of an intruder, they'd abandon the house, cover their tracks, and HMRC would be no nearer to linking the cannabis factory with the drug barons behind it.

What I desperately needed was a diversion. Perhaps if I were to.... Two strides took me back into the kitchen, giving me a few precious seconds out of sight from the top of the stairs. I picked my way across to the sink, careful not to crush any of the plants. Seizing the pump sprayer, I pointed the lance at one of the battery of lights, turned my face away, closed my eyes and pressed the trigger.

BANG. The accompanying blinding flash was visible through closed lids. I opened my eyes. Pitch-black. With the fans out of action, the silence was unnerving – and dangerous. Any sound I made now would announce the presence of an intruder.

I pulled out my pencil torch and shielding the narrow ray with my fingers, tiptoed silently to the back door, any sounds masked by the stream of curses coming from the man at the top of the stairs, now plunged into darkness. Once behind the blackout curtain, I played the beam on the locks and in ten seconds was relocking the door behind me.

To avoid disturbing the sleeping dog at number 33, I made my way back to the car by crawling through the straggly hedge separating number 32 from 31. Twenty seconds later I'd left the scene.

By 3 a.m. I was parking the car in the forecourt of the Lodge. I let myself into my apartment, reflecting how unforgivably careless I had been: I should have taken into account the strong possibility that in addition to Selkirk Properties' twice-weekly visits, there'd be a live-in gardener. I'd been fortunate indeed to get away with it.

Gorgonzola had again taken possession of the forbidden pillow, but I was too tired to remonstrate. I took a quick shower, swooped on her, changed the pillowcase and fell into a deep sleep that not even a petulant paw could disturb.

It was a faint scrabbling at the front door that woke me. I opened one eye and brought the alarm clock into focus. I'd been asleep for not much more than three and a half hours.

'You're not getting out *that* way, G!' I groaned. 'Stop–'

At that moment her face loomed between me and the clock, whiskers tickled my cheek, a rough tongue licked my forehead. I lay there, staring into her eyes, instantly fully awake. *Scrabble scratch*. If Gorgonzola wasn't making those noises, who was? Someone was using a picklock on the front door. It was even more unnerving when the noises stopped. Was someone even now creeping up the hall?

Shoving G aside, I swung my legs over the bed and looked round for a weapon. The only suitable object was the bedside lamp, but its flex ran out of sight behind the low base of the four-poster bed: impossible to unplug the lamp without moving the heavy bed.

I seized one of my trainers from the floor, took up position behind the half-open bedroom door and waited. Seconds passed … no stealthy movements … no sound of someone breathing. Nothing.

G stared at me, scratched vigorously at her ear, then padded out into the hall. From the kitchen came the clang of her bowl being upended and pushed about the floor.

I took a deep breath and let it out in a long sigh. There *was* no one in the hall. After the tensions of last night, I'd jumped to the wrong conclusion, added two and two and made five. Someone, however, *had* been out in the corridor. I put on my robe and opened the front door. An A4 sheet of paper had been neatly taped to one of the panels.

Have <u>some</u> consideration for your neighbours.
DO <u>NOT</u> SLAM CAR DOORS IN THE NIGHT!

The reprimand was written in red felt pen. It was unsigned.

A wave of rage swept over me. Yes, I'd come in at an unearthly hour of the morning, but I'd certainly *not* slammed the car door, or as the note implied, indulged in a noisy spree of door-slamming. Something brushed against my leg. I glanced down to see G gazing anxiously up at me, worried that I was about to go out and forget to feed her.

I bent down and tickled her ears. 'Whodunnit, G?'

The most likely candidate to have pinned up the notice was somebody whose apartment faced onto the forecourt – Clive Baxter or one of the St Clairs. My bet was that it had been Maxine. Yes, the St Clairs must have heard my car arrive at 3 a.m., but what if it had been *Baxter* who had pinned up the notice? I'd have to have a story ready if he had heard my car in the early hours. I tore the notice off and stuffed it into my pocket.

'Ah, you've seen my note.' I turned to see Maxine bearing down on me, the glint of battle in her eye.

I drew myself up to my full height under the faux silk, faux designer robe and addressed her in haughty Dewar-Smythe tones. 'I think you've pinned your notice on the wrong door, Mrs St Clair. I did come in very late, but I took *particular* care to close the car door *quietly* so as not to wake *anybody*.' And that was true. I certainly hadn't wanted to draw attention to my comings and goings.

She gave this a moment's thought, then swept on. 'Be that as it may! The Major's a very light sleeper, a necessity for a military man. He was out of bed and at the window just like that!' A snap of her fingers. 'And *this* time *you* were walking away from your car.' With a peremptory, '*If* there's another occurrence, you can be sure that I'll be making a formal complaint to Mr Collins.' She turned to go, then swung on her heel to glare down at Gorgonzola. 'Shoo, cat!'

She marched off along the corridor.

Thoughtfully I watched her go. Who else had slammed their car door in the night? I decided it wasn't worth going back to bed: I wouldn't sleep.

After I'd cleared the table of breakfast things, I spread out the Ordnance Survey map of Fife and looked for Shell Bay, the site of the *Harvester*'s next pick-up. My finger traced along the coastline south of Anstruther. Pittenweem ... Elie ... Earlsferry ... and a mile further on, Shell Bay. Access was either by a narrow road branching off from the main road down to a camping and caravan site on the sands; or on foot from Earlsferry via the Fife Coastal Path, marked by a string of red dots along the shore. I'd be sure to find guidebooks to that area in the Lodge's small library. No time like the present for some research.

I pushed open the door of the residents' lounge. It would be another hour before residents wandered in for morning coffee, so at this time of the day I had the place to myself. Dust motes danced in a shaft of sunlight that slanted through the large windows, releasing rainbows from the crystal prisms of the chandelier. On my previous visit to the lounge I hadn't investigated the library, which turned out to take the form of two bookcases, a standard lamp with fringed shade, and two stuffed-leather armchairs, their backs turned to the room to establish a boundary. For some, the library might have been a bit of a disappointment as most of the books were thin volumes devoted to the lives and achievements of historical figures connected with Fife: Mary Queen of Scots, the many kings by name of James, novelist Sir Walter Scott, architect Robert Adam.... But I found exactly what I was looking for on the next shelf – guidebooks covering the nearby areas of Fife, the Lothians and Edinburgh.

I selected *Along the Fife Coastal Path*. The map on the facing page of Chapter 5, *Largo Bay (Leven to Elie)*, confirmed that this section of the walk included Shell Bay. I settled down comfortably in one of the armchairs and started to read. Loud in the silence, the ormolu clock on the mantelpiece *tick tocked* the seconds away....

'Thinking of exploring the Coastal Path?'

I woke with a start. A shadow had fallen across the pages of the book open on my knee. I tilted back my head to see Clive Baxter smiling down at me from behind my armchair.

'Oh, oh yes, but I'm not a great walker. Any advice on an easy but interesting part of it?' Stifling an involuntary yawn, I held up the book, taking the opportunity to close it as I did so.

He came round to sit down on the other armchair. 'Had a late night?'

Not a casual question, the eyes behind the rimless glasses were watchful. Was he aware of my early morning arrival, or had he heard my altercation with Maxine?

When in doubt, tell the truth, a lie can be a trap. 'Yes.' I was unable to stifle another betraying yawn. 'I didn't get in till three o'clock.' But now he'd fish for information as to where I had been. And I didn't have a story ready.

Before I could say anything to divert him from that dangerous topic, he said, as if casually, 'Night club in St Andrews?'

A 'yes', and he'd ask which one. *Any* answer would dig me into a deeper hole. I waved a hand airily. 'A couple....'

Too late, I realized that might very well have made things worse. If he'd heard me leave at 1a.m. and return in two hours, my nightclub story didn't fit. Best thing was to change the subject and deal with the probability that he had seen the guidebook on my knee open at the pages dealing with the area round Shell Bay.

I said quickly, 'You know the region well. I've been wondering which way to walk along the Coastal Path. Do you think it's more scenic round Largo Bay or towards Pittenweem and Anstruther?'

'Oh definitely the two and a half miles from St Monans to Anstruther. There are fine views of the Isle of May and plenty of history you can read up about in that guidebook.' An answer that would keep me at a safe distance from Shell Bay.

'St Monans it is, then.' To divert him from returning to the topic of nightclubs, I set about probing his cover story of being an antique dealer. 'On your many visits to the area to search for Wemyss pottery, Clive, you must make some interesting finds?' Was there an almost imperceptible hesitation before he answered?

'It's mainly run-of-the-mill stuff, but if I come across something like a large cat painted with cabbage roses, I'll get five thousand pounds for it. Generally, it's the painted decoration that makes the difference....' He trailed off like an actor who has forgotten his lines and is desperately waiting for a prompt. In a getaway attempt, he pressed his hands down on the arms of the chair and began to lever himself to his feet.

Not so fast, I thought, and placed a restraining hand on his arm. 'Five thousand pounds! Wow! What Wemyss Ware decoration should I look out for next time I'm at a car boot sale?'

Reluctantly he subsided once more into the armchair. 'Er ... gorse and white heather are extremely rare.' Then more confidently, 'The decoration's usually cabbage roses, but the rarer the flower the higher the price. The dog rose is definitely more valuable.' He got up quickly, but not quickly enough to evade my next question.

'I know this is silly, but I presume a cabbage rose is called that because it looks like a cabbage – though not green, of course.' I giggled. 'But you can't say a dog rose is called that because it looks like a *dog*, can you! Pure clear yellow is my favourite colour. Have you found Wemyss pottery featuring a yellow dog rose?'

'On a previous trip, yes, but nothing this time. I've a picture I could show you, but I'm afraid I've got to dash … meeting someone....' He made for the door in what could only be described as a half-run.

I looked after him thoughtfully. Dog roses are usually pink, sometimes white. And from my research on Wemyss Ware I knew that the pottery featured pink dog roses, but not yellow ones. It seemed that Clive Baxter was almost as ignorant about Wemyss Ware as I was.

Just as I was congratulating myself that I'd caught him out, he turned at the door. 'Found that venue for your exhibition yet, Vanessa?'

I sighed theatrically. 'I'm beginning to give up hope. Looks like I'll just have to be a non-participant this year.' That should let me off the hook.

He delivered his bombshell. 'Cheer up! I've had a word with someone who says he can find one for you.'

'That's *wonderful*, Clive! Where?' I jumped to my feet, smiling broadly, heart sinking. I had nothing to exhibit.

'Haven't time to go into it now. See you later.' The door swung to behind him.

No longer in the mood for research, I returned the guidebook to the shelf. It looked like I'd have to put on some kind of exhibition after all.

Back in the apartment I set about composing the text message that would stave off an immediate summons back to Edinburgh. The report on my investigation of the cannabis factory would need careful wording. I'd have to send it before Attila's next furious message reached me – and every second might count. Deep in thought, I stared at Gorgonzola. She shifted uneasily under my gaze, no doubt recalling some as yet undiscovered act of which she knew I'd disapprove.

'That's it!'

At my self-congratulatory snap of the fingers, G's eyes widened, thinking I had read her mind. She wandered casually over to the doorway and disappeared – out of sight was out of reach.

Smiling, I reached for my phone. My previous text had given the impression that I'd sent it when I'd been on-site investigating. I texted Attila the address of the cannabis factory in Pittenweem, and added the message, *Whole-property factory with gardener. Selkirk Properties check it Tues and Fri.* Then I added the carefully chosen words that would prevent any further communication from him. *Under deep cover.* These three little words meant I had infiltrated the Selkirk organization and that any text message from him would endanger my life. However much he wanted to get in touch with me, his hands were tied. I pressed *Send.*

Only one thing could put paid to the breathing space I'd just won for myself. If Mandy had connected my foolish 'late night' remark with the wetsuit hanging in my bathroom, the occupant of apartment 4 would feature in her report on the residents at the Lodge. But she would want to confirm her suspicions. On her second visit tomorrow, she'd check for supporting evidence. That's what I would do myself.

So I set about providing an innocent explanation for the wetsuit. I did an internet search for 'watersports clubs Fife', looking for somewhere near at hand. It didn't take long. The nearby holiday resort of Elie fitted the bill, offering waterskiing, windsurfing and equipment hire. Minutes later, I was placing the print-out beside the telephone, where Mandy couldn't fail to see it when she arrived in the morning to do her cleaning.

In the event, I needn't have bothered.

CHAPTER FIFTEEN

Mandy, real name Pat Robertson, stared at the rain streaming down the windows of the bus. She'd look like a drowned rat by the time she'd walked up that long drive to the Lodge. Though Andrew Tyler had made it clear that a car was incompatible with her undercover role as a lowly agency cleaner, on a day like this she'd been tempted to disobey his instructions. But, of course, she hadn't. It didn't pay to get on the wrong side of Andrew Tyler, more than her life was worth! Through the arc cleared by the windscreen wiper she saw her stop approaching and pressed the button.

For a moment she stood watching the bus draw away, its wheels throwing out a curtain of spray. Cursing Tyler's nit-picking caution against her use of a car, she pulled up the collar of her coat, and head bent to shield her face from the driving rain, set off on the long trudge up the drive.

As a distraction from the raindrops trickling down her neck, she went over in her mind the report she would send in this evening. Tyler would be pleased with her: Monday's cleaning visit had proved fruitful. Already she'd identified one definite suspect, the man Baxter in apartment 3. A piece of luck that he'd been out, and lying there on the table had been his laptop, not protected by a password either. There'd even been a folder named *Selkirk*. Carelessness like that made her job easy. A file in the folder listed places and dates, a pity she hadn't had the time to copy it onto her memory stick. The sound of his key in the lock had been a real heart-stopper, but by switching on the vacuum cleaner she'd managed to cover up the chime of the laptop closing down. If he was out again today, she'd make sure to copy that folder.

And then there was the woman in apartment 4, the woman with the cat. The damp wetsuit hanging in the bathroom didn't mean anything in itself, of course. She looked the sporty type and could very well have been waterskiing the previous day. But in that case, the suit would have been almost dry. This, together with the remark the woman had made about having had a late night....

Absorbed in her thoughts, Mandy failed to register the soft purr of the engine as the car closed in on her from behind. With an accelerating roar, the car leapt forward. She spun round. Too late. Much too late.

A glimpse of the driver hunched over the wheel. Rimless glasses, black curly hair sprinkled with grey—

I stared at the rain streaming down the windows. Not a good day for walking round the harbour at Anstruther as I'd planned. Even G had made reluctant use of the litter tray rather than brave the deluge outside. But the bad weather was the chance to mug up on Shell Bay and the section of the Coastal Path from which Clive Baxter had so slickly diverted me.

'I'm going along to the residents' lounge, G. Pillows and worktops are Out – of – Bounds.' I emphasized each of the last three words with a shake of the finger. 'Agreed?'

One eye opened a slit and closed again, signifying, 'Maybe yes, or maybe no'.

'Yield not to Temptation, G,' I said firmly, and closed kitchen and bedroom doors. I had little confidence in her will to resist.

As I approached the lounge, Terry Warburton was coming down the stairs carrying an A3 portfolio under his arm.

'Morning, Terry. Those the photos for the exhibition?'

'Yep. I'm off right now to Edinburgh. Running late, got to rush.' With a parting wave, he headed for the front door.

I seated myself in one of the armchairs in the library corner and had just opened the guidebook at the page on Shell Bay, when I heard Maxine's voice raised in another complaint to the long-suffering Collins. With eyes on the text and ears tuned to hear if it concerned the car-door-slamming occupant of apartment 4, it was impossible either to take in what I was reading or to make out more than an occasional word of what was going on in the entrance hall. Curiosity got the better of me. I left the guidebook on the arm of the chair and eased open the door.

Maxine was in full flood. 'I hear what you say, Collins. But it's *just* not good enough. An agency's only as good as its cleaning staff. Nine o'clock, I said to her. And it's now half past.'

So Mandy was late. Not surprising, considering the weather.

'What do you want me to do about it, Mrs St Clair?' Collins sounded fed up. 'As I've said, I could contact the agency, but there could be several explanations for her being half an hour late on a day like this. The bus, for instance, could—'

'Then she should have taken that into account,' Maxine snapped.

The telephone rang in the office, giving him the excuse he needed to break off the conversation. 'Just a moment, Mrs St Clair. I'll have to answer that. Might be the agency.'

I was easing the lounge door shut with the intention of returning to my seat to pick up the guidebook, when I heard, '*What!*' Collins's voice was breathless with shock. 'What's *that* you're saying, Terry? Hit-and-run? I'll come at once.'

I flung open the door. He was running out of the office, shrugging on his jacket and calling back as he went, 'There's been a terrible accident on the drive. Terry's called an ambulance. It appears that the cleaner's been—'

The heavy wooden entrance door banged shut behind him, cutting off the end of his sentence. Maxine stared after him, for once silenced. Heart thumping, I too started to run.

I caught up with him as he was getting into his car. 'I know a bit about first aid. I might be able to help.'

He motioned me into the passenger seat and moments later we were heading down the drive. The *swish swish* of the windscreen wipers ticked off the passing of precious seconds. Neither of us spoke. Halfway down, just round the first bend, we came upon Terry's car, abandoned. The wide-open driver's door blocked out the scene of the accident. Though the car was still moving, I flung open the door and jumped out.

Mandy was lying half on the grass verge, half on the tarmac, one arm outflung. A dumpy Russian doll, face upturned, the rain trickled down her plump cheeks as if she was weeping for her life cut short. I knelt down beside her, but it was clear that there was nothing I, or anyone, could do.

I stood up with a sigh, and for the first time noticed Terry standing several yards down the drive, white-faced, the shoulders of his fawn jacket dark with rain, hair plastered to his head.

'She was just lying there when I came down the drive. I thought it best to stay here to stop any cars coming up in case ... in case ...'

'Yes,' I said.

He cleared his throat. 'Do you think we should cover her up?'

'No, leave it to the police and the ambulance men. They'll be here any moment.'

The dead don't feel discomfort, only the living. I was conscious of the rain soaking through my thin jersey.

Collins spoke from behind me, voice tight with anger. 'The bastard's been driving too fast for the conditions. He's seen her too late. Didn't stop, just left her.'

I nodded. But that wasn't how it had happened. If it had been an *accident*, even a hit-and-run driver would have braked instinctively. I could see no skid marks, no tyre tread left on the tarmac, nothing to show he'd braked, nothing at all. No, the driver *had* seen Mandy. She had been his target. Somebody had wanted her dead.

Lost in our thoughts, we stood in silence, listening to the urgent note of the distant siren. I was conscious of the hum of traffic on the main road, and a steady *drip ... drip* from the overhanging trees. The siren was louder now ... louder ... louder ... till suddenly, blue lights flashing, ambulance and police car swept up the drive.

Time seemed to stand still as I watched the paramedics kneel beside Mandy, then stand up shaking their heads. After a brief consultation with the two policemen, they closed the rear doors and the ambulance drove slowly off.

One of the policemen came over to where we stood.

'Why didn't they take her away?' Terry burst out. 'Aren't you even going to cover her up?'

'Just waiting for forensics, sir. They'll bring a tent.'

He produced a notebook, took a brief statement from me, and after he'd ascertained that I was a mere bystander with no information to offer, I was allowed to go.

The rain had reduced to a fine drizzle as I set off up the drive, more determined than ever to bring Spinks and his organization to book. In front of me something glinted in the short grass of the verge. I stooped and picked up a pair of steel-rimmed glasses. Mandy's. I held them up. The lenses were plain glass. If this attempt to make herself appear harmless and of no account had been noticed, that would have been enough.... Sadly, I placed the glasses back where I'd found them.

Perhaps it was something else she'd done, through inexperience made a mistake that had drawn attention to herself in some way. Was one of the residents responsible? I'm a good judge of people, my life depends on it. Anyone is capable of killing if they have sufficient reason, but I could fairly certainly rule out Major and Maxine St Clair. Likewise Terry Warburton. His car bore no signs of damage to the wing, head-lights, bonnet or windscreen.

Knowing what I did about Nicola Beaton's scheme to swap the cannabis packages, I certainly couldn't rule her out. She had a motive for murder if she thought Mandy had discovered something incrimi-nating. Even so, I didn't think Beaton had it in her to cold-bloodedly run someone down. Besides, there'd never been a car in her parking place. Each time I'd seen her leaving the Lodge it had been by bus.

My bet was that the broken glass from a headlight and the piece of windscreen wiper lying on the drive would be from the car of that charming antique dealer, Clive Baxter. Yes, he had to be Mandy's killer. It must have been in *his* apartment that she'd made her fatal mistake. The fact that his car was not in the forecourt supported my theory that his was the hit-and-run vehicle, and if I was right, he'd have left early enough not to be connected with the incident. He'd have waited for Mandy to get off the bus and start walking up the drive. As cover, some time in the afternoon he would arrive back at the Lodge bewailing the fact that his car had been stolen from where he'd parked it in town.

G and I would pay his apartment a visit on the off-chance that Mandy had seen something there that had aroused her suspicion. But I'd have to be very careful indeed not to leave any trace that I'd been there, or I'd end up as she had. Dead.

CHAPTER SIXTEEN

When I got back to my apartment, G sensed my sombre mood, rubbing herself sympathetically against my uncomfortably damp trouser legs. I changed out of my wet clothes and set about composing a text to Attila that would inform him of Mandy's death, without revealing my whereabouts at the Lodge.

Substitute cleaner killed in hit-and-run. NOT accident. Am investigating.

Satisfied that the wording said all that was necessary without revealing everything, I sent it. My 'under deep cover' status would remain in force till I informed him otherwise, so he would wait for me to contact him again. And I wasn't going to do that until it suited me because then he would inform me that a substitute for Greg was in place. When Attila had assigned me to work with Greg, he had made it very clear that the important decisions – *any* decision – would not be mine to make, that I would have merely a supporting role. And supporting roles are not for me.

Baxter hadn't yet returned to the Lodge. It was an ideal opportunity for a little investigation. When, as I'd hoped, there was no reply to his doorbell, I went back to my apartment and took my picklocks and G's working collar out of the safe.

'Job for you, G,' I said, lifting her off the sofa.

Together we crossed the corridor to Baxter's door. With the picklock inserted, I hesitated. He might come back unexpectedly and catch me in the act. Was it worth the risk? Yes. What Mandy had discovered had been important, worth killing for. There was one thing that puzzled me, however. *Her* death didn't bear the Spinks hallmark: murder cleverly passed off as unfortunate accident. Had Baxter panicked, acted on impulse without Spinks's knowledge? Perhaps he'd been careless, left something incriminating for Mandy to see, something he shouldn't have.

When you worked for Spinks, one mistake was one mistake too many, and Baxter would know that.

The pins of the lock turned and we were in. I set G to roam and headed straight for the lounge. The room was as the property developer's stylist had left it: nothing had been added. I'd expected to find examples of Wemyss Ware bowls, pigs or cats decorating the tops of bookcase and sideboard, but these surfaces were bare of all items, and the books in the bookcase were the same standard issue as in mine. There was no sign of a laptop. Baxter hadn't been as careless as I'd hoped.

I turned my attention to the safe. From studying the one in my own apartment, I'd a good idea of which picklock to use. The door of the safe swung open. Inside were several bundles of £50 notes and a laptop. I lifted it out, careful not to disturb the money. If that laptop had been lying out on the table for Mandy to see, and if it hadn't been password protected....

No password. The screen came to life displaying three folders: *Wemyss Ware*, *Tide Times*, and *Selkirk*. The one of particular interest was the last, but I didn't make the mistake of opening it to view the content. If Baxter had suspicions that a file had been opened, he would check the file properties to see the last time it had been accessed. Could that have been the slip that had betrayed Mandy? Copying it would also be a giveaway, but there was a very good chance that Baxter would rely on the laptop being secure in the safe, be sure that no one could possibly have gained unauthorized access, and not bother to check. I inserted my memory stick, copied the whole folder, closed down, and had the laptop back in the safe in less than a minute.

There had been no crooning call from G to indicate any trace of drugs as she searched bedroom and bathroom. She came into the lounge and I watched her sniff around the furniture, then leap up onto the sofa. After a cursory sniff at the cushions, she sat down and scratched at an ear. Nothing to interest me here, she was saying. Or me either, I thought. I'd got what I'd wanted. Time to go. Never push your luck. I checked that everything in the lounge was as it had been, signalled to G to follow, and left.

Back in my own apartment I opened the *Selkirk* folder on my memory stick. The times and places of cannabis shipments were all there: next on the list was Shell Bay, scheduled for the early hours of

Friday. I returned the laptop to my safe, satisfied with a good morning's work.

But like Mandy, I too had been careless, though I didn't know it at the time.

It was just before 6 p.m. when Clive Baxter let himself into his apartment. How easy it had all been. Though he'd made a point of looking out for the spot where he'd run the woman down, there'd been little trace, only some flattened grass. He'd made a real song and dance to Collins about the bastard in St Andrews who had stolen his car, and about how he'd had to get the bus back to the Lodge and walk up the drive in the drizzle. He had put on a good act, tut-tutting when Collins had told him about the accident. The silly fool had been quite upset.

Yes, how easy it had all been. Well-satisfied with himself, he hung up his wet coat in the hall. He would go to the residents' lounge tonight to celebrate, treat himself to an 18 year-old Highland Park whisky and give out that he was drowning his sorrows.

He looked at his watch – he was just in time to catch the local six o'clock news. There might well be something about the hit-and-run and the progress the police were making in tracing the car. Brilliant idea to report it stolen ... they'd never be able to prove he'd been the driver. He was in the clear.

He sat down on the sofa and reached for the remote control. It was then that he saw the single red hair on the cushion. Where the hell had that come from? He'd had no visitors, red-haired or otherwise. He picked it up between finger and thumb. Looked like the hair of a dog – or a cat. The woman across the corridor had a red-haired cat with a silly name, a scruffy creature she had the nerve to pass off as a pedigree. But how could it have got in? Had he left a window open? Not in here. Or the kitchen. Or the bathroom. Or the bedroom.

Sweat broke out on his forehead. The hair on the sofa could mean only one thing – that the cat had followed the woman into his apartment. For a long moment he stood, paralysed by shock. *Had she broken into the safe and taken the laptop and the money?* Heart racing, he rushed to the wardrobe. The safe was shut. With shaking hands he examined the lock and found no sign of tampering. He opened the safe. The laptop and the money were still there. The intruder hadn't got at them.

If only he had kept the laptop in the safe when the cleaner had been around.... The chime of the laptop closing down – that was what had given the nosy woman away. She'd been looking at the files. He couldn't take a chance on her just being a harmless busybody, could he? Yes, he'd had to get rid of her. If the American, Mr Martin as he called himself, got to hear that he'd allowed someone to see what was on his laptop, he'd end up like the guy Forrest in Pittenweem.... He shivered.

He closed the safe, went back to the lounge and sat staring at the blank TV screen, the six o'clock news forgotten. What was he going to do about the woman with the cat? She had let herself in by picking his door lock, so she was a professional. A professional from ... the police? Revenue & Customs? A rival gang? Or was she just a professional *thief*, preying on the wealthy, a twenty-first-century version of Raffles, someone with an upper-class lifestyle who stole from the rich for the sheer thrill of doing so? That was it. That would explain why she had been prepared to pay such an expensive rent for a trial period at the Lodge. Her plan would be to suss out small high-value items in each apartment and then vanish overnight. The St Clairs, now, they'd have plenty of jewellery for her to get her hands on. That bitch Maxine was forever prancing around with gold dripping from her. Come to think of it, the Vanessa woman was probably behind the theft of Warburton's camera. The thief hadn't been an outsider at all, it had been Vanessa Dewar-Smythe!

Well, there would have been nothing to interest her in *this* apartment. She hadn't got into the safe, hadn't seen the money, hadn't seen the laptop. Hadn't found anything. He relaxed....

That evening I headed for the library to continue reading about the Coastal Path in the guidebook. My heart sank when I met the Major and Maxine coming out of the residents' restaurant.

She put a restraining hand on his arm. 'Just a moment, Spencer. I want a word with Vanessa.' She turned to me. 'You're just the person we want to speak to!'

I wasn't in the mood for confrontation. 'I'm sorry, Maxine, but I'm in a bit of a rush,' I lied. 'I want to catch Collins before he goes off duty.'

She planted herself in my path, effectively blocking any attempt to sidle past. 'I know that this is of somewhat trivial importance in view of the tragic death of the cleaner, but we must ask you *once again* to show *some* consideration for your neighbours.'

'It's an ultimatum. Let's be blunt, my dear.' The Major's moustache bristled aggressively.

'I'm afraid I don't know what you mean.' I was genuinely at a loss.

'This morning, at about seven o'clock—'

'At 0700 hours precisely,' the Major snapped.

Frowning at the interruption, Maxine swept on. 'Yes, well, as I was saying, at the crack of dawn this morning we were roused from sleep by the slamming of a car door. Yours.'

'But—'

'It's no use denying it. I'm not mistaken. First the car door—'

'And then the engine,' the Major barked, determined to have his say.

'It definitely wasn't me!' I flared, aggrieved at the injustice of the accusation. 'It could have been *any*body. Have you spoken to Terry Warburton or Clive Baxter? Did you look out of the window? The sound of the car door first and then the engine, you said? That means the car was *leaving* the car park.'

They looked at each other, a niggle of doubt creeping in.

'*Harrumph.*' The Major turned to Maxine and muttered, 'Unconfirmed sighting.'

Maxine cleared her throat. 'Er ... we *may* have jumped to the wrong conclusion, been a trifle hasty, Vanessa.'

The Major nodded stiffly. 'Sorry, *if* we're mistaken!'

'That's quite all right.' I said graciously.

Their faces reddened and Maxine stepped aside from my path. Recalling just in time that I was supposed to be in a hurry to see Collins, I walked briskly in the direction of the office.

I poked my head round Collins's door. 'About the accident this morning, it has just occurred to me.... Could a delivery van have been responsible?'

He glanced up from the computer screen. 'The police asked that too.' He shook his head. 'No, there was nothing scheduled at that time and the post van doesn't come till eleven o'clock. I'm afraid the police will have their work cut out. Terrible business, terrible business.'

I sighed. 'Let's hope they'll find the vehicle soon and trace the driver.'

The police might not yet know his identity, but I knew. And thanks to the encounter with the St Clairs, I knew how he'd planned the hit-and-run: he'd left the Lodge at 7 a.m., lain in wait near the bus stop and followed Mandy up the drive. It went against the grain to delay informing the police. Unfortunately, the success of the HMRC operation was of more importance. If Baxter was arrested now, the subsequent police investigation would cause Spinks to go to ground.

My first concern must be to find out if the information on Baxter's laptop was still accurate. My bet was that the dates, times and places of the drug drops would remain unchanged. Baxter would not have dared to tell Spinks that he'd made the mistake of allowing the cleaner access to his computer.

Confident that I was right, I headed again for the library to consult the road atlas on how to get to Shell Bay. The fire was crackling in the grate and although it was still light outside, the table lamps were lit. According to the map, a minor road led to the caravan site on the shore. At shipment time Spinks's men would be watching it for any sign of police activity, so it would be better to go on foot by the Coastal Path. I ordered a Laphroaig whisky and crossed over to one of the settees beside the fire.

The Coastal Path ran from Earlsferry along the top of a cliff, but an even more unobtrusive alternative was by the beach along something called the Chain Walk. According to the guidebook, the Chain Walk consisted of horizontal or vertical chains to enable walkers to cross the inlets and headlands of Kincraig Point, one of the arms of Shell Bay. *Strenuous, exciting ... danger of falling rocks and being cut off by the tide ... no escape up the sheer cliffs....* I sipped a whisky and stared into the leaping flames. From the sound of it, the Chain Walk was a bit too adventurous. The easy route along the top of the cliff – that's the way I would go.

CHAPTER SEVENTEEN

The next morning I made my preparations for a daylight reconnaissance of the Coastal Path at Shell Bay – sunhat, walking boots, rucksack, sweatshirt, picnic lunch, binoculars and guidebook borrowed from the Lodge library. Gorgonzola was preparing for *her* day by selecting, rejecting, and reselecting a sunny patch of carpet in front of the French doors. Finally, choice made, she lay down on her side anticipating several hours of cat dreams. Her eyes closed, her whiskers twitched, her side rose and fell....

I let myself out and clumped my way through the entrance hall. The plastic map case hanging round my neck showed the Ordnance Survey map folded to display the path from Crail to St Monans, the opposite direction intended. It was just as well that I'd taken this precaution as Baxter was standing outside the office in conversation with Collins.

'... bloody expensive having to hire a car,' Baxter was saying. 'It's the state mine might be in when they find it that worries me.'

As I passed, I waved and called cheerily, 'St Monans to Crail today.' That should allay any suspicions Baxter might have that my destination was Shell Bay.

Collins responded with, 'It's a good day for the Coastal Path.'

Baxter said nothing, but there was something in the way he looked at me that suggested he might know of my visit to his apartment. That was nonsense, how *could* he know?

I took the bus to Earlsferry and set off along the Coastal Path towards Shell Bay. Though it was only half-past nine, the sun was already warm. From the edge of the village a grassy track led over a low headland past the ruined gable of what had been a tiny church. In the far distance across the Forth was the hazy outline of the Bass Rock and behind it, just visible, the cone of Berwick Law. I followed the recommended guidebook route, taking to the sand round the edge of a golf

116

course. Fifty yards on from a signpost reading *Coastal Path*, steps cut into the earth led steeply upwards to the top of the cliff. Halfway up I rested on a makeshift wooden seat to look out over the bay towards Earlsferry. Two tiny figures and a dog wandered along the sands far below, and on the smooth velvet green of the golf course three players bent over their clubs.

I continued on up a narrow earth path. On my left a grassy slope fell steeply down to rocks, on my right a high bank sprinkled with the white, yellow and purple of wild flowers rose to the skyline. Bordering the path and glinting silver in the sun's rays, the dried seed heads of daisy-like flowers swayed in a stiff breeze. In the centre of one, the red dot of a ladybird nestled like a tiny jewel. Beauty and peace. For the moment I could push to the back of my mind the reason I was here.

At the top of the cliff the path skirted a large circular concrete pit, the remains of a World War Two gun emplacement. War ... death ... the murder of my colleagues Greg and Mandy. The spell was broken – this was no carefree holiday ramble in the sun amid beautiful scenery. I could no longer push to the back of my mind that I was on a reconnaissance for tonight's surveillance at Shell Bay. I walked on....

I turned off the main path to follow a trail trodden in the waist-high grass towards a low flat-roofed building, a wartime bunker, positioned perilously close to the edge of the cliff and surrounded by concrete posts. It was just the sort of place Selkirk's gang might use as a signalling station or look-out post. The door hung drunkenly on its hinges, and inside, in the subdued light from two glassless windows, I saw the usual evidence of vandalism: walls disfigured by graffiti, a scatter of empty beer cans and cigarette butts. I picked up a crushed Marlboro cigarette packet. Spinks smoked Marlboro ... I visualized him standing at the window keeping watch. There was no proof that he had actually been here, nevertheless....

I crunched my way over the litter to a window, rested my arms on the sill and looked out. A red admiral butterfly fluttered among the silky heads of the tall grass on the few yards of cliff top separating the bunker from a sheer drop to the sea, in the distance the gentle curve of Shell Bay, and beyond, faint in the pale haze, the turning blades of the wind turbine at Methil and the hump of Largo Law.

Voices cut through the *wheep* of seabirds and the *wassh* of waves against the base of the cliff far below. At the point where the path climbed up from Shell Bay, two men came into sight. I caught my breath. There was something familiar about the taller of the two figures. I reached into my rucksack for my binoculars. The thin features of Hiram J Spinks leapt sharply into focus beneath a white golfing cap. And the man struggling to keep up with him, cheeks red with exertion, was none other than Clive Baxter.

With shaking hands I lowered the binoculars, stuffed them back into the rucksack and ran for the door. Their destination could only be the bunker. There was nowhere to hide. What better place than this cliff top for Spinks to arrange one of his little 'accidents'?

I had five minutes, perhaps not even that, before they reached the cliff top and would be able to see along the full length of the path. A fleeing figure would be sure to attract their attention, but there was no alternative. I set off at a run in a race against time to reach the wartime fortifications and the bend in the path that would hide me from view.

Panting, I rounded the bend in the path. It had taken four minutes. Had they seen me? A glimpse would be enough for Baxter to remember the combination of white sunhat, black rucksack and green shirt – and know that I'd deliberately lied about where I was going.

Lying flat on the ground, I parted the tall grasses growing between the tumbled concrete blocks and, heart beating fast, looked back towards the bunker. For a few moments there was no one in sight, then the white cap of Spinks appeared, joined after a short delay by the unfit Baxter. Nothing in their behaviour indicated that they'd seen me. I watched as they turned off the path and disappeared into the bunker. Against all the odds I'd got away with it.

Ten hours later I made my second visit to Earlsferry, this time by car. At an hour before midnight there was still a vestige of light left in the sky, enough for me to make my way up the steps to the wartime fortifications without the use of a torch. In black outfit and with blackened face, I flitted like a shadow along the cliff top path towards the bunker, the only sounds the *slap slap* of waves against the rocks below, the eerie call of some night bird, the soft *pad pad* of my feet. Spinks and Baxter's visit to the bunker made it probable that they were keeping to the schedule I'd copied to my memory stick, but probability was not enough. I had to be a hundred per cent certain before I informed HMRC when and where to make their swoop.

The shape of the bunker loomed up, dark against a sky washed the palest of greens. I stepped off the path and crouched in the long grass that bordered the bunker. There seemed to be no one inside, no glimmer of light from a shaded torch, but I took no chances, straining eyes and ears for any human sound or movement. Satisfied that there was no one in the bunker, I lay down to wait....

... Now that all light had drained from the sky, the outline of the bunker had merged with the night. I shifted from one hip to the other. It had been a long hour. It might be better to move to a point on the cliff top where I could look down on Shell Bay and keep watch for the bobbing torch of someone coming up the path. That would give me more than enough time to take up position on the Earlsferry side of the bunker. As soon as I'd established it was being used as a signal station, I'd retreat. Yes, I'd do just that. It was a spur of the moment decision that I came to regret.

I stood up. Away from the glare of street lights the stars glittered, ice crystals in a blue-black sky ... belted Orion ... the tilted W of Cassiopeia ... the square hook of the Plough.... I picked my way along the path as far as two benches sited at the top of stone steps that led down into darkness. From this height the distant lights of the Fife coastal villages were clusters of yellow beads, but all I could see in the darkness below me was a broken white line where small waves dashed against the rocky shoreline. A figure seated on a bench would be clearly silhouetted against the lighter night sky if anyone looked up from the Shell Bay path, so I felt my way halfway down the steps and sat down. Time enough when I saw the light of an approaching torch to retreat up to the cliff top, keeping low, and conceal myself near the bunker.

It was not from the direction of Shell Bay but from the steps above me, that danger came. The soft scrape of a boot and a muttered curse were the only warnings. Heart hammering, mouth dry, each moment anticipating that a torch would nail me in its beam, I leapt to my feet and felt my way down one ... two ... three ... four steps. At the eighth step I risked a backward glance. No torch beam at all.

The glowing tip of a cigarette butt arced through the air, dying in a trail of sparks on the step I'd just vacated. From above came a grunt and the rasping splutter of a match being struck. I edged on down ... nineteen, twenty steps.... He'd stopped at the benches. He'd not come down the steps because, like me, he was looking out for whoever was coming from Shell Bay and hadn't switched on a torch because he didn't want to advertise his presence on the cliff top.

Twenty-nine steps ... thirty. At last, my foot found sloping path. And then my luck ran out. Ahead, I saw the bob of torches. Spinks's men were coming along the path from Shell Bay on their way to send the signal from the bunker. I couldn't retreat up the steps, I was trapped.

I tried to remember what I had seen on either side of the path when I'd leaned out of the bunker window this morning. Inland, on my right, was a thick impenetrable hedge cutting off any access to the fields. On my left was a track that led down towards the sea. I shuffled forward as fast as I dared in the dark, searching for that track. It had to be close-by....

The torches were nearer now. I didn't have much time. At a crouching half-walk, half-run to lessen the chance of being seen, I followed the barely visible edge of the path. Beside a ghostly patch of white campion flowers, the long grass gave way to shorter turf. I'd found the track leading down to the sea.

I stumbled towards the glint of water, the sound of my footsteps covered by the *waassh ... waassh* of the tide against rocks. The path came out onto a grassy shelf above the beach of a small cove. A thin crescent moon had risen above the sea. It wouldn't be long before the signal was sent for the ship to make its run into Shell Bay. I'd be safe enough here till I heard the signal party returning from the bunker, then I'd go back along the cliff top to Earlsferry, mission accomplished.

Low voices passed nearby, and a couple of minutes later a quiet greeting drifted down from the man stationed at the top of the steps. I sat on a flat-topped rock and peered up at the outline of the bunker on the cliff above. I didn't have long to wait until three brief flashes of light pricked out from that dark rectangle.

I heard the faint hum of a ship's engines growing steadily louder ... voices coming down the steps ... passing the end of the path. The signallers were on their way back to Shell Bay. I relaxed. From out at sea came an abrupt change of note as engines throttled back. Suddenly the bow of a small ship loomed out of the darkness, heading not for the sandy beach of Shell Bay, but for the narrow confines of the cove where I sat.

I leapt to my feet, cursing my stupidity, as I heard voices coming down the path towards me. *Of course* they wouldn't load packages of cannabis onto a boat within yards of the caravan park. I gazed wildly round for an escape route. On my right was the sea and the approaching ship, on my left, the sheer slate-grey face of the cliff. Straight ahead across a narrow tidal inlet, a metal chain hung down the rock above a broad ledge – the Shell Bay end of the Chain Walk.

I tried to recall what I had read in the guidebook, but all I could remember was that the route was particularly dangerous when the tide was coming in, as it was now. But it offered my only chance of escape. A wave slapped hard against the back of the inlet, warning me that it would be a race against time to make my way to Earlsferry at the other end of the chains. I hesitated.

On the path to the cove someone stumbled and cursed. My decision made, I plunged into the icy chest-deep water of the inlet. Half-swimming, half-wading, I reached the other side, hoisted myself onto the ledge and grabbed hold of the chain. Hand over hand, bracing my feet and feeling for footholds, I climbed to the top of the rocky ridge that formed one arm of the inlet and threw myself flat. I was just in time. Pools of torchlight wavered on the beach of the cove, bobbing torches and dark figures advanced to the water's edge. The fishing boat was nosing slowly forward, trailing behind it the squat shape of an inflatable. While it was still short of the entrance to the cove, the anchor splashed into the water.

A low voice called from the shore, 'There's been a delay getting the quad bike and trailer. Give it an hour.'

The words carried clearly across the water, bringing the burst of activity on deck to a halt. An hour before loading commenced, perhaps an hour and a half in total till they'd finished loading. My heart sank. If I wanted to avoid the Chain Walk and return to Earlsferry by the cliff top path, I'd have to stay where I was till they'd gone. I thought about it for a moment. After lying in my wet clothes for that length of time, I'd be on the verge of hypothermia, might not have the strength to clamber down the chain and swim back across the icy waters of the inlet. By that time, too, it would be high tide, the waves would be dashing against the cliff. There was no alternative, I'd have to risk the dangers of the Chain Walk. If I went now, it should just be possible to get to Earlsferry before high tide.

I squirmed back from the skyline and studied what lay on the other side of the ridge: a sliver of pebbly beach and two caves, their mouths gaping like empty eye sockets. I grasped hold of a short vertical chain and scrambled down into the tiny bay. The first cave was just a shallow scoop in the rock; a brief inspection with my torch of the other one revealed a tunnel running back several yards into the cliff, its floor worn smooth by millennia of waves. A ring of plastic flotsam was trapped at the far end and the walls were slimy with seaweed above head height. No refuge there if the tide forced me to turn back from the Chain Walk.

I'd spent only a few minutes inside the cave, but when I emerged a thin layer of water had already covered the pebbles of the beach. The tide was coming in fast. Stamping firmly on misgivings about being able to reach the end of the Chain Walk before the route became impassable, I grabbed hold of the horizontal chain above a ledge barely wide enough to take my boot. Face pressed to the rock, I inched round a buttress, feet just clear of the incoming tide.

I stumbled on ... another small bay, slabs of rock already awash ... a long chain ... a short chain ... a chain and steps ... a chain and toeholds.... Each time it took more effort, each time my hands were colder, legs shakier. Bracing my feet against smooth rock, I pulled myself wearily up yet another vertical chain attached to a metal post on top of a rocky ridge to find myself staring at moonlight glinting on small waves rippling across the surface of a wide bay. On the headland above was the rectangular silhouette of the wartime gun emplacement overlooking Earlsferry. Not far to go now.

But was there something horribly familiar about that silhouette? Relief gave way to despair. I'd been scrambling over rocks and up and down chains for over an hour, and all that time I'd merely been working my way round the bays and inlets of Kincraig Point, one of the arms of Shell Bay. What I was looking at was not the gun emplacement but the bunker. Cold, wet and exhausted, I clung to the metal post, fighting back tears. In the night sky above, the pinpoint stars continued on their silent journey, emphasizing just how alone I was and far from help. Out at sea, in the darkness the light on the Isle of May blinked once ... twice. Then all was darkness once more.

It was anger that came to my rescue: Greg and Mandy were dead, murdered, and if I sat here whimpering I'd die too, from hypothermia or drowning. Spinks would win. On that previous mission, as he'd shoved my head beneath the water he'd gloated, 'Those who try to get one over on Hiram J Spinks don't live to regret it.' He'd got it wrong. I had lived. But he was still at large, free to make millions from drugs that brought untold misery and death to others.

'Mustn't give in, mustn't give in,' I muttered as I waded waist-deep between what bizarrely appeared to be sections of fluted Roman columns, rocks that had fallen from the basalt organ-pipe formation on the cliff face above. As if to give me encouragement, the going suddenly became easier: underfoot was as smooth as a pavement, the water merely knee-deep. I splashed forward at a high-stepping, slow-motion run. A mistake: pebbles rolled beneath a boot and, arms windmilling wildly, I lost my balance and fell backwards. I staggered to my feet spitting out seawater and waded on, this time feeling cautiously for what might lie unseen beneath the surface. Progress slowed to a snail's pace. What I'd taken to be smooth rock was booby-trapped with mini potholes and loose pebbles. I fixed my eyes on the far arm of the bay and trudged on, forcing one foot in front of the other, body and mind numb. Mustn't give in, mustn't give in....

A rocky ridge rose ahead of me. It should have been an easy scramble, but in my weakened state it took all my strength. I collapsed at the top and lay there, for I don't know how long. I'd stopped shivering, a bad sign. With an effort I reached up for the long horizontal chain that stretched out of sight round a rocky buttress. One arm looped over the chain and face pressed to the rock, I worked my way slowly, slowly, along the broad ledge, dreading what might lie round the corner.

Lights. I could see the lights of Earlsferry twinkling beyond the golf course. So close, so close. But there was one final barrier: a narrow strip of dark water, its surface moving in a slow, sullen swell. Half a dozen strokes would take me to the far side. Half a dozen strokes. Just half a dozen strokes. But did I have the strength? I plunged in.

One stroke, two strokes, three ... fear stabbed as the swell pulled me towards the cliffs and away from the shallow steps cut in the barnacled rock. I flailed my way back towards the steps, and seconds before the next surge plucked me away, reached out to grab hold of a jutting rock. I clung on desperately as the swell rose up ... up over my head ... then slowly fell away. With the very last of my strength I flung myself forward, wedged a knee on a step, and in a state of collapse heaved myself above the reach of the waves.

I'm still a bit hazy about how I managed on shaky legs to make it back to my car at Earlsferry – put it down to the psychological boost of having survived that nightmare traverse of the Chain Walk. I sat slumped, heater going full blast. The car filled with the smell of damp clothes, the windows steamed up; I sipped at a cup of hot tea from the thermos and felt myself gradually thaw until I had the strength to rub the black camouflage from my face. Body warmth escapes from the uncovered head, so after a moment's thought I delved in the glove compartment for the balaclava kept for night prowls, rolled it up into a beanie hat and jammed it down over my wet hair.

Buoyed up with the thought that the schedule on the memory stick was correct, that tonight hadn't been a total disaster, I turned the key in the ignition. I'd established what I'd set out to do.

It was nearly 4 a.m. when I drove up to the Lodge. In the grey predawn light its walls were drained of colour, giving the building a melancholy air, but high up on the stepped gable a blackbird was in full fluting song. As I switched off the ignition, I glanced anxiously across at the St Clairs' bedroom window. The curtains remained firmly closed. I relaxed.

I'd climbed stiffly from the car and put my hand out to ease the door shut, when without warning a knee buckled. As I lurched forward, my outstretched hand slammed the door shut. *CLUNK*. The sound bounced off the building, bringing the blackbird's song to an abrupt halt. After a moment's silence, the *chook chook chook* of its alarm call pierced the still air, a strident call guaranteed to alert not only its mate but, more disastrously, the light-sleeping St Clairs.

If I could disappear round the side of the building before they leapt to the window, they wouldn't be *absolutely* sure who had been the culprit, so would be reluctant to challenge my vehement denials after the embarrassment of their false accusation two days ago.

Their curtains were still closed. I set off at a half-run, aching legs slow to respond. Seconds later, the beanie balaclava began to slip slowly down over my eyes. At that very moment the St Clair curtains were tugged apart. Two irate faces glared out, their furious eyes met mine. Two fingers spread, I desperately pushed up the hat to shove it clear of my eyes. Forcing a friendly grin, I fled.

It was only as my head hit the pillow that I realized that the gesture of pushing up the balaclava beanie might well have been – would almost certainly *have* been – misconstrued by the St Clairs as a contemptuous two-fingered salute, the V-sign, and my friendly grin as nothing but sheer brazen insolence.

CHAPTER EIGHTEEN

I slept the dreamless sleep of utter exhaustion for ten long hours. I'd taken the precaution of shutting the bedroom door in anticipation of the patting paw, Gorgonzola's routine to wake me up, so it was early afternoon before I finally surfaced. I lay drowsily contemplating the wording of the message I would send to Attila now that I'd confirmed the places and dates of Selkirk's drug shipments. The grudging praise I'd earn from that should go a long way to offset the revelation that I'd failed to obey his initial order to take up the job of cleaner at the Lodge.

Yes, things were looking good. I sat on the edge of the bed, grinned at my reflection and gave it a cheery thumbs-up. The grin faltered and faded as it triggered the memory of the trouble I was undoubtedly in with the St Clairs. Nothing I could say would persuade them it had all been a misunderstanding. Their complaint would have already winged its way to Collins, so I'd just have to wait and see how he'd react.

I sighed. Gorgonzola was another one I'd offended and would have to placate: I'd failed to provide her with both breakfast *and* lunch. Last night, knowing that I'd be incommunicado for hours past her breakfast time, I'd put out an extra bowl of food when I came in. But she'd just have viewed that as an extra, a well-deserved compensation for being left alone all night. To her, breakfast was the bowl put down at breakfast time. And she was still waiting for it. Before I showered and dressed, I'd make her a breakfast-lunch.

As I tucked into my own, I had to accept that my days here at the Lodge were numbered. Profuse apologies to the St Clairs and a suitable explanation for last night's unfortunately timed gesture *might* do the trick. But sooner rather than later, I would be guilty of another unpardonable offence. It was just a matter of time. They would complain to Collins, invoking the deeds of condition, and though he was all too aware how difficult and unreasonable the St Clairs were, forever pounding on his office door with trivial complaints, to protect his own position he would have to ask me to leave.

Time to make plans to explain to anyone who asked why I was remaining in the area once I had left the Lodge. I'd have to rely on my cover story of would-be exhibitor at the Pittenweem Festival. There was a weakness in that story that would have to be remedied, however. Two days ago in the library Clive Baxter had shown a disturbing interest in my supposed quest for a venue and I hadn't done anything about finding one. Any time now he might ask me which places I'd tried. To admit that I hadn't, in fact, approached anybody would confirm all his suspicions. Perhaps if I offered a generous sum towards rental costs, I could persuade a venue in Pittenweem to provide a little space for me.

That posed another problem: how was I to pay for it? After some thought, I had the answer. Play my cards right and I could prise out of Carla a £3,000 refund for the three weeks' unused accommodation at the Lodge. The part-rent of a venue would cost a fraction of that. And what is more, the one week I'd already spent here in luxury living would hopefully bring the operation to a successful conclusion. Cheap at the price. So how could HMRC Accounts complain about a piddling little bit of venue rental? Optimism restored, I set off for Pittenweem.

A single heavy raindrop spattered the windscreen as I parked the Mercedes. Half a dozen more darkened the pavement as I locked the car, leaving Gorgonzola sprawled out in possession of the rear seat. There was a feel of thunder in the air, that heavy stillness that precedes a sudden heavy downpour. With only a week till the start of the Festival, Pittenweem was busy with its preparations: strings of red and blue bunting criss-crossed the High Street and blue placards bearing large white numbers had appeared outside doors to indicate the properties housing exhibitions.

After studying the map supplied by the Festival organisers, I started down a flight of steps leading to a narrow wynd where dusty-pink valerian and other garden escapees had taken root in cracks on the top of high sandstone walls that shut out any view except a leaden sky and a pewter sea glimpsed between pantiled roofs ranging in colour from a bright orange-red to weathered-with-lichen green.

The door of the first venue in the wynd was firmly closed and there was no answer to my ring. At the next venue marked on the map, the up-and-over garage door was raised. Inside, stacked three deep against the whitewashed walls, were oil paintings of rocky shores and sunset waves.

'Hello?' I called. 'Hello?

A young man with a neat Vandyke beard poked his head round an access door in the back wall.

'Yep?' he said.

'I was wondering if—?'

'Nope.' He withdrew his head. The access door clicked shut.

Two venues tried. More than a hundred venues left to try. Looking on the bright side, that was a hundred opportunities for success.

The wynd narrowed as it continued steeply downwards. Without warning there came a long rumble of thunder, the *splat splat* of heavy raindrops. Then the heavens opened in a torrential downpour. Stair-rods of rain bounced in spurts off the ground, soaking my jacket in seconds. The only place that could offer shelter was the garage with the oil paintings. Just as I turned back to seek refuge, the garage door tilted down and slammed shut. With rain running down my face and dripping off my nose, I ran on downhill, feet splashing through puddles, hoping to find somewhere to shelter lower down the wynd.

A short distance ahead the wynd turned sharply to the left. I rounded the corner to see a huge blue-and-white golf umbrella advancing uphill towards me on short sturdy legs, the legs clad in black fishnet tights. The effect was quite startling. As the umbrella suddenly whirled side-on, I caught a glimpse of a small, chubby woman with shoulder-length henna-dyed hair. She closed down the brolly, gave it a vigorous shake and disappeared backwards into the open doorway of Venue 102.

I rushed after her and found myself in a short stone-flagged passage. I stood for a moment peering out at the downpour and the water streaming down the stone-flagged surface of the wynd, then followed the trail of wet footprints to a closed door, adding my own drips to hers. The previous encounter with Vandyke Beard had taught me that coming slowly to the point got nowhere. Money talks. I knocked.

'Care to go fifty-fifty on the cost of this venue, Ms ... er?' I called.

The door flew open.

'Sapphire McGurk. Seventy-five per cent paid by you, twenty-five by me. Cash on the nail.' She too was a woman who believed in coming straight to the point.

*

The St Clair counter-attack, when it came, was by stealth. When I got back to the Lodge, the missile had been sneaked through my letterbox. It lay on my hall carpet, a time-bomb ticking away. I opened the envelope. It had the Royal Stewart tartan edging of Lodge stationery, but it wasn't the expected communication from Collins.

The Major had escalated hostilities to a higher level.

Ms Dewar-Smythe,

This is to inform you that I have written to Selkirk Properties in Anstruther to bring your reprehensible behaviour to the attention of the management. I have requested that the contract for your tenure here at the King James Hunting Lodge be cancelled forthwith.

Spencer St Clair, Major (Retired)

The words jumped out like bullets fired at point-blank range. Rage fought with consternation for supremacy. Rage won. I scrumpled the letter into a ball and hurled it down the hall. Before it could hit the carpet, Gorgonzola shot from the lounge, front paws extended like a basketball player reaching for the ball. Pat … swat … pat … pounce. She gave it the treatment it deserved.

'Atta girl, G,' I murmured, and went to fix myself some food.

While I ate, I pondered the fallout of the Major's latest action. Whoever was in charge in Selkirk's office at Anstruther might take action, might even come in person to investigate. It was most unlikely to be Spinks, but even so I couldn't afford my face becoming known to anyone high up in the Selkirk organization. In addition, the Major would have undoubtedly taken the opportunity to fully catalogue each and every one of my offences. My earlier decision that it was time to move out was correct. Staying on here was out of the question now. There was every chance that Spinks might hear about the woman and her scruffy Persian cat at the Lodge, so near the centre of his money-laundering and drug-shipment operation. And that might trigger a memory of his encounter with the HMRC agent who owned a cat. I had no option but to leave the Lodge – forthwith, as the Major had so bluntly put it.

In the words of Gerry Burnside, my erstwhile controller, 'There's always a silver lining to the blackest situation.' After a little thought I found it – in fact there were three silver linings. The brightest was that it would be advisable, anyway, to leave the Lodge. Staying on here was an unnecessary risk now that I'd obtained the schedule of shipments from Baxter and achieved what Attila had sent me to do. Secondly, leaving wouldn't hamper my investigation into Beaton's regular visits to St Andrews – I could lie in wait at the bus station and follow her from there. And thirdly, as I'd already calculated, a reasonable explanation for cutting short my trial residency should enable me to reclaim the next three weeks' rental of a thousand pounds a week.

Yes, the King James Hunting Lodge had served its purpose. And Vanessa Dewar-Smythe would depart in style – before she was summarily and ignominiously ejected. I laid my plans. I'd leave this very afternoon, a good twenty hours before the Major's letter could arrive at Selkirk Properties. That way, the St Clairs would find to their chagrin that they'd launched their attack too late: the enemy had marched away as bold as brass, without even having the decency to slink shamefacedly away under cover of darkness. To pile chagrin on their chagrin, I picked up the envelope and carefully stuck down the flap again so as to make it appear I had not opened the letter and read their belligerently penned message.

At precisely five o'clock each afternoon, the Major and Maxine, creatures of habit, would sally forth from their apartment to take afternoon tea in the residents' lounge. At one minute before five o'clock I stood poised outside my doorway, in one hand the faux designer suitcase, in the other, the envelope and Gorgonzola on her lead. As soon as I heard the St Clairs' door open, I moved forward at a pace designed to meet up with them in front of the residents' lounge. At the sight of me the St Clairs hesitated, their eyes sending an unspoken message to each other.

'Come along, *do*, Smootchikins,' I cried loudly, giving a quite unnecessary tug at G's lead.

Her reaction, as I knew it would be, was to perversely dig her claws into the thick pile of the carpet. I tugged again, and when she put up even more resistance, I picked her up, allowing the envelope to slip from my fingers. Out of the corner of my eye I saw it float down to lie on the carpet, its tartan edge drawing the St Clairs' eyes like a magnet. Pretending not to notice, I rolled the suitcase in the direction of Collins's office. One step ... two ... three....

'Just a moment, Ms Dewar-Smythe. You've dropped this.'

I turned. Maxine was advancing towards me, the letter in her hand. They'd be hoping that I would open the envelope in their presence.

I put Gorgonzola down. 'Thank you *so* much, Mrs St Clair,' I fluted in a gracious manner calculated to irritate. 'I didn't notice I'd dropped it. Since the phone call this morning,' – I was deliberately vague, unnecessary details can later prove to be tripwires – 'I've been in *such* a rush getting my things together that I've not even had time to open the mail, just gathered it up as I came out.' I noted with some considerable satisfaction the covert glance they exchanged. 'I'm sorry to leave this gorgeous place, but must dash.' I grasped the handle of my suitcase. 'This way, Smootchikins.'

I continued across the entrance hall to say my farewell to Collins. A few minutes later, formalities completed, I turned to manoeuvre my suitcase down the front steps and glimpsed the St Clairs disappearing into the office, avid to find out if I was gone for good. I stowed my luggage in the Mercedes, strapped G into her harness, and with a royal wave of the hand for the benefit of the Major and Maxine, pulled out of the car park in my ostentatiously upmarket Mercedes.

At the spot on the drive where Mandy had met her death, I paused for a brief moment. Then left the King James Hunting Lodge for the very last time.

When I arrived in Anstruther the tide was out, leaving the harbour floor patterned with seaweed, dark mud, and isolated pools of water linked by meandering channels; in the middle of the harbour, seagulls wheeled and circled with hauntingly mournful cries over a huddle of sailing boats listing at awkward angles, their keels sunk deep into the wet sand.

I parked the car and crossed the road to Selkirk Properties. There was no sign of the fine photographs that Terry Warburton had handed in, the window display remained unchanged: the same crow-stepped and turreted King James Hunting Lodge, the same white sand bay and impossibly blue sea were making an unanswered siren call to passers-by.

Carla was not behind her desk when I pushed open the door, though the acrid smell of nail polish hung heavy in the air.

'Hello-o, anyone there?' I called.

There was no reply. The piece of paper propped up on the desk spoke for her. *Back in five minutes.*

A temptation like this was impossible to resist. I went to the door and looked both ways along the street. There was no sign of an approaching ash-blonde head. Satisfied, I moved round to the back of the desk and slid open the top drawer. Inside were a bottle of fuchsia-pink nail varnish, a packet of tissues and a couple of fashion magazines. The second drawer contained application forms and a pile of envelopes. The desktop was bare except for a small notepad (blank), promotional leaflets and a reconditioned old-style telephone with a pull-out tray for lists of telephone numbers. Presumably such an instrument was felt to be in keeping with Selkirk's pre-twentieth-century properties. I moved round to stand in front of the desk so that my body concealed what I was up to, swivelled the telephone towards me and pulled out the tray.

Even someone as empty-headed as Carla might notice indents on the surface of the notepad so I tore off the top sheet, and rested it on the desktop. I'd jotted down four names and phone numbers from the list in the pull-out tray and was scribbling down the last number, when behind me, I heard the click of the door latch accompanied by the appetising aroma of fish and chips liberally sprinkled with vinegar. In one swift movement I swivelled the telephone back into its former position and turned round. Carla stood in the doorway, pink nail-varnished finger and thumb in the process of applying a bottle of Coke to her fuchsia-pink lips.

'Why there you are, Carla!' I cried, adopting the aristocratic tone I'd used to impress her on my first visit. 'I was just penning you a note.' I smiled, holding up the piece of paper, blank side towards her. 'Needn't have bo-thered, now you are here.' I crumpled the paper into a ball and thrust it into my pocket, then sat down on the chair in front of her desk and fished in my bag. 'I'm here to hand in the keys to my ap-aht-ment at the Hunting Lodge.'

For a few seconds the bottle remained poised at her lips as she took in what lost commission on the sale of apartment 4 at the Lodge would mean for the Carla Windsor bank account and the future purchase of designer accessories.

Then she rallied. 'I'm sorry to hear that, madam.' She moved swiftly to sit behind her desk. 'Has madam fully considered how much she'll miss the ambience, the luxury, and....' Suddenly conscious that the Coke bottle did nothing for the prestige of the King James Hunting Lodge, or for that matter, her elegant image, she slid the offending bottle out of sight, camouflaging her movement to deposit it on the floor behind the desk by leaning forward and fixing me with earnest eyes. 'Not to mention, of course, that you'll be *losing* the guaranteed rental income of *a hundred thousand pounds...*?' The pink-nailed fingers wrote £100,000 in thick black marker pen on the pad and pushed it towards me to bring home to me the magnitude of my loss.

I sighed heavily. 'Ah, yes. You're so *very* right.'

Carla brightened.

Slowly and regretfully I traced round the zeros with my finger. 'But, you see, my partner phoned this morning and issued me with an ultimatum – live with him in Cannes, or live without him at the Lodge. So what was I to do?'

Her expression said plainly, 'No contest. Toss him and take the cash!'

I sighed again. 'My mind's made up. You see, he's a multi-millionaire, so I'm afraid that I'll have to sacrifice the Lodge.'

This time it was Carla who sighed. That was a decision she thoroughly understood.

CHAPTER NINETEEN

One of Anstruther's claims to fame – for some, the major one – is its award-winning fish and chips. Since I'd slept through break-fast, and lunch had consisted of merely a sandwich, I wasn't going to miss the opportunity of giving my verdict. But first I'd get rid of the distinctive Mercedes. I couldn't afford to draw attention to myself with that car.

'Make the most of your luxury transport, G,' I said as the Mercedes whispered its way to St Andrews.

I returned the car to the hire company in St Andrews and reverted to HMRC's somewhat elderly Ford Focus that never rated more than a passing glance. From a wi-fi café I sent the cannabis shipment schedule to Attila by encrypted email, adding the information, *New cover will be ceramics exhibitor at Pittenweem Festival, Venue 102.*

That should satisfy him, keep him off my back for a short time at least. Not, of course, that he would ever be completely satisfied with anything *I* did.

At 9.30 that evening the takeaway queue stretched along the street outside the famed Anstruther Fish Bar on the quayside. I shuffled my way forward in the line, keen to put its award-winning claims to the test. Brass, glass and class summed up the brightly lit interior: shiny brass rails, etched glass panels and stainless steel serving counter. No cats, of course, were allowed in the restaurant, hence my long wait in the queue for a takeaway. At last I stepped in through the doorway, to be welcomed by a life-sized statue of a fisherman clad in yellow oilskins and holding a large fish by the tail. The interior décor was equally nautical, not to mention fishy: a fearsomely-toothed metal wall sculp-ture, a ship's bell and wheel, and a TV showing a film of trawlermen hauling in the catch soon to be on the Fish Bar's menu.

Clutching a cardboard tray of haddock and chips, I crossed the road to the car park and slid into the back seat of the car. Holding the package out of G's reach, I spread its wrapping paper on the seat.

'If you don't like the "secret recipe" batter, G, I'll have it all. Here's a very small piece of fish for you to try.'

A sniff, a delicate nibble, and it was gone. Verdict delivered.

'My turn now to do a food test.' With a plastic fork I broke off a large piece for myself, all too aware of her expectant eyes and the drip of saliva from the corner of her mouth.

Together we finished off the fish. I lifted the last chip to my mouth and gazed through the car window at the late evening scene. Perhaps when this operation had been brought to a successful conclusion, I too would be wandering beside the harbour as a tourist hearing the musical *tink tink* of rigging, with nothing more on my mind than looking at the boats.

I took my mobile phone from my pocket and sent a message to Attila. *Seeking out other cannabis factories. No longer under deep cover. As ceramics exhibitor at Pittenweem Festival exhibits needed. Send half a dozen ceramic sculptures plus the ceramic statue of the white lady in my apartment to Venue 102.*

He would be infuriated that I was taking matters into my own hands rather than awaiting orders from him, but when an agent in the field makes a request, it cannot be ignored. With considerable satisfaction I closed the phone and slipped it back into my pocket.

Tonight I was booked into The Waterfront hotel. I'd be gone from Anstruther in the morning, long before elegant Carla draped herself behind the desk in nearby Selkirk Properties. I bought a local newspaper to scan the pages for any update to the police inquiry into Mandy's death and found what I was looking for in a small news item near the foot of a page.

HIT-AND-RUN DEATH: CAR TRACED

The car involved in Tuesday's fatal hit-and-run accident at the King James Hunting Lodge was found yesterday abandoned in a suburb of St Andrews. It had been stolen from the car park where the owner had left it earlier in the day. Police enquiries are continuing.

Mandy's murder must have been hastily planned, so I didn't think that Baxter would be able to convince the police that he wasn't involved: his story, whatever it was, would be riddled with contradictions and inconsistencies. Handcuffs were about to snap over Baxter's wrists, I was sure of it.

A cat litter tray was not a standard hotel accessory, so I clipped on G's lead and we wandered along the waterfront in search of a suitable patch of earth. At ten o'clock it was still twilight with a luminescent blue-green sky, and once G had found her toilet spot, I sat on a seat near the lifeboat station with her on my knee, enjoying the contrast to daytime noise and bustle, aware of faint sounds that would have passed unnoticed during the day: the *scutter* of an ice cream wrapper blowing up the road, the *clunk* of a car passing over a grating, the gentle *lap lap* of water against the harbour wall as the incoming tide crept slowly into the basin and round the huddle of sailing boats, now aground on a waterlogged sandbank.

Further along, outside the pubs and takeaway shops on the brightly lit area of the waterfront, groups were still hanging about, most of them in shirtsleeves or T-shirts, seemingly oblivious to the cool wind that had sprung up. I pulled up the collar of my jacket and lifted Gorgonzola onto the ground. Time to go back to the hotel.

I had just got to my feet when a burly man pushing his way through the drinking and chatting groups caught my attention. There was no mistaking that oily slicked-back hair and bristling black moustache. Bert Mackay! As he approached a white van parked outside the Waterfront restaurant, its indicators winked orange. I sank down again onto the seat, thankful for the poor lighting at this section of the harbour. If I had the opportunity to follow him, I didn't want Bert to remember that he'd seen me here on the quayside. He seemed to be a man on a mission and I was determined to find out what that mission was. He slid the driver's door open and got in. I rose to my feet, and at a leisurely pace that wouldn't attract his attention, walked the short distance to my car.

By the time I'd hastily strapped G into her harness, the van had completed a U-turn and driven off in the direction of Pittenweem. At this time of night with little traffic on the road, I was confident that I would be able to catch up with him again, but he was travelling fast and I'd passed through Pittenweem before the van came into sight. Across the estuary of the Forth, light pollution caught in layers of cloud streaked the dark night sky above the string of twinkling orange dots marking the street lights of the Lothians from North Berwick to Edinburgh. I dropped back to follow the van's rear lights at a discreet distance towards the fishing village of St Monans through undulating farmland, passing a windmill and a ruin silhouetted against the silvery gleam of the sea.

The van sped on through the holiday township of Elie, and past the road leading to Shell Bay and its caravan park, confirmation that wherever Bert was heading, a cannabis consignment wasn't scheduled there for tonight. The white lines marking the edge and centre of the road swept by ... moths, white fireflies, rushed towards my headlights to vanish upwards in the slipstream.

The sugarloaf cone of Largo Law loomed a darker bulk against the sky, a sign I was approaching the village of Upper Largo. The van slowed, made a right turn and headed off along a narrow unsigned road. I dropped further back. Driving with dipped headlights in the unlit countryside between villages hadn't been too difficult on the main road with its markings, but on this narrow road I was forced to drive on side-lights since dipped beam would attract Mackay's attention. The distance between us increased: several times I lost sight of his rear lights, but his main beam cutting through the darkness ahead reassured me that he hadn't given me the slip.

After about ten minutes, the van's brake lights glowed red as it slowed down and stopped four hundred yards ahead, alongside barred gates set in a high concrete wall. I braked hard and switched off my lights. Mackay couldn't have been checking in his rear mirror to see if he was being followed, for without a backward glance he got out of the van, walked up to the gates and with an odd sideways twist, disappeared from sight.

I couldn't leave the car on the narrow road without lights, a hazard to other drivers. Besides, when he returned to his car, even the slow-witted Mackay would be suspicious of a car parked near the gates. I switched on dipped beam and drove past, casting a quick glance sideways as I did so. The gates were closed and padlocked but two of the bars had been wrenched wide apart, forming space enough for even a beer-belly like his to squeeze through.

I was in luck: a short distance past the end of the wall, a track wound into a belt of trees. I bumped along it until hidden from the road. Behind me in the back seat, Gorgonzola lunged against her harness, eager to pit her wits against the local night-life.

'Sorry, G. I'm afraid you'll have to sit this one out.'

I released her from the harness and slipped out of the car before she took in the fact that she was being left behind. There was enough light in the sky to make my way back along the track to the road without stumbling. If Mackay were to re-emerge through the gates, he'd be looking towards his van, giving me vital seconds to throw myself into the long grass and weeds at its base. I'd intended to keep close to the high wall, but after a few steps I realized that wasn't a good idea: a trail trampled through the nettles and ragwort would leave a tell-tale sign that someone had been snooping. From then on I kept to the tarmac road, on edge that he might appear at any moment. A movement on the top of the wall set my heart racing, but it was only the wind stirring the racemes of a buddleia that had rooted into the coping.

I never let an opportunity pass by to snoop, so on the off-chance that Bert might have left his van unlocked, I tried the driver's door. It swung open. An empty beer can, a couple of cigarette packets and several expired parking stubs littered the floor-well on the passenger side. I found nothing of interest in the door pockets or the map compartment. Oh well, it had been worth trying. I stooped lower for a final glance under the seats – and spotted the corner of a piece of paper, just visible, wedged between the driver's seat and the gear housing. I slid my hand down into the narrow gap and with some difficulty extricated the paper. It was an unopened Oxfam charity envelope, presumably an unwanted and discarded postal delivery, subsequently used as a handy piece of paper to jot down a phone number. The effort was worthwhile, for it bore Bert Mackay's name and Pittenweem address. I thrust it into an inner pocket and turned my attention to his means of entry through the gates.

I slipped through the egg-shaped gap between the vertical bars. Judging by its size and rectangular shape, the building facing me had once been manufacturing premises, but now the windows were boarded up, the concrete walls stained green from broken guttering and rising damp. In a gust of wind, a loose strut of the framework attaching the faded *For Sale* notice to the padlocked double entrance doors *tap tapped* a message of dereliction and decay. But appearances can be deceptive. If I was right, Bert's visit here meant that the building was in business once more.

The area devoted to plants in cannabis factories can vary in size from a wardrobe to a room, or even a small house such as I'd tracked down in Pittenweem. Here the cannabis-growing was on an industrial scale. Behind those boarded-up windows would be a sophisticated pumping and ventilation system with its accompanying ducting, fans and powerful lights. Outside the temperature was fifteen degrees Celsius, inside it would be nearer forty degrees. A place this size would generate a cash crop of millions of pounds a year, something that would certainly attract the attention of Hiram J Spinks.

The rusty padlock on the double doors had obviously hung there undisturbed for years. My rubber-soled shoes made no sound as I moved along the front of the building in search of the door Mackay must have used. Suspicions weren't enough evidence that this abandoned building was in fact a cannabis factory. Halfway along the front of the building was a small door, unpadlocked. I'd ease open the door a crack and the superheated air inside and the whiff of that distinctive cannabis smell would be sufficient proof.

I was within a couple of yards of the door when I heard the hum of an approaching car. Was it about to pull up at the gates? If one of Spinks's gang came into the yard, he'd see me. I tensed, ready to run to the corner of the building. If I didn't round it before a shout raised the alarm, I'd be trapped within the high walls without a chance of escape. The engine sound was closer now. Lights flickered across the bars of the gate ... and passed on.

Now I was at the door. Its blistered and peeling paintwork, graffiti-scrawled panels and rust-pitted handle gave no indication that it had been opened in years. Shading the pen-torch with my cupped hand, I studied the plate round the keyhole: small scratches glinted in the torchlight, evidence of recent use. Gently, very gently, I turned the handle and eased the door fractionally open. As it cleared the jamb, a razor-thin line of light ran along the top and side of the door. I pressed my cheek to the tiny gap and got the proof I needed: hot air against my skin, the pungent smell of cannabis in my nostrils.

I was about to ease the door shut when the *hummm* of a car being driven at high speed cut through the silence of the surrounding countryside. Headlights on full beam picked out the tracery of branches and leaves in a line of trees. I dismissed it as just another passing car and concentrated on closing the door, slowly, infinitesimally slowly.

I whirled round at the squeal of brakes. The headlights of a car drawn up outside etched the shadow of the barred gate on the cracked and worn tarmac of the yard. I snatched my hand away as if the door handle was red hot. Released from the pressure, the catch disengaged with a soft *click* and the line of light round the door reappeared. Heart in mouth I raced for the corner of the building. The car door slammed. I had five, or at most ten seconds, before my moving figure caught the eye of whoever came through the gates. And I didn't have those seconds.

Against all my instincts, I stopped running, dropped to the ground and lay on the cracked tarmac, face shielded by my arms, awaiting the shout of discovery. Now the silence of the night was my enemy: my fast breathing, loud in my ears, threatened to betray me to whoever was making his way across the yard. I rested my forehead on my folded arms, straining to hear the soft sound of approaching footsteps. Nothing.

Suddenly, very close, a voice swore softly. 'The bastard that left the door open is gonna catch it in the butt!' The accent was American, the voice one I knew well, one that sent a chill through me. Hiram J Spinks was standing a few yards from me. I lay absolutely still.

Seconds later I heard the click of the door closing. Had he gone inside or was he standing peering into the darkness, sensing that something was not right? The seconds ticked by.... Then a yawn, the faint scuff of a shoe as he shifted position, told me he *was* still there, watchful, suspicious.

The door opened, saving me from almost certain discovery.

'That you, Mr Martin?' Bert Mackay's whisper, whining, subservient. 'After you phoned, I came as quick as I could.'

'I told you to keep this bloody door locked. Shut and *locked*. You left it open, Mac.'

'I didn't.... It wasn't me, must have been—' The sentence ended abruptly in a strangled gasp.

'Quit passing the buck. Guys who work for me don't goof up.' The menace in his voice made his meaning clear: the payoff for any mistake was final, the wages of sin, death. 'The bum who's been messing me up over the consignments from the King James is gonna find that out PDQ. You hearing me, Mac?'

'I–I d-don't know what you mean, Mr Martin. I—'

I heard a heavy thump as of a body being shoved violently against the door, followed by a spluttering gurgle. I didn't have to see what was going on to know that Spinks's hand had a firm grasp on Mackay's throat.

'I'll spell it out, so there'll be no misunderstanding, bud. Last week I found some smartass had been pulling a fast one palming off garbage as skunk. I'm asking myself if the swap's being done here at the factory – which would mean that right now I'm looking at the son-of-a-bitch making the swap.'

'No ... *ugghh.*' Another choking gurgle.

'Or could be it's being done at the Lodge while the goods are waiting collection. Any ideas, bud? If you don't come up with who the hell's fleecing me, I'll have to figure that it's Bert Mack-kay.'

'It–it must be that woman, that woman at the Lodge.' It came out as a croak.

Ah, he was putting the blame for his little scheme on Nicola Beaton. Anything to save his own miserable skin. Bastard!

'She's English. Moved into apartment 4 a week ago.'

My heart missed a beat. It wasn't Beaton he was fingering. It was *me*.

Eager to convince, he gabbled on. 'Nikky says that the woman's giving it out that she's here for the Pittenweem Festival. Why would she pay all that cash to stay at a place like the Lodge when she could get cheap digs in Pittenweem? Something fishy there.' He warmed to his theme. 'And just a few days ago I heard from Nikky that the woman's been hanging about on the golf course near the bunker where the stuff's—'

There was the sound of fist making contact with flesh.

'The moment you have *any* suspicions about *anything*, you tell me. Understood?'

A whimpered, 'Ye-e-ss, sir, Mr Martin.'

'This woman, what else d'ya know about her? What she look like? I'll get someone to pay her a visit.'

Silence.

I held my breath. My description fitted half the women of my age in Scotland: medium height, medium brown hair, features easily forget-table. But if Bert blurted out that the woman had a cat, Spinks would make the connection with the cat belonging to HMRC agent Smith. To save my life on that previous encounter with him, I'd conned him into thinking I was Deputy Controller HM Revenue & Customs in Scotland, something he'd not forget. A lie that might now prove my undoing.

'Well? Do I have to shake it outta you?'

'S-sorry, Mr Martin.' In Mackay's voice a thin quaver of terror. 'I've–I've never seen her. You–you said I was never to go to the Lodge.' The quaver strengthened to a whine. 'But Nikky will know all about the woman. I'll phone her and find out first thing tomorrow.'

A pause, then Spinks delivered his verdict. 'You're off the hook – for now, Mac. Meantime you and me are gonna do a little spot check on the next consignment.'

The door opened and closed. The factory yard was once more silent and dark. When I'd arrived, my priority had been caution and stealth, now it was speed. Time to get out of here. Truth to tell, the shock of suddenly finding myself so close to Spinks had left me more than a little shaken. The moment I heard the door click shut, I was on my feet racing for that gap in the bars of the factory gate.

Drawn up a little way beyond Mackay's white van was a dark-coloured hatchback. Screened by the vehicle, I hunkered down and risked a quick flash of my pencil torch to memorize the number plate before I ran back up the road to the woodland track where I'd left the car.

Gorgonzola was crouched on the parcel shelf, face pressed against the glass of the rear window, tantalized beyond measure by the nocturnal scurryings of little creatures. With one quick movement, I whipped open the door, slid behind the wheel and pulled the door shut while she was still in the process of scrabbling down the upholstery of the rear seat.

'When needs must, a girl has to do what a girl has to do, G,' I said, leaning over to attach her harness and ignoring the mews of protest.

I didn't drive past the factory gates, but took a long circuitous route back to Anstruther and The Waterfront hotel. Plenty of time, therefore, to think over what to do. Forewarned is forearmed. Mackay and Beaton would take care that no more packages went missing from the bunker. And with my sudden departure from the Lodge, I'd played into their hands: Spinks would be convinced that I was indeed responsible for switching the packages of cannabis. The dice were loaded against me. The one thing in my favour was that Mackay hadn't mentioned the woman's cat. His failure to do so had bought time for Vanessa Dewar-Smythe and her cat to go to ground, disappear, vanish into thin air. And I knew just how to make it happen.

CHAPTER TWENTY

Early next morning, long before Bert Mackay would have got round to making that phone call to Nicola Beaton, I checked out of The Waterfront hotel and headed for St Andrews. I was feeling a bit more optimistic: she would certainly supply Bert with the name of Vanessa Dewar-Smythe, but I'd already ditched that identity. To Sapphire McGurk I was Kirsty Gordon. True, Beaton would describe my appearance, but a description that fitted thousands of women wouldn't be of much help to Spinks. Nevertheless I wasn't taking any chances.

I left the car in a shady spot in St Andrews, its feline occupant still sulking after my refusal last night to let her go 'roaming in the gloaming' as the Scottish Harry Lauder song put it – or as I would have said, 'wandering in the half-light of a summer night.'

It didn't take long to find what I was looking for, a hairdressing salon. *Appointments not always necessary* announced the notice hanging in the window of What A Snip! I pushed open the door. When I emerged from the shop an hour and a half later, gone was the straight-haired brunette, Vanessa Dewar-Smythe; in her place was curly-headed Kirsty Gordon with raven-black hair and fantastically long (false) eyelashes. I paused for a moment to study my reflection in the salon window. Was that really me?

Gorgonzola's reaction when I peered into the car was gratifyingly hostile. Back arched, eyes round, pupils wide, she edged away to the far side of the car seat. I opened the door.

Psschh.... A spitting hiss was cut short as she caught my scent.

'It's the new me, G,' I said, as I got behind the wheel. 'And soon it'll be the new *you*.'

I was confident that I looked sufficiently different now, but red Persians are not common and that, combined with G's scruffy coat, could link her with the new me. That was another reason I had come to St Andrews. It took several enquiries before I found a hairdresser for Gorgonzola in the form of Josie's Pet Parlour, a tiny shop that promised, *Trims while U wait. Satisfaction guaranteed.*

With G clutched firmly in my arms, I breezed in. A young woman looked up from blow-drying the silky coat of a leggy Afghan hound. Both of them eyed Gorgonzola.

'It's an emergency,' I cried. 'My mother's been taken ill and I have to leave my cat with a friend. I just *know* she'll forget to brush her.' My voice rose to a wail. 'Last time this happened, Fluffy's coat became so tangled and matted that I had to take her to the vet.' I kissed the top of Gorgonzola's head. 'Didn't I, Fluffy?'

'Fluffy?' Josie and the Afghan studied G's patchy coat.

Keeping a wary eye on the Afghan, I put G on the floor. 'What I was hoping was that you would trim her coat very short, give her a sort of crew cut, you might say. I'd be *ever* so grateful.'

'I'm afraid we don't—'

My face crumpled. 'You see the state of her coat? The thin patches are where the tangles were. They were so bad that the vet had to take them out under anaesthetic. If it happens again, she'll have no coat left.'

The Afghan looked down its long nose at Gorgonzola and tossed its silky head. I didn't know what Josie was thinking, but I was pretty sure about the Afghan. I played my ace. With a loud sniff as of stifled tears, I picked G up and shoulders drooping dejectedly, made my way slowly towards the door.

My hand was on the latch when she relented. 'OK, then. Come back in fifteen minutes when I've finished with the hound.'

'Is that really you, G?' I said, surveying Josie's handiwork.

A short-haired ginger cat gazed grumpily back. Nobody would now recognize her as the bunker-polluting Smootchikins. We both had new identities.

Now that Vanessa Dewar-Smythe had departed from the Lodge and vanished into thin air, there was no necessity to continue with my cover as exhibitor at Pittenweem, but to Sapphire McGurk cash in her hand was cash in her bank, as she'd made very clear. There was no chance of her agreeing to cancel my arrangement with her: the word 'refund' was not in the McGurk vocabulary. Besides, a venue located in the same street as Mackay's house might prove very useful. That would be my justification when the cost was queried by HMRC Accounts.

With a week to go to the Pittenweem Festival, next on my agenda must be to find accommodation, somewhere within easy reach of Pittenweem, but far enough away to avoid a chance meeting with Carla or one of the residents of the Lodge. It would be easier to vanish from view in a town the size of St Andrews, but the possibility of encountering Spinks – or Nicola Beaton on one of her visits – ruled that out.

Last night when I'd followed Mackay's van towards the disused factory, I'd driven through the outskirts of Upper Largo and, during my research of the Fife Coastal Path, I'd read about the village of Lower Largo. It was famous as the birthplace of the real-life Robinson Crusoe, one Andrew Selkirk, after whom the late unlamented owner of Selkirk Properties seemed to have been named. Lower Largo would fit my requirements exactly: hidden away off the A915, the tourist route to the fishing villages of Fife, and about twenty minutes' drive from Pittenweem. I was in luck: a phone call secured a couple of nights' accommodation at the Crusoe Hotel.

From the village of Upper Largo I turned off down a steep, narrow road passing under a picturesque arched viaduct. Ahead lay a tiny tidal harbour formed by the mouth of a river, and beside it the Crusoe Hotel, a centuries-old two-storey building rising from the rocky beach itself. A modern extension with port hole windows and hanging baskets of purple and white petunias stretched out to meet a wooden landing stage. The hotel had made inventive use of the Robinson Crusoe connection: arms of a signpost pointed to the *Juan Fernandez Lounge and Family Bar*, the *Castaway Restaurant*, and to *Juan Fernandez Island 7,500 miles*. A fourth arm with a heart and the sign of a footstep pointed along the road to the Crusoe memorial. I let G out to roam, aiming to collect her later and smuggle her into the hotel.

My room was in the extension, its window looking directly over the Forth to the Bass Rock and the town of North Berwick. That tiny white dot might be the Seabird Centre with its camera, silent witness to the murder of Drew Selkirk on the Isle of May.

I had my lunch in the Crusoe-themed lounge bar: walls lined with vertical half-logs in a cabin effect and in the floor a square of glass covering the print of the barefoot of Man Friday. The small window beside my table gave a view of the sea lapping against seaweed-fringed brown rocks and a narrow strip of white sand. Around me was the buzz and chatter of couples and families on holiday, at leisure, relaxing, doing nothing much. It took an effort of will to remind myself that I was not on holiday like them: this afternoon I had a rendezvous with my Festival co-exhibitor, Sapphire McGurk.

There was no answer to my tap on the door when I arrived at Venue 102. I tried the handle. Four o'clock, she'd said, but the door was locked. Could she have forgotten I was coming? I went back along the passageway and peered through the window that looked out onto the wynd. At first, reflections and the dimness of the interior of the room made it difficult to distinguish anything. I pressed my forehead to the glass and made out a low *chaise longue* against the side wall, on it the purple-covered mound of Sapphire's hips. By angling my head a bit more, I could see her head resting against the back of the *chaise*, mouth open, eyes shut. An arm hung limply over the edge. I rapped sharply on the window.

Her eyes snapped open, the mound heaved. When I tapped on the window again, less sharply this time, she sat upright, swinging her legs to the floor and flickered her fingers in a little wave. After her little power nap, Sapphire McGurk was wide awake and ready to do business.

She opened the door, yawning and running a hand through her hennaed hair. 'I was just mulling over a few design ideas, Kirsty.'

I smiled. '"When upon my couch I lie in vacant or in pensive mood", as the poet Wordsworth said.'

'I was not vacant, definitely pensive.' The sharpness a rebuke. 'Now, to our little agreement. You pay seventy-five per cent, I pay twenty-five.'

I nodded.

'That proportion, of course, *also* applies to the allocation of space, entitling you to – a quarter of the room, and myself to three-quarters.'

Like a conductor bringing in a section of the orchestra, she waved her hand round the small room crammed with net storage bags full to the brim with coloured wools. Her green eyes bored into mine, challenging me to object, dispute, argue the toss for a fairer share. There was no use protesting: I was desperate and she knew it.

Inwardly fuming at this shameless behaviour, I too waved an airy hand. 'That'll be fine by me. I need only a little space. This is my first festival and I just want to gauge the public's reaction, see if it's worth giving up my day job.' I surveyed the ramparts of wool. 'Now where do you suggest I set up?'

Sapphire's lips pursed into a scarlet heart. 'Well ... my knitting machine goes here.' She stood in front of the window and spread her arms wide. 'And then, of course, my skeins of natural-dyed wool will be hanging here and here.' She spread her arms again to indicate the whole of the wall behind the chaise, and the adjacent wall. 'And the finished knitted garments will be displayed on the chaise longue. So that leaves *you* with....'

My turn to purse my lips. 'The table.'

The allotted table was far too small to house my own sculptural creation, the two-foot long Henry Moore-style White Lady, as well as the few small ceramics Attila was sending. Anyway I'd shown Clive Baxter a photo of the White Lady – it was something not easily forgotten – so I couldn't now exhibit it. I sighed, visions of spectacular acclaim fading fast. Yes, for Attila's six small sculptures it would be just fine. I looked up from eyeing the table.

Sapphire was gazing at me speculatively. 'You'll not be bringing in your pieces for a few days yet?'

'Well, I don't know exactly.' How long would it take Attila to commandeer some suitable sculptures? 'You see,' I improvised, 'I had to wait till I'd secured a venue before having them sent up. So, er....'

Sapphire pounced. 'You won't say no, then, to giving me a little hand in the meantime.'

'I will, yes,' I said. Then I realized that her question had been admirably phrased with the deliberate ambiguity of the Delphic Oracle for both 'yes' and 'no' to mean the same thing and accord with her wishes. To make it clear that I had no intention of helping her, I added hastily, 'I mean, no.'

Deliberately misreading my reply, Sapphire beamed. 'Well, that's very good of you, Kirsty. I thought you could make a start by helping me decide which colours are the most effective for attracting people to the venue. I need someone tall to hang up my sample skeins.' She darted across to the bags of wool. 'What do you think of this?' She held up a soft blue for my inspection. 'My latest experiment with natural dyes.'

I edged towards the door. 'I really must—'

Her cry of, 'Yes, it's a winner,' isn't it?' drowned out the end of my sentence. The word 'go' sank without trace.

I tried again. 'What I meant was—'

'I understand. *Everyone* struggles to find the exact words to describe the amazing shades I've managed to create.' From the bags of wool she plucked dusky reds and oranges, a creamy white, smoky greens and blues, a cornfield yellow and a twilight grey. 'Now let's see which colours look best together in natural light.'

Beckoning me to follow, she vanished through the doorway, the *click click click* of her heels loud in the flagged passage. I trailed after her, plotting a chance to escape. Spending the next few hours at the beck and call of Sapphire McGurk was not something I'd bargained for.

She was waiting for me in the wynd, ready to give me my instructions. She thrust the wools into my arms before I could make an excuse and leave.

'You stand here beside the venue notice, and I'll go down the wynd a bit. When I've decided which colours show up best from a distance, I'll call out their order to you and you can nip up the ladder and hang them on the hooks above the door.'

I sneaked a look at my watch and sighed. Bert Mackay's house was somewhere further down this wynd. I consoled myself with the thought that it wouldn't take me long to find it once I escaped from Sapphire's clutches.

From twenty yards away she called, 'Right, Kirsty, hold up the reds and blues....'

Half an hour later I was still going up and down the ladder hanging up different combinations of wools: once she'd made a decision, she'd wait for somebody to pass by to ask their opinion, and then it was all change again ... and yet again.

Nobody had come along for some time and I was hoping she was making the final choice of colours, when hurrying footsteps sounded on the flagstones higher up the wynd. Any minute now Sapphire would accost whoever was coming round the dog-leg corner. My heart sank, but perhaps I'd be in luck and they wouldn't pause to give a verdict.

A man and a woman came round the corner. The people I least wanted to see – Nicola Beaton and Bert Mackay. Casually I turned away and made a show of looking up at the skeins, pretending to straighten one of them. Would my disguise fool Beaton? I caught a glimpse of Mackay hurrying past, paying me no attention at all.

I could feel Beaton's eyes upon me. 'Stop, Bert!' I've seen—'

Despite having steeled myself to show no reaction, heart thumping, I clutched at a skein pulling it off its hook.

'No, *no*, Kirsty!' Sapphire's voice was sharp with irritation. 'I haven't told you to take that one down. Put the red back where it was.'

'*Wa-ait*, Bert!'

My cover was blown, the new disguise a wasted effort.

Beaton's hand came over my shoulder and fingered the skeins. 'These wools are such *unusual* shades.'

I breathed again.

'Can you tell me—?'

My heart missed another beat. If I spoke, she'd be sure to recognize my voice. If I changed my voice by adopting a Scottish accent, Sapphire would be sure to call out, 'Why on earth are you speaking like that, Kirsty?' That would draw Beaton's full attention to me. My new hair-style and colour would not be enough, she'd see straight through my disguise.

Sapphire's swift call of, 'Can *I* help you?' came to my rescue.

With surprising speed for one of her build, she advanced from her position further down the wynd, elbowed me aside and launched into a well-rehearsed sales pitch. The fish was nibbling at the hook, and real-izing that my knowledge of natural dyes was zero, she wasn't going to allow me to mess up a sales opportunity. 'Indeed they are *very* unusual. You'll not find colours like these anywhere else – all natural dyes from native plants based on my own techniques after years of experimenta-tion.'

Beaton touched the wool to her cheek. 'It's so *soft*. And, of course, no toxic chemicals.'

Down the wynd Bert Mackay tapped his foot impatiently and glanced at his watch.

Ignoring these hints, Sapphire gestured toward the passageway leading to her studio. 'Do come in and see the wonderful range of colours available.'

'No time for that.' Mackay strode up, seized Beaton's arm, and hustled her away. The fish had been snatched from the hook.

'Preview evening next Friday,' Sapphire called after them. 'Your chance to get first pick. If you wait till the Festival opens on Saturday, they'll have been snapped up.'

They didn't look back. Too busy bickering.

Seizing my chance to escape, I made a dash for the dog-leg corner up the wynd. 'See you in the next couple of days when the box of sculptures arrives,' I called over my shoulder.

I didn't look back either.

CHAPTER TWENTY-ONE

It was 4 a.m. when Gorgonzola decided that an urgent visit to the loo was required. She signalled this with a leap, not onto the bed, but onto my midriff as I lay on my back in deep sleep, triggering a nightmare reliving of the occasion when Spinks's henchman, the Silent One, had pressed down on me with his boot as he interrogated me on the Isle of May. *Ooooph.* Air whooshed out of my lungs. A terror-driven twist of my body upward and suddenly the weight was gone.

A *waagh*, a *thump* and my sleep-dulled brain sluggishly registered that I was lying on a soft mattress, not hard concrete. There was no Silent One looming over me. No Spinks saying coldly, 'Kill her.' I sat up. Grey dawn light was seeping through the small window, imprinting a faint four-paned image on the far wall of the room. Of course ... I was in the Crusoe Hotel.

Two large furry paws rose from the pool of darkness at floor level and clamped themselves to the edge of the duvet. In between them appeared G's indignant face. When she saw she had my attention, the paws unclamped and she sank back into the gloom, only to reappear on the windowsill. The message was plain. Grumbling, I padded over to the window and pushed it open. In the air was the tang of salt, mud and seaweed, and from the other side of the harbour wall came the soft *shhsh shush* of waves washing over rock and sand. Our two heads looked down at the tarmac of the car park below, a drop of fifteen feet with no accommodating ledge or projections.

'No exit for you that way, G,' I said.

But I was speaking to thin air: she was already over at the door, looking back at me impatiently. As I was about to close the window, my attention was caught by a fishing boat beached at an acute angle on the mud flats in the tidal harbour. Dark-painted wheelhouse ... on the bow facing me, star-shaped damage to the hull ... I was looking at the *Selkirk*

Harvester. There was no glimmer of light in the wheelhouse or spilling from the hatch, so this was the chance to poke around below deck. I pulled on jeans, dark T-shirt and jacket. Sleep and comfortable bed, if not forgotten were pushed into second place.

I crept cautiously down the stairs with Gorgonzola scampering lightly ahead and glancing back constantly to check my progress. There was no one at reception. A low-wattage bulb and the light in the sky from a window made it possible to make my way to the outside door without bumping into anything. With a pat at my pocket to check that I had the pass-key issued to guests for an after-hours return, I turned the latch, stepped outside and closed the door quietly behind me.

Far from dashing off on her urgent mission, G waited till she was safely out of grabbing reach, then stretched lo-o-ng and slowly, and with a cheeky twitch of her tail, strolled out of the car park towards the stone arches of the old railway viaduct spanning the river, the only thing on her mind the hunt. I'd been well and truly conned.

I crossed to the edge of the jetty. The *Selkirk Harvester* lay aground only a few yards away. In the hotel behind me and in the houses across the tidal flats of the river, blinds were down and curtains pulled firmly shut. Tide out, water in harbour, river only a couple of inches deep, and an iron ladder fixed to a metal plate on the stonework reaching to the bed of the river. Who could resist? Certainly not DJ Smith.

I stuffed one shoe into each trouser pocket and seconds later was stepping off the bottom rung of the ladder. Sand and slimy seaweed oozed between my toes as I splashed over to the *Harvester*. Clambering aboard was easy enough: the angle of the boat put the gunwale within reach. A stretch upward, a leap, a scrabble, and I was kneeling on the steeply sloping deck.

The wheelhouse door was locked, the windows cloudy with salt. I cleared a tiny area down near the bottom of the frame just big enough for an eye to look through, not large enough to attract attention, and peered into the dim and shadowy interior at a console with dials, a rolled-up chart, an oilskin on a hook ... nothing out of the ordinary, nothing of interest to me.

I yawned ... three more hours in bed was a much more inviting prospect than investigating the smelly depths of an empty hold. Stepping over a couple of orange buoys and a coil of rope, I edged my way back down the sloping deck to the gunwale. With one leg over the rail, I paused, eyeing the two hatch covers on the deck. One was padlocked. Would anyone bother to secure an *empty* hold? A drug consignment wouldn't be left unguarded overnight. Was it worth investigating?

I stifled another yawn. The lure of the Crusoe's comfortable bed was strong. And yet ... that new, shiny padlock had been fitted very recently. It had not been dulled and pitted by months of exposure to salt water. To a thief or burglar, and to me also, a padlock is an unerring indication of something worthwhile within. Perhaps there *was* something worth investigating, after all.

I swung my leg back over the rail and knelt down on the deck beside the hatch cover held in place by the padlocked metal strap. I felt in my jacket pocket for my picklocks. It wouldn't take long to open the padlock, lift off the cover and find out what was important enough for someone to keep secure.

A couple of twists, a click, and the padlock swung clear of the hasp. I shoved it in my pocket to keep it safe and lifted the heavy cover onto the deck. Gripping the coaming, I bent down to look into the hold. The white beam of my pencil torch probed the darkness below, picking out wet floorboards ... a wooden compartment holding a mini-mountain of ice ... a stack of empty fish boxes. Empty fish boxes weren't worth keeping under lock and key. So what *was*? I made another sweep round the hold with the torch.

The narrow ray of light passing across the surface of the crushed ice transformed it into a heap of glittering diamonds. I swung the beam back and steadied it. Whatever was being kept safely under lock and key must be hidden under the ice: a consignment of cannabis, heroin or cocaine, rather than a haul of lobsters or fish. In a trice I was down the short ladder, the lure of comfortable bed forgotten.

I scraped away a layer of ice, shifting it aside to left and to right. Only more ice. I excavated more vigorously, deeper and deeper ... six inches ... twelve inches ... still nothing but ice. I withdrew my numb red hands from the hole and blew on my fingers to warm them while I stepped back and studied the pile. I had possibly another two feet of shovelling, before I could be certain that there was nothing hidden there.

My hands were aching from the cold and the spoil heap of cast-aside ice had begun to cascade onto the floor, when at last a faint grey shape appeared beneath the layers of crystals. I excavated a small hole to enable my fingers to touch the object. Cloth, not the waterproof wrapping used for drug packages. Cloth? Puzzled, I enlarged the cleared area. It was definitely dark blue cotton, with a small button and, a couple of inches away, another. *Shirt buttons.* I snatched my hands away, mind trying to deny the sinister truth.

I took a deep breath, steeling myself to push aside more ice. A trouser belt. I stared at it. I knew now the purpose of the padlock on the hatch. It had been to conceal the body of the man lying under the few remaining inches of ice. A shiver ran through me. At the cannabis factory not so very far from where I now stood, I'd heard Spinks threaten Mackay, 'If you don't come up with who the hell's fleecing me, I'll have to figure that it's *you*.'

Was it Bert Mackay under the ice? There was only one way to find out. The face must lie under the spoil heap I'd built up on the left. I scooped up the ice, but almost immediately had to stop and thrust my aching hands into my armpits to warm them. Returning circulation increased the pain fourfold. I'd have to find something to protect my numbed hands ... an empty fish box would do. I snatched one up and got to work shovelling the displaced ice onto the floor. No need for care: the already exposed belt and shirt buttons told me when I would reach the face.

When I'd dug down to a within a few inches of where I estimated the head to be, I laid the fish box scoop on the floor, and gritting my teeth against the pain in my hands, set about removing the final layer, brushing away the icy rubble with careful fingers as delicately as an archaeologist uncovering a precious artefact. Shirt collar ... neck ... *face.*

The man staring up through sightless eyes at the thin beam of the torch *was not Bert Mackay*. Entombed in the ice was Clive Baxter, antique dealer. Without his glasses, skin bleached of colour, hair, beard and moustache rimed with ice, he was now a very ex-antique dealer.

Perhaps under Spinks's tough questioning over why his car had been involved with a hit-and-run, Baxter had blurted out exactly why he had been suspicious of the cleaner, thinking that Spinks would endorse the murder. That would have been a big enough mistake to ensure *his* murder. Spinks didn't tolerate mistakes, one small mistake was one too many. And Baxter had made not one mistake, but four: he had allowed Mandy access to his laptop, left out and unprotected by a password; he had tried to cover this up by killing her; he'd drawn the attention of the police to himself by using his own car for the hit-and-run; and by running her down on its drive, made the King James Hunting Lodge, site of one of Spinks's drug operations, the focus of unwelcome attention. Yes, by arranging Mandy's murder, Baxter had arranged a watery grave for himself. For him, the River Forth had become the River Styx and the *Selkirk Harvester* Charon's ferryboat taking his soul from this world to the next.

Spinks had a very good chance of passing off Baxter's murder as a tragic accident. My guess was that, unconscious or drunk, Baxter's head had been held underwater to accord with drowning in case his body was found fairly quickly. In most cases, drowning is accidental, so without signs of force or other evidence to indicate foul play, murder wouldn't be suspected. Dumped far enough offshore, however, the body could take months to wash up, if it ever did.

In one of the gardens on the other side of the harbour, a dog barked, galvanizing me into action. Time was running out: early risers in the village would soon be drawing back their bedroom curtains and would see me scrambling out of the open hatch. Of more urgency was the realization that the tide must now be coming in, and the crew would return as soon as there was enough water to float the boat. If I didn't remove all traces of my visit and get out of here quickly, I would be sharing this icy tomb with Baxter. I grabbed up the fish box, feverishly scooped the ice from the floor back into the stall and replaced the box in the corner with the others. I crushed underfoot any ice left on the floor till it melted into the wet of the floorboards.

But it was caution, not speed, that governed my departure: I stopped on a rung of the ladder and swept the torch beam round the hold. Satisfied that I'd left no sign that I'd been there, I peered over the top of the coaming. No passersby on the road ... bedroom curtains still firmly closed in the houses across the harbour ... the staff of the Crusoe Hotel still in their beds. The hatch cover back in position, I retrieved the padlock from my pocket, and hatch secured, slid down the sloping deck. I swung my legs over the rail and splashed down into water already more than knee-deep.

The only eyes that saw me leave the *Harvester* were Gorgonzola's. She was sitting primly upright on the edge of the jetty licking busily at a paw. As soon as she caught sight of me, she darted across to the doorway of the hotel and sat there, back towards me, message plain: night roaming over, soft duvet bed (mine) demanded *now*.

In my room I lay under the duvet with G curled up against me and drifted off to sleep. But my dreams were restless and troubled ... I stood knee-deep in the waves of Pilgrims Haven Bay amongst the assorted junk that nudged the half-submerged body of Drew Selkirk. All at once, the pallid face of Clive Baxter spiralled wraith-like upwards from the salty depths. In spite of my efforts to fend his body off with a fish box, it floated towards me ... nearer and nearer.... A tall thin figure bent over the drowned man. Spinks. Slowly, the figure turned and beckoned. His lips mouthed, 'You're next', the words themselves rendered inaudible by the screams of wheeling gulls.

CHAPTER TWENTY-TWO

Yawning, I stumbled out of bed and drew back the curtains. The tide was in, boats were bobbing at anchor in the little harbour and the *Selkirk Harvester* with its grim cargo had gone. Spinks had meted out to Mandy's murderer a sentence more severe than that permitted by law. I had no regrets about my failure to alert the police, for that would have jeopardized HRMC's operation and achieved little.

I wandered into the bathroom and stood at the mirror gazing with satisfaction at my still-unfamiliar appearance. Before my transformation I'd been worried that during the Festival one of the residents at the King James Hunting Lodge would visit Venue 102, recognize me and spread the news. How worried should I be now? I ticked the residents off on my fingers. Nicola Beaton had been fooled by my black-and-curly hair and those wonderful eyelashes. Clive Baxter was dead and now the only venue *he* would be visiting was Davy Jones's Locker. The prickly St Clairs' readily identifiable voices and their loud commentary on a venue they'd just visited would give me enough warning of their approach to make myself scarce. As for manager Steve Collins, during the day he'd be busy with his duties at the Lodge, and anyway he wouldn't be interested in seeking out a venue featured in the Festival guide as a display of natural-dyed knitting yarns. Photographer Terry Warburton wouldn't be roaming round the Pittenweem venues, camera at the ready, for on this occasion he was safely out of the way in distant Edinburgh, busy with his own exhibition.

A plaintive *miaow* came from the doorway. G was hungry.

'Breakfast served fresh from the tin to your travelling bowl in fifteen minutes,' I called over my shoulder and turned on the shower.

After my own late breakfast in the restaurant, I crossed the road to The Railway Tavern. G's little escapade in the early hours of this morning had made it imperative to find accommodation that would allow us to roam freely day and night. The young woman wiping down the bar counter greeted me with a smile.

I ordered a cappuccino and got down to business. 'I don't suppose you know of any self-catering vacancies in the village?'

As she operated the coffee machine, she said over her shoulder, 'You might be in luck. All I'm saying is you'll have to pay ready cash.' Steam hissed through the milk. 'Mr Tomlinson was in last night sounding off about losing three weeks' rental. He was waving a letter from a couple of holiday renters announcing that they were not going to turn up today after all. Seems they wanted to be in Edinburgh for the Festival Fringe and that Lower Largo was too far to travel.' She slid the cup towards me. 'When you've finished your coffee I'll give you directions to his cottage. It's not far along the shore from the hotel.'

I came to a satisfactory arrangement with Mr Tomlinson and an hour later had rolled my faux designer suitcase into his traditional fisherman's cottage. In the back garden, beyond a border of purple lavender and spiky thistle-like blue flowers, a gate in a low wall gave access to the beach via a short set of wooden steps. Through the small-paned kitchen window I could see Gorgonzola taking half-hearted swipes at passing bees, her mind on how to con me into dishing up her next meal before it was due. On *my* mind was when to inform Attila of Baxter's murder. Should it be now ... or later?

To inform Attila *now* was definitely out of the question as interception of the *Selkirk Havester* would alert Spinks to the fact that his organization was under surveillance. In any case, Baxter's body had probably already been dumped to commune with the fishes somewhere out in the vast expanse of the North Sea. The police would search the boat and find nothing and then....

Yes, it was tempting to avoid the flak by keeping him in the dark for the moment about my discovery of Baxter's body, since the success or failure of the operation did not depend on me reporting it. Tempting, but unprofessional: the police search for Clive Baxter would continue, wasting police time. And if my failure to disclose this did come to light....

So I'd have to tell him sometime. I sighed. At my debriefing on the conclusion of the operation, Attila would certainly make the most of the fact that I'd disobeyed orders by failing to turn up in the role of cleaner at the Lodge. I could visualize the scene all too clearly. Stony-faced, he would stare at me, letting the silence lengthen. Without warning his fist would crash down on the desk.

'The replacement operative met her death as a direct consequence of your *blatant* disregard of my order to present yourself at the Lodge in the undercover role I'd assigned to you.' The imputation being that I was *totally* responsible. Unfair, but I had to admit that in a small way I had been. '*And*,' he would continue, 'because you did not report your suspicions that the man Baxter was involved, he is – still – at – large.' The last three words emphasized by a stab of the forefinger.

At that point I'd have to confess that Baxter, too, was dead and that I'd withheld this information as well. Which, of course, would invite further severe recriminations on the lines of, 'Smith, it is *your* duty to apprise me of *every* piece of information you uncover, it is *my* decision on whether to act upon it.'

My name would feature once more in Attila's black book. But if I had by that time successfully wound up the mission, the matter would end there. Further musing was brought to an abrupt end by a call to my mobile.

'*Kirs-staay*! He-e-lp! *Come at once!*'

The piercing shriek almost made me drop the phone. The voice was so distorted by hysteria that I barely recognized it as Sapphire McGurk's. In the background were the sounds of grunts and heavy breathing followed by a crash and a woman's scream. Then silence. The call ended.

For a moment I stood there stunned, staring at the phone. I thrust it into my pocket, shouted out of the window, 'You're on your own, G. Back soon,' and minutes later was on my way to Pittenweem as fast as legally permitted. In the quarter of an hour it took to get there, I tried to work out what could have occurred, conjuring up one possibility after another, only to reject them all: there was no reason that I could think of for Sapphire to have made that call.

I found a parking place at the Fish Market down beside the harbour. As I took the steep steps of the wynd two at a time, I again tried to contact Sapphire on my mobile, only to hear the ringing tone and an automated response. 'The person you are calling is currently unavailable. Please try again later.'

Heart pounding, I increased my pace, eyes down to avoid missing my footing on the steps. When the steps became a flagstone slope, I looked up. Opposite Venue 102, six very large wooden packing cases almost blocked the narrow wynd. A burly man in overalls was struggling to manoeuvre a seventh, smaller, wooden case through the passageway that led to Sapphire's door.

From within the passageway on the other side of the case, a voice grunted, 'No use, Danny. Bloody thing's gone and jammed against the wall again. Passage is even narrower from here on.'

Sapphire's distraught face appeared at the small window giving onto the wynd, her henna hair a fiery tangle. 'I told you! *I told you*! It's *far* too big to get through there. I've been telling you for twenty minutes that it's all a terrible mistake. I *begged* you to take them away. But would you listen? *No*! Now this one's stuck. Admit it.'

The burly man stopped heaving and pushing in order to wipe the sweat from his brow. 'Orders were to deliver it here at this address, luv. More than our job's worth to take it away. Don't you worry. Me and Harry'll have it into that studio of yours in a jiff.'

He applied a shoulder to the end of the packing case. From further inside the passageway came the scrunch of wood against stone and a muffled oath.

Sapphire caught sight of me hovering in the background. 'Kirsty!' she screamed. 'What the *hell* does this mean? Sculptures to fit on the table, that's what we agreed! There was I, generous enough to let you share my studio and you duped me, that's what you've done!'

Who was *she* to talk about duping! And who was being generous! Hadn't I paid seventy-five per cent of the cost of her rental of the studio, and been meanly allotted not three-quarters of the studio area, not even half, but the small space occupied by a *table*! The meanness, the injustice of it! I saw red.

'*Really*, Sapphire!' I raged. 'Money-wise you got the best of the deal. What's more, you're hogging the whole studio, leaving me with only the table. What makes you think these packing cases have *anything* to do with—?'

Seven ceramic sculptures in total, I'd said to Attila and there were seven packing cases. Realization dawned that these might indeed be the sculptures I'd sent for. I *had* specified that the sculptures were to be *small*, hadn't I? These packing cases were huge. What on earth had possessed Attila to source such large and presumably cost-a-lot statues?

On past operations he'd been reluctant to sanction even the minimum of expenditure.

Cr-a-ack. Splintering wood galvanized me into action. The contents of this case were in imminent danger of being broken. I'd be in even more trouble if HMRC were to receive a hefty bill for damaged artwork.

I leapt forward. 'Stop!'

A second too late. Packing case and Danny vanished from view with the suddenness of a blockage disappearing down a drain, a blockage impelled by vigorous thrusts with a plunger. Just as suddenly Sapphire too disappeared. One moment she was gesticulating angrily from the window, the next she was gone, the swaying curtain the only sign she'd been there. From inside the studio came a wail of, 'Not there! Not *there*! Put it on the table,' followed by the heavy thud of the packing case being dumped down.

The two men emerged from the passageway dusting their hands with the satisfaction of a difficult job well done and stood surveying the six remaining packing cases semi-blocking the wynd.

Danny scratched his head. 'Not a snowball's chance in hell of getting any of the others in. That one was the smallest. What do you want us to do with the rest of the load, luv?'

I sighed. 'You'll just have to take them back to the sender. They can't stay here.'

'No can do. We've got drop-offs all the way up to Inverness and each time we'd have to unload these cases to get at the stuff behind.'

'Ee-r....' I racked my brain for a solution. Perhaps they could be left in the back garden of the fisherman's cottage in Lower Largo? No, that was far too small and access to it was through the house via doorways even narrower than here, or via a trek along the beach and up wooden steps too flimsy to take the weight of packing cases and men. My mind went blank. 'Ee-r....' I said again.

Harry looked at his watch. 'Don't want to hurry you, luv, but we've got a schedule to keep to and time's money.'

With rising panic I surveyed the packing cases. The one now taking up the whole of Sapphire's table might or might not be my White Lady, but whatever it was, it would have to do as an exhibit. Judging by the size of these other wooden crates, the large sculptures inside wouldn't be out of place in the grounds of a mansion house. The Lodge, *that* could be the answer! The courtyard surrounding its lily pond, the pride and joy of the St Clairs, *was* rather bare and would most certainly be improved by some classy statues to complement the Major's prize koi.

'How much to take them to the King James Hunting Lodge? It's not far – only twenty minutes from here.'

They exchanged £-sign looks. Then Harry slowly shook his head. 'It was one thing to trolley 'em down this lane, it'll be another to shove 'em up it.'

'With all them steps up to the High Street.' Danny clapped his hand to the small of his back, wincing to indicate the likelihood of severe injury to one whose muscles had already been strained by the struggle to ram the first packing case through the impossibly narrow entrance to Sapphire's studio.

'You could take the crates that way.' I pointed to the steps leading down towards the harbour.

To give himself time to invent another excuse for jacking up the price, Danny took out a cigarette, tapped it on the back of his hand, stuck it between his lips and rummaged in his overalls for a lighter.

'I know it's asking a lot,' I wheedled. 'How much to make it worth your while.'

Another exchange of glances. Another rapid calculation of how much they could squeeze out of me.

Holding the cigarette between first and second fingers, Danny blew a perfect smoke ring. 'Fifty–'

'That's just for taking them down all these steps,' Harry broke in swiftly. 'And fifty more to take them to that Lodge place you're talking about.'

I frowned. 'A hundred pounds? That's pretty steep.'

Danny threw his cigarette down and ground it under his heel. 'No gain without pain, luv.'

I forced a smile. 'It's a deal. Just give me a few minutes to get to the cash machine.'

Half an hour later the last of the packing cases were being loaded into their van. Danny climbed into the cab and stuck his head out of the window.

'Need a name to make the delivery.'

'They're for a Major St Clair. Just leave them beside the lily pond in the entrance courtyard.'

I watched the profiteering pair drive off with a self-celebratory *toot*

toot, then climbed back up the steps of the wynd congratulating myself that I'd found the perfect solution for those embarrassing packing cases: I visualized the Major and Maxine rushing out to inspect the surprise gifts. They'd walk round and round them and wonder what they contained. In some excitement they'd break the cases open to reveal the six classy sculptures that had cost Attila a tidy sum to hire. And what's more, the Art Works would be safe at the Lodge till Attila sent for them with the excuse that their delivery had been in error.

All this time Sapphire had been conspicuous by her absence. It was odd that she hadn't come rushing out of her studio while I was negotiating with Danny and Harry. I panted up the wynd to the studio only to find the door closed – and locked. I tried the handle again. Definitely locked. Inside, I could hear movement.

I knocked loudly. The movements stopped. 'Sapphire! It's me.'

'I know it's you, Kirsty, and you're – not – getting – in. You've broken our agreement. The terms will have to be renegotiated.'

An impasse. And it was broken only by offering her even *more* cash....

The packing case occupied the whole of Sapphire's table-top. When I prised it open, I was relieved to find that it was indeed my White Lady, reposing demurely inside. She had managed to survive Danny and Harry's rough handling with no evidence of chips or cracks. This would have to be my one exhibit for the Festival. Fortunately, the mistake I'd made in showing Baxter its photograph didn't matter now.

Behind me, Sapphire gave it a disparaging sniff and a snide, 'Are these two bulges her boobs or her bum?'

I wasn't wounded. Henry Moore and Picasso have had their critics too.

CHAPTER TWENTY-THREE

Frosty relations were the order of the day on both sides until a week later. Then the frenzied preparations on the Festival Preview Night forced a détente when Sapphire required an assistant to hang up a display of yarns outside the studio. Her request to get the ladder out was just what I'd been waiting for, as standing on its top step gave me an excellent view of Bert Mackay's front door, otherwise hidden behind his garden wall. My frequent scaling of the ladder on the excuse of rearranging the skeins to better advantage did much to thaw the atmosphere.

Someone like myself desperate for exhibition space must have persuaded Mackay to rent out one of his rooms at the last minute, for a couple of days previously a banner proclaiming NEW VENUE had sprouted on the wall. That had given me an idea. Mackay might very well take himself off somewhere to avoid all the people who would be crowding into his house on the busy preview evening. That would give me the ideal opportunity to do some snooping in the private part of the house, and Sapphire wouldn't notice if I slipped away while she was in the midst of a sales pitch and demonstration.

My presence wouldn't be necessary at my own exhibition or to be more brutally accurate, exhibit. Kirsty Gordon's name didn't appear in the Festival brochure on the Artist and Venue list or among the accompanying thumbnail pictures of the artwork, so nobody would be seeking me out with a view to commissioning a similar statue. People coming to the venue to see Sapphire's yarns would assume the White Lady statue was part of her display.

At eight o'clock on Preview Night, an hour after the venues opened, I could see from the top of the ladder that a small queue had formed in Mackay's garden indicating an overflow of visitors to that exhibition. I looked across to where Sapphire was busy demonstrating the various dyes obtained from herbs, leaves, bark, onion skins, tea and coffee.

She was saying, 'For all dyes, you need a fixative. For berries it's salt, and for plant material it's vinegar. Now you've also got to remember that....'

This was the opportunity I'd been waiting for. I slipped away and walked down the wynd to Mackay's house. Pinned to the gate was a large poster:

Photographic Exhibition
Predator and Prey

Below was a full-colour close-up of a blowfly, an iridescent blue-bottle, clinging precariously with one leg to the bright green lip of a carnivorous pitcher plant, its tumble to a death by drowning imminent. The photographer certainly had talent.

I joined the queue in the garden. The photos on display in the house must have been worth more than a quick glance, as it was some time before I could edge my way into the exhibition itself. Inside, immediately to the left of the front door, narrow stone steps led to the upper floor. A short corridor led to the kitchen where I glimpsed a worktop laden with an impressive array of wine glasses, bottles and plates of crisps. No sign of Mackay there.

Two ground-floor rooms had been cleared of furniture for the exhibition and the walls hung with poster-size photographs. I filtered through the knots of people in the crowded exhibition room clutching the glass of wine thrust into my hand, stopping now and again to study the photographs. No sign of Mackay here either. I'd make my way confidently upstairs as if I had every right to be there and if challenged, I'd apologize for my mistake in thinking the exhibition continued on the upper floor. As a final check, I'd first poke my head into the kitchen and ask where he was. If I was told he was upstairs, I'd nod my thanks and nip out the front door and away.

I'd just abandoned my glass on a table preparatory to putting this plan into action, when I was stopped in my tracks by one of the black-and-white photographs. A seagull stood at the water's edge preening its feathers, seemingly unaware of a cat in predatory mid-air pounce. It was the dramatic action photo of Gorgonzola taken by Terry Warburton.

'Hi, there, Vanessa, glad you could make it! What do you think of my exhibition?' The shout rose above the hubbub in the room.

I whirled round in dismay.

A grinning Terry Warburton was advancing towards me. 'That shot I captured of Smootchikins in action perfectly illustrates the theme of *Predator and Prey*, eh?'

I saw Nicola Beaton staring at me over the intervening heads. She was mouthing, 'Vanessa? Smootchikins!' as realization dawned that here at last was the woman Bert had so opportunely fingered to let the two of them off the hook. On her face was growing excitement that Vanessa Dewar-Smythe was still around. If she gave Bert my new description to pass to Spinks, she and Bert would no longer be in danger of being blamed for the missing cannabis packages.

It had been a disastrous mistake to come here.

'Terry!' I gasped. 'What a surprise! I had no idea that this was *your* exhibition. I thought you were in Edinburgh.'

'Yes, it was a surprise to me too. It was completely unexpected for me to get a venue at the last minute like this, but my show in Edinburgh finished on Monday and I took the chance of asking around.'

I became all too aware that Nicola Beaton had sidled closer, and under the pretext of making a close study of a nearby photograph, was listening intently to every word.

Terry was studying me. 'New hairstyle, new colour. But the way you hold your head is the same. That's what a photographer remembers. How come you're not still staying at the Lodge?'

'Blame it on my partner,' I laughed as if I had nothing to hide. 'I'm about to start a new life with him in Cannes.' Conscious of Beaton's listening ears and that any changes I made in the story I'd spun to Carla at Selkirk Properties could catch me out, I added, 'Would you believe it! After *all* that he promised, he didn't fancy coming to live with me at the Lodge! So there was no use spending more money on rental with a view to buying, was there?' With a bit of luck Terry would be distracted from commenting further on my changed appearance. Unfortunately, he wasn't.

He was looking at me, eyebrows raised. 'But why the expensive make-over? Doesn't that man of yours go for straight-haired brunettes any more, then?'

'Thought I'd surprise him,' I said. 'If he doesn't like me like this, I'll change back to the old me.'

Nicola Beaton had come to a decision. Choosing that moment to straighten up from an over-long inspection of the photograph of a sea eagle with talons outspread, a millisecond away from the strike, she turned towards me, performing an exaggerated double-take of surprised recognition.

'Why, it's Vanessa … Vanessa Dewar-Smythe … isn't it?' A feigned moment of doubt was indicated by the hesitations and a frown. 'It was the voice that did it. When I heard you speaking just now, I *thought* I recognized the voice. But … but … you left the Lodge a week ago. I didn't expect to find you still here in Pittenweem?' The question in her voice artfully designed to elicit a reply.

Blissfully unaware of the danger he was putting me in, Terry chipped in with, 'Let me guess – you're helping out at an exhibition at the Festival.'

I was on the verge of denying it, spinning a story that I was staying in Edinburgh and had just come all the way here for the buzz of Preview Night, when I saw a change in Beaton's expression. The words 'helping' and 'exhibition' had obviously triggered the memory of a woman hanging up natural-dyed yarns at the venue further up the wynd. A woman with short, black, curly hair just like mine.

It was a Catch 22 situation. Beaton would know if I lied about being at Venue 102 and be sure to inform Mackay. The lie would confirm that the woman who had so suddenly scarpered from the Lodge must indeed be up to something. Spinks needed no proof before he acted to eliminate someone. Suspicion was more than enough.

If I *did* admit to helping at Venue 102, that would more than confirm Beaton's suspicions because I'd pretended not to recognize her when she was standing beside me. Even more suspicious was the fact that I had answered to the name of Kirsty. What reason could there possibly be for these actions other than that I had something to hide? Either way Beaton would waste no time in hastening to tell Mackay her news. The damage would be done.

There was one possible way to retrieve the situation. If Mackay thought I could be located at Venue 102 for the rest of the week, there was just the chance he might delay reporting me to Spinks until tomorrow. And by tomorrow I would be long gone from there.

I nodded. 'Yes, you're right, Terry. Until the end of the Festival I'm helping Sapphire at the venue just up the wynd. We weren't busy so I took the chance to look in here. But I'd better rush back. Congrats, Terry, I'll pop in again later in the week.'

With a wave to both of them, I made my escape, conscious all the way to the door of Beaton's eyes boring into my back. Had I given myself a breathing space, time to disappear again?

Sapphire was still in full flow when I arrived back at the studio. '... but if you find these natural colours a little subdued for your taste, I'll let you into a Sapphire McGurk secret. For brighter colours, chalk or rainwater is the answer, depending on the colour you're working with....'

Unnoticed, I slipped into the room – and came to an abrupt halt. Sapphire had converted my beloved Work of Art into a display mannequin for her wares. My White Lady statue was no longer reclining in naked splendour on the table. She was now artfully festooned with skeins of wool in muted shades of blue, green and lavender. Only her face and one large foot were still visible. I stared at the White Lady who gazed demurely back.

I put out a hand to snatch off the offending wool, then thought better of it. I wasn't going to come anywhere near this venue again. And that was going to present me with a big problem: the statue was too heavy for me to carry away tonight. Why not leave her in Sapphire's clutches till the Festival was over, giving me a week to make arrangements for the uplift?

I turned to sneak away. Too late, I'd been spotted.

A peremptory, 'Kirsty, where *have* you been!' was the prelude to two hours of slavery as I was set to work holding up skeins, mixing up buckets of coloured water, chopping plant material, straining tea and coffee grounds, and *ugh!* scouring wool to remove grease and oils.

Closing time of ten o'clock couldn't come too soon. At last, hot, tired and rebellious, I flung off my apron ready to slump on the *chaise longue*. Sapphire beat me to it, sinking down with an exaggerated sigh.

'A very successful, but exhausting evening, Kirsty. I think that calls for a little refreshment.' A languid wave towards the wall cupboard. 'You'll find glass and bottles in there.' She closed her eyes and held out a plump hand ready to receive. 'Ice right to the *top*.'

On a shelf in the cupboard reposed a half-full bottle of Bombay Sapphire blue gin, two small unopened bottles of tonic water, two lemons, a tiny knife, an insulated ice bucket and, in solitary splendour, *one* large glass. It was clear that my role was to be waiter to the waited-on, orderly to the general, flunky to the mistress of the house.

In mutinous mood, I tipped ice cubes into the glass.

Her eyes opened enough to inspect. '*Right* to the top.'

'How much gin, Sapphire?' I gritted.

'I think on this occasion, a *very* generous amount.' Her eyes closed once more to indicate a woman overcome by utter exhaustion.

My voice crackling with suppressed anger, tone barely civil, I ground out, 'And tonic? How – much – tonic, Sapphire?'

'As much as the glass'll take, Kirsty.' A frown. 'And on no account forget the squeeze of lemon.'

I shot her a quick glance – her eyes remained closed, hand outstretched in blissful anticipation. I took a couple of surreptitious sips. Just as I raised the glass and was about to indulge myself with a third, her eyes snapped open.

Quickly I held the glass up higher and narrowed my eyes as if to judge the level of liquid. 'Is this enough, Sapphire?'

A pout. 'Full to the brim, I said, dear. A glass three-quarters full is a glass a quarter empty, is it not?' An imperiously beckoning finger was a clear demonstration that she'd been kept waiting far too long.

Her hand closed round the glass. With each sip a slow smile spread across her face. She didn't see me tiptoe out. Sapphire's order for a refill would fall on empty air.

CHAPTER TWENTY-FOUR

The next morning, Saturday, I went to ground in the holiday cottage at Lower Largo. The drug shipments' schedule I'd seen on Baxter's laptop had convinced me that Spinks was soon about to bring his operation to a close. But I didn't have enough information for HMRC to locate him before he moved on. I had to remain in the area, yet couldn't take the risk of being seen in any of the East Coast villages by Beaton, or for that matter another resident of the Lodge who might mention the meeting to her. All day Gorgonzola and I stayed indoors. From now on it was going to be safety first.

I have to admit that by six o'clock in the evening, I was bored, browned off, fed-up to the back teeth with being cooped up in the cottage staring out of the window, ignoring those frequent and increasingly strident voicemails from Sapphire demanding my presence to help her in the studio. It was the last of her string of messages that weakened my resolve to stay indoors.

'Kirsty, damn you! Where the *hell* are you? I know you harped on ad infinitum about going off to see the torchlight procession and fireworks display. But the procession doesn't even *begin* till 9.15. That will give you two and a half *hours* to help me. You saw how *busy* it was last night. After all I've *done* for you, you *owe* it to me to come and help in my hour of need.'

That did it. It wasn't the vision of an overwrought, perspiring and hassled Sapphire that changed my mind about staying put in the cottage, it was the reminder that I had been looking forward to the torchlight procession and the firework display since I'd first heard about the Festival. What harm would it do to go and watch? It would be dark and I'd just be one of the hundreds milling around.

*

At Venue 102 the handle of the studio door turned. A red-faced man and a woman, her hair scraped back behind her ears in a most unbecoming style, stood framed in the doorway looking around. Sapphire McGurk glanced up crossly from straining a messy concoction of roots and bark into a bucket.

'I'm not open for another ten minutes,' she snapped.

As if they hadn't heard, the couple advanced into the studio. Sapphire frowned. Who did they think they *were* to come bursting into her studio like this?

She slowly enunciated as to persons not well-versed in the English language, 'Read – my – lips. *Not* – open – for – ten–' She stopped abruptly. Was this not the woman who had shown such a gratifying interest in her natural-dyed wools a week ago? It wouldn't do to antagonize a potential customer. The frown vanished to be replaced by a forced smile. 'As you see, I'm not *quite* ready yet. Can I possibly ask you to come back in ten minutes?'

The man strode forward. 'Back in ten minutes. No bloody way!'

Sapphire's eyes opened wide in disbelief, her mouth even wider to splutter, 'Bugg—'

The woman dug a sharp elbow into the man's ribs.

'Of course we can come back. I can see that you're in quite a bit of difficulty having to manage everything on your own. Where's the girl that was helping you the other day? Has she let you down?'

Touched in a raw spot, Sapphire flung down the sieve. 'Yes, she *has*! Kirsty's taken the *whole* day off because she knew if she came in tonight, I'd not let her go off to see the procession and the fireworks.' To vent her frustration, she lifted the sieve up again and banged it down hard. The couple glanced at each other, oblivious to the brown droplets spattered over their clothes.

'Oh! She *told* us she'd be here.' The woman turned away, muttering, 'We'll catch up with her later.' At the doorway she swung round. 'So you think we'll find her watching the procession, do you?'

Sapphire grabbed some skeins of wool and dunked them savagely in the sieved liquid. 'Sure to! Or at the fireworks. She certainly went on enough about both.'

It was only after the couple had gone that it occurred to her that the very same woman who only a week ago had so admired the natural-dyed wools for their unusual shades, softness and freedom from toxic chemicals, had rushed off without showing the slightest interest in them.

I left it till twilight before driving to Pittenweem, confident that it would then be safe to mingle with the crowds at the gathering point for the firework procession. Under the street lights on the promenade a brisk trade was being done in decorative Mickey Mouse balloons, green, blue and pink glow sticks, and despite the cold wind, ice creams.

I chose the location with care, taking up position in a doorway to watch the procession move purposefully off. Bagpipes and drums struck up a stirring Scottish medley; laughing children fenced with luminous glow sticks; light and shadow from flaring torches flickered over the sea of faces. The river of fire flowed past the harbour, moved slowly up the steep Abbey Wall Road, and was lost to sight.

Sorely tempted as I was to join in, I resisted: Beaton, Mackay, and even Spinks could very well be among the spectators lining the route. To keep the lowest of low profiles was the condition I'd laid down for myself when I'd made the decision to leave Lower Largo. And I was going to stand by my decision.

Once the procession had wound its way back in half an hour, the fireworks would begin. Till then I'd keep well away from any brightly lit areas. Head down, face half-hidden by the upturned collar of my warm jacket, I wandered along the promenade and stood leaning on the railing looking down on the waves washing over low-lying seaweed-covered reefs. The darkening waters of the Forth stretched out unbroken to a horizon marked by the twinkling lights of the East Lothian coast. In a pale sky with clouds still flushed pink, a moving pinpoint of white light marked a plane on its course for Edinburgh airport.

A peaceful scene, and I should have been soothed, but I was still on edge over how little time there was to bring the operation to a successful conclusion. Criminal organizations and drug barons are experts in judging how long they can run a scheme. If there is danger of a more powerful rival organization muscling in or of the authorities getting wind of it, they pull out. So when Spinks's suspicions had been aroused by my undercover colleague Greg Findlay, I'd have expected him to make one final shipment to wind up his operation. He'd already had another warning that the writing was on the wall for his current scheme when a mysterious woman at the Lodge had tampered with the cannabis consignment in the bunker. That Spinks hadn't pulled out by now indicated that whatever he was up to was on the verge of completion and far too important for him to abandon.

But time was running out for another reason. Never patient at the best of times, once Attila had decided he'd given me more than enough leeway to track down the man behind the cannabis ring, he'd intercept the next consignment on the list I'd given him. And Spinks would cut his losses and go, no matter how lucrative the final shipment.

I leaned back against the rail watching a little girl choose a blue dolphin from the balloon seller and walk proudly off with it bobbing on its string. A couple of hundred yards ahead of her there was a ripple of movement among the knots of people waiting for the highlight of the evening to begin. A man and woman were pushing their way through the crowd. What drew my attention to them was that they were not looking ahead, intent on reaching some objective. As they elbowed their way through the crowd their heads were turning from side to side, scanning faces, as if looking out for somebody. The glint of streetlight on the man's oily slicked-back hair sent my pulse racing. Despite the poor light and the distance, I was sure that the man was Bert Mackay and that the woman must be Nicola Beaton. The person they were looking for was *me*. They knew I was somewhere in the crowd.

They approached a solitary figure leaning on the railing looking out to sea – just as I had been doing only a short while before. If I stayed where I was, they'd home in on me. The crowd would be no protection. In a less public place Mackay wouldn't hesitate to use force to drag me off with them, but though they couldn't do that here, their tactic would be for Beaton to keep me talking while Mackay went off to contact Spinks. They'd keep me under close observation till Spinks could make arrangements, then a knife-point dug into my ribs or the barrel of a gun jammed painfully into my back would ensure I came quietly.

For the moment their attention was on the figure by the railing. I could drop onto the beach only six feet below in the hope that they'd not notice me and hurry past. Or I could thread my way through the people on the promenade and try to make an escape up the nearest wynd. I'd have to make my decision *now*. A figure hurrying away from the scene would draw the very attention I hoped to avoid, so I chose the beach.

No one was taking any interest in me. I slipped under the railing and dropped onto the narrow strip of sand below. I sat there, arms loosely clasped round knees as if waiting patiently for the fireworks to begin. Had I moved fast enough? Would Beaton poke her head over the railing with a cry of, 'Look, it's Vanessa! Whatever are you doing down there?'

I pulled back the sleeve of my jacket to look at my watch. Seconds, slow as minutes, passed.... The faint strain of pipes and drums drifted down from the promenade above, increasing in volume as the torchlight procession approached. The loud chatter of voices overhead indicated that the promenade was rapidly filling up with spectators. Safety in numbers, they say, but it was safer to remain here, sitting on the sand.

It's essential in my line of work to be honest about admitting blame, so I spent the next quarter of an hour in self-recrimination. What had *possessed* me to risk the HMRC operation, my life, *everything*, for a few minutes' enjoyment of flaming torches and colourful pyrotechnics? To give in to temptation was unprofessional and I was paying the penalty.

It's also essential to analyze *why* things have gone wrong. How was it I'd been so mistaken in thinking that there would be little risk in mingling with the crowds? It was clear that Beaton and Mackay knew I was going to be here, yet I hadn't told anybody. It had been a spur-of-the-moment decision taken only a couple of hours ago, so how could they *possibly* have known?

Sapphire! They must have learned from Sapphire that I was going to be at the fireworks. Only yesterday I'd asked her about the route of the procession and the time of the fireworks and made it clear that she couldn't expect my help tonight. She hadn't taken this very well, and I suspected that if I had indeed turned up at the studio, her demands on me would have made it impossible to get away. Beaton and Mackay must have called there. They would have only have had to say that they were looking for me and Sapphire would have let fly about how her assistant had let her down by going off to see the fireworks. Yes, that's how it must have been. That was something I should have foreseen.

But the clear thought necessary to survive in a dangerous situation is sabotaged by dwelling on the past and there's no point regretting something you can't fix. I sighed. Oh well, I'd have an uninterrupted view of the fireworks set off on the outer pier of the harbour. After that, it would be a matter of judging when best to leave my refuge on the beach to mingle with the crowds making their way back to the car park and bus stops.

Swooosh. With a fiery trail, a starburst of white light and a fusillade of bangs, the fireworks began. For the next quarter of an hour the displays colour-washed sky and sea. To a stirring rendition of *The Ride of the Valkyries*, yellow, green, and red chrysanthemums blossomed, white comets streaked their trails heavenward, orange and green fire-balls curved a trail over sea and promenade. BANG – a vertical line of glittering tinsel hung in the sky. *Pptt pptt pptt* – showers of golden rain pittered down. *Crackle crackle crackle* – white stars fizzed and sparked. A curtain of smoke hung in the air after each burst of fireworks, eddying and drifting in ever-changing patterns towards the promenade.

Swoosh BANGBANGBANG. The display climaxed with three elegant palm trees drooping their amber fronds slowly down ... down ... down, trunks and fronds slowly fading into the smoke that now hung like a dense sea haar over promenade and quayside. Above me I could hear the shuffle of feet, the buzz of voices as the crowd dispersed to make their way back to the car park or to prolong the evening with a fish supper or a convivial drink in a pub.

I stood up, easing my stiffened muscles as I calculated how best to haul myself up onto the promenade.

A head poked over the railing. 'I *thought* it was you, Vanessa.'

Startled, I took a step back, heart thumping, till I recognized the smiling face.

'Terry! I should have known you and your camera would be around here somewhere.'

'Want a heave up?

I held up my arms.

He grabbed my wrists. 'Jump at the count of three.'

I tensed my muscles.

'One ... two ... *three.*'

He'd underestimated the combined power of my spring and his own strength. He thought the woman he was pulling up was the pathetically unfit Vanessa Dewar-Smythe whose sole idea of exercise was an easy stroll with her cat on a lead – the image I'd cultivated at the Lodge. I was a physically fit, gym-frequenting HMRC agent. The result was that I rose up the wall from the beach with unexpected speed.

BANG. A blinding FLASH.

A rocket exploded where my back had been only seconds before.

CHAPTER TWENTY-FIVE

A ring of concerned faces was looking down at me. I lay on the promenade, shaking from the reaction, ears ringing from the blast, but otherwise unhurt. Before I'd set out for the fireworks that evening, I'd decided that standing around in the cold wind watching the torchlight procession and the firework display would be a chilly experience: this Scottish August evening merited warm trousers and boots rather than light summer clothing and flimsy sandals. Scorched and blackened wool and sooty, pitted leather proved it was a decision that had saved me from severe injury.

Terry was kneeling at my side, lips moving like an actor in a silent film.

'Can't hear what you're saying, Terry. But I'm all right. Be OK in a minute.' My lips were moving. Words without sound. Were they just in my head?

The wall of bystanders parted as two paramedics in green coveralls pushed their way through the crowd and I was carried off to an ambulance stationed at the Fish Market to receive casualties. Superficial burns dressed, hearing gradually returning, and now only slightly shaky, I attempted to persuade the paramedics I was fit to be released.

Pursing his lips, the older of the two shook his head. 'It's not as simple as that, lass. There could be delayed shock.'

'Aye, we can't take the chance, Joe.' The other man laid a restraining hand on my shoulder, gently pushing me back down on the stretcher. 'Shock can lead to a medical emergency.' Synchronized nods. 'How are you feeling?' Synchronized words.

The truth was that I was feeling pretty scared. While they'd been attending to my minor burns, I'd come to realize that the stray rocket had not been an unfortunate accident: it had been a deliberate attempt to maim and kill. Mackay and Beaton had given Spinks the description of the suspicious woman at the Lodge and told him that she would be among the crowd watching the firework display. He must have taken up position on the outer pier where the fireworks were being set off, a position directly opposite the main viewing area of Mid Shore. He'd have scanned the crowd through powerful night binoculars, and as a lone figure sitting on the sand, I had made it easy for him. He'd have recognized me as his old enemy at once: my face would have been imprinted on his memory, just as his was on mine.

'How are you feeling?' Joe asked again. 'Let's see. I'll just take your pulse.' He reached for my wrist. 'Tell me, is there anyone waiting for you outside?'

Terry, perhaps. Spinks, almost certainly. He'd want to find out how successful he'd been. The thought set my heart racing.

'Pulse rate's high, Mike,' Joe murmured. 'Sweating too....' They exchanged glances. He eased himself up from the bench. 'Better if you have a check-up. Nothing at all to worry about, my dear.' The rear door closed behind him, then opened again. 'Chap out here wants to know how you are. Says he's with you.'

Was it Terry outside? Or was it Mackay? I played safe.

'Tell him I'm OK and that I'll be in touch tomorrow.'

I sank back and closed my eyes.

When the ambulance arrived at Kirkcaldy Hospital's Accident and Emergency Department, I was a lot calmer, and by the time I was attended to, calmer still. My pulse rate was almost back to normal, and with none of the symptoms of shock in evidence, it was decided that I needed no further treatment for the minor burns on my legs.

While waiting for attention in Casualty, I'd come to a decision: Attila's search for cannabis factories would have to wait, I'd concentrate on locating Spinks. 'Those who try to get one over on Hiram J Spinks don't live to regret it,' he'd said. Before he nailed *me*, I was going to have to nail him, and it would have to be soon. I'd worked out a plan, and it involved Terry Warburton.

Feeling more than a little conspicuous in trousers cropped to below the knee by paramedic scissors, boots scorched and pockmarked, and calves wound round with bandages reminiscent of the puttees worn by soldiers in World War One, I made my way to reception to phone a taxi to take me back to Lower Largo – another claim on my expenses that would be sure to catch Attila's attention and require explanation.

*

It was nearly 2 a.m. when I arrived back in Lower Largo. After a wary sniff at my scorched boots and bandaged legs, Gorgonzola sat back, looking up at me, wide-eyed. A long *mi-a-o-w*, without even a glance in the direction of her empty food bowl, conveyed her sympathy for my fragile state of health.

It was late midday before I surfaced from a deep sleep. Sensitive as ever when I was in a low mood, G had solicitously refrained from trampling over my legs in the night or from waking me up for her breakfast. I walked slowly along to the newspaper shop and came back with a Sunday paper heavy with supplements. I like to skim through a newspaper while munching on my toast and marmalade, cup of tea at my elbow.

After breakfast, feeling much restored, I mulled over the plan I'd worked out in Casualty. Terry had a lucrative business taking action photographs of golfers on the Old Course or with their caddies in world-famous locations on the Course, like the Swinton Bridge, the notorious Road Hole Bunker, or the eighteenth hole in front of the Clubhouse. Camera-shy as he was, even Spinks might have succumbed to the temptation of posing for one of Terry's photographs. It was, to use a golfing metaphor, a long shot, but if he *had* ordered a photo, Terry would have a note of the name and address Spinks was using.

A convincing reason for asking to look through the photo library would be to tell Terry that I was an undercover tax inspector looking for a man guilty of tax offences, a man who adopted various aliases, a man who was a golf fanatic and who, I had reason to believe, was at present in the St Andrews area. If I recognized Spinks in one of the photos, I'd naturally want to know the name and address. That settled, I poured another cup of tea. Gorgonzola was curled up on my lap, purring contentedly. I nudged her aside and fished in my pocket for my mobile to phone Terry.

There was, I thought guiltily, another phone call I should be making: the tricky one to Attila to report the discovery of Clive Baxter's body. As if he had read my thoughts, at that moment a text message came in from Attila. *Phone SOONEST. Mandatory. T.* It ended with the code word signifying 'extreme urgency'.

An instant reply would demonstrate that I was a model operative, on the alert to receive orders, and by implication, carry them out.

He answered immediately. 'This is a welcome surprise, Smith. Ten days have passed since your *last* communication asking for statues to be supplied to assist with your new undercover role.'

I said nothing. What was there to say? He knew very well that an operative reported in only when there was something of substance to report, and only when it was safe to do so.

He broke the silence. 'HMRC spent a considerable amount of money on those statues. Would you care to update me on whether it was money well spent?'

I visualized the statues now adding an elegant touch to the courtyard at the Lodge. 'Yes, I can truthfully say they are just what is needed.'

'Good. Now that the Festival's over, I'll see that they are uplifted shortly. The reason I'm making this call is that there has been a new development re the death of our agent sent as cleaner to the Lodge. An arrest warrant has been issued for a Clive Baxter, a resident at the Lodge and the owner of the car involved in the hit-and-run. Two weeks ago you sent in a report that the cleaner's death was not a simple hit-and-run, that it was, in fact, murder. Would you care to enlighten me as to why you came so early to that conclusion?'

There was no way out of it: I'd have to make a full confession not only that I'd held back vital information, but that I too had been a resident at the Lodge.

He heard me out in silence. Then, 'Let me get this clear. You had the opportunity to stay at the Lodge, where you became suspicious of Baxter. You failed to warn our agent about him, though you could see she was inexperienced. What is more, for two whole weeks you have known the identity of her murderer. Is that correct?'

'Yes, Mr Tyler, that is correct, but I can expl—'

He cut me short, tone icy. 'Baxter has disappeared, gone to ground. If, *at the time*, you had communicated to me what you knew, he would now be under arrest. Thanks to your misguided disregard for this rule of procedure, he's got away scot-free.'

I closed my eyes and took a deep breath. 'Well, he hasn't, not exactly,' I said. This was turning out as I had predicted, but without the successful outcome to the mission which would have led to my breach of the rules being forgiven, if not forgotten. I told him of my discovery of Baxter's body in the hold of the *Selkirk Harvester*.

The tirade began. 'I'm speechless, Smith, *speechless*.' If only he had been. It was several minutes before he ended with the words, 'I'm taking you off the operation, Smith. At the end of the week I'll arrange a session for you to brief your replacement.' He cut the connection.

CHAPTER TWENTY-SIX

For a long moment I stared at the mobile, then relieved my feelings in an outburst to G who was snoozing on the rug in a patch of sun.

'The man's an idiot taking me off the case when I'm *so* close to tracking down Spinks! How unfair is *that*, G!' I slammed the flat of my hand down on the table hard enough to make the cup rattle in its saucer.

Startled, Gorgonzola raised her head and stared back at me, eyes wide.

'Surely the objective of this operation is to catch the shadowy figure behind the cannabis factories, wouldn't you say, G?'

She must have thought that the anger in my voice was directed against her. She sprang up and came over to twine herself round my legs, purring loudly, well aware that fawning and flattery were a sure way out of trouble.

I warmed to my theme. 'Attila's blinkered, got it all wrong. He refuses to believe that Hiram J Spinks *is* that shadowy figure. I know what I *saw*: Spinks pushed Selkirk to his death. I know what I *heard*: I recognized his voice at the cannabis factory. And I *won't* let him get away this time. I just *won't*.' I thumped the table again. Mewing piteously, G redoubled her efforts to placate.

That got my attention. Full of contrition, I bent down and stroked her curved back. 'Sorry, G, I'm not angry with *you*.' I seized one of the supplement sections, tore out a page and screwed it up into a ball.

'Catch!' I sent it rolling across the carpet in front of her.

A leap, a pounce, a pat pat pat. *Smack*! The ball was expertly dispatched. She crouched, waiting expectantly. I reached for the supplement to rip out another page. A headline caught my eye. *BEATON'S BOOK ANOTHER WINNER*

I skimmed the paragraphs, then sank back in the chair and slowly reread the article. It seemed that in London, yesterday evening, the novelist Nicola Beaton had been scheduled to give an after-dinner talk at a well-known London hotel to celebrate the launch of her latest historical novel, set in the time of James V. Yesterday. In London. At more-or-less the same time that I'd glimpsed Beaton and Mackay searching for me among the crowds on Pittenweem Mid Shore.

When I'd first come to the Lodge, I'd visited her website as part of my research into the residents. I'd pushed aside lingering doubts over a discrepancy between the Beaton I'd met and the photograph on the website, putting it down to a very different hairstyle and to the fact that authors and publishers often favour a youthful appearance in an author's publicity photograph. It now seemed more than likely that the Nicola Beaton of the Lodge and the author Nicola Beaton were not one and the same person.

I stared at the newspaper article that had delivered the bombshell. Why would someone who had been put in place at the Lodge as part of Selkirk's cannabis and money-laundering organization choose to adopt the identity of a *real* author? Pretend to be a novelist engaged in research, yes, but why take the risk of exposure as an imposter when any false name would have done? Could she be related, a sister, perhaps, or a cousin?

'Puzzling, eh, G?'

A *miaow* and an impatient tap on my foot indicated that my deliberations had gone on too long. I tossed her another crumpled-up paper ball and stared out of the window, deep in thought.

The fact that Spinks had tried to kill me at the Pittenweem firework display supported the conclusion I'd already reached: that he was aware the authorities were closing in, and that he needed more time to organize the final lucrative shipment of his cannabis enterprise. I came to a decision. My last hope of tracing Spinks rested on Terry having taken a photo of him on the Old Course. If he didn't have a photo, I'd slip the damning newspaper article and an anonymous note through Beaton's letterbox to try to panic her into leading me to Spinks before he went to ground.

I picked up the phone. 'It's Vanessa, Terry. ... No, no, only shock and a few minor burns. I'm fine now. I need to ask you a favour. Could I come over this afternoon and have a look at your photos of golfers? Here's why....' I launched into my story of being a tax inspector on the trail of a tax dodger.

*

It was frustrating that I couldn't go straight to the Lodge and start looking through the photos. First I had to catch the bus to Pittenweem and make my way to the Festival car park where I'd left my car when I'd driven to see the fireworks.

It was a tense moment when I drew up outside the Lodge alongside Terry's somewhat ancient red Vauxhall. I'd set the appointment with him for the afternoon, when Beaton would be away on one of those mysterious Sunday visits of hers to St Andrews. If the anonymous note accompanying the article was to work, it was vital that I didn't encounter her. My aim was to induce alarm, lead her to think that by meeting the anonymous writer she could somehow resolve the matter without Spinks finding out that she'd aroused suspicion. When we met, I'd pressure her to tell me all she knew about Spinks in return for my silence. There was, of course, the possibility that if I misjudged her reaction to the anonymous note, I'd be turning up for that meeting with Beaton only to find I had a rendezvous with Spinks, but the risk of that was minimal. She'd be too afraid to incur the wrath of 'Mr Martin'.

I had been looking forward to seeing the improvement the six imposing Works of Art had made to the ambience of the Lodge. So it was rather a shock when I saw the six statues that now graced the entrance courtyard and its lily pond. 'Graced' was perhaps not the most accurate of words, 'dominated' being more apt. The size of the crates had indicated that the statues would be large, but I'd somehow expected them to be in classical Greek style – tastefully draped maidens, or perhaps a Rodin-style Thinker. But these were of the ultra-modern Henry Moore-cum-Picasso School, and against the backdrop of the corbel-stepped and turreted Lodge were alien blobs dropped from outer space. Far from being impressed, the St Clairs would have been utterly aghast. It was comforting that they would have no way of knowing that I was responsible.

Unfortunately they were at home, as evidenced by the Major's tank-like 4x4, precision-parked in the exact centre of his assigned space. This had to be a stealth visit, my entrance to and exit from the Lodge unseen. If they saw me here now, they would be sure to rant on to the other residents, Beaton included, about my reappearance.

Shielded by the bulk of the Major's car, I took stock: nobody in the courtyard, nobody on the front steps, no twitch of the curtains at the Major's windows. However, there was just a chance that someone might now be occupying my ex-apartment, charmed into the purchase by the elegant Carla of Selkirk Properties; there was just a chance that Beaton might have stayed at home 'working on a novel' and had not gone off as usual to St Andrews. But there was no chance whatsoever that Baxter was in *his* apartment cataloguing his Wemyss Ware – or doing anything at all for that matter. His French doors would be my means of entry.

Seconds later I had rounded the corner of the building and was standing outside the French doors of the late unlamented antique dealer, picklocks in hand. Though all his furniture and personal possessions were as he had left them, the rooms had an eerie, empty air as if the apartment had sensed the owner would never be coming back. I left by his front door, having first listened for voices or movement in the corridor outside. In order to get unseen to Terry's apartment on the upper floor I made use of a narrow stairway behind an unmarked door, in former times designated for the use of servants.

My meeting with Terry didn't work out as I'd hoped. He believed my story that I was on the trail of a golf-fanatic tax-dodger and lost no time in sifting through his golfing photos with me. Unfortunately none of them featured Spinks.

'Oh well, Terry,' I sighed, 'it was worth a try. If you could let me have a look at the next set of photos you take, perhaps he'll be in one of them. Thanks anyway.'

After leaving Terry's apartment, I made use of the servants' stair identical to the one on the other side of the building, slipped my note through Beaton's letterbox and, retracing my route, made my way back to my car without encountering anyone.

Nicola Beaton frowned down at the envelope lying face-down on her hall floor. Her mail had arrived before she set off for St Andrews, so somebody at the Lodge must have pushed it through her letterbox. Probably that little pipsqueak the Major, or his busybody wife, wanting to rope her in to some so-called charity event. She picked it up to toss it in the kitchen bin.

Stunned, she stared at the scrawl on the front of the envelope.

Are you Nicola Beaton? I think not!

She turned it over and over before plucking up the courage to tear it open. It contained a newspaper cutting and a half-sheet of cheap notepaper. The words burned themselves into her brain.

It wouldn't do for others to find out, would it? Meet me at St Rule's Tower, St Andrew's Cathedral, at 3 pm tomorrow or I go to the police.

She ran her tongue over dry lips, and with hands that shook smoothed out the newspaper cutting on the worktop. She read it twice, the first time quickly, and again more slowly, then collapsed onto a chair and stared out of the kitchen window. Outside the sun was shining in a cloudless blue sky, but for Nicola Beaton the outlook was dark indeed. She reached out a hand for the phone. Mr Martin, he would know what to do.

CHAPTER TWENTY-SEVEN

I'd set up the meeting with Beaton for three in the afternoon to give me the opportunity to inspect the vicinity of St Rule's Tower for potential ambush places. I was pretty confident that Beaton didn't have the ruthlessness to recruit Mackay for a surprise attack, but I always prepare for the unexpected, so at nine o'clock the next morning I was making my way towards the ruined cathedral. Ten minutes later I was standing at the foot of the eleventh-century St Rule's Tower, a solid heavy-looking construction compared with the graceful airiness of the thirteenth-century cathedral gables.

I stood with my back to the tower looking about me. A sea mist was creeping in, shrouding the tombstones, veiling all that remained of the once-imposing grey stone needle of the West Gable rising into a sky heavy with cloud. A supporting flying buttress on one side and the slender stone tracery of an arched window on the other, reinforced the impression of a space rocket prepared for take-off at Cape Canaveral with the weathered vertical tombstones standing around as silent spectators.

There was just the possibility that Beaton would have turned to Bert Mackay for help, but at three in the afternoon when there would be a number of tourists wandering around with cameras, there'd be no need to worry about the beer-bellied Mackay lying in wait for me behind one of the memorial headstones.

Before making my way back to the car park, I paused for a while at the memorials to the world-famous champion golfers, Tommy Morris and his son Young Tom, then stopped off at a teashop in Market Street. I sipped my coffee, well satisfied with my plan to panic Beaton into turning informer.

When I returned to Lower Largo, Gorgonzola turned her back on me in a pointed demonstration of her displeasure at being shut in the cottage tedious hour after tedious hour on such a fine day. She jumped onto the window seat and stared meaningfully out of the window at the gulls preening their feathers on the sea wall. Were there not birds to stalk, mice to hunt, dogs to goad and torment?

An unreserved apology was expected and given. 'I'm sorry, G. It was *really* thoughtless of me to be away for so long. I meant to be back long before this, but you know how it is....' I opened the door to the back garden and let her out.

I turned my thoughts to Nicola Beaton. I always arrive at a rendezvous at least two hours in advance, but this time I was dealing with an amateur criminal, so an hour would be more than sufficient. If I left at half past one, that would be time enough to drive to St Andrews and find a position where I could keep the entrance to the tower under surveillance and ensure there were no nasty surprises. To soften her up, I'd let Beaton stand looking round nervously for a couple of minutes before I made my approach.

A lot rested on this afternoon's meeting: if it didn't lead me closer to Spinks, I would be reporting for another assignment at the end of the week and he would have won again. With a sigh I sat down at the table and began writing up the notes that would be needed to put my successor and Attila fully in the picture.

Waaaaaghh GRRRUUFF GRRRUUFF hsssss GRRRR hssssss

I shot out of my seat and rushed to the window. Gorgonzola was standing on the sea wall at the foot of the garden, stiff legged, back arched. Aggression, not fear, in every bristling hair of her newly cropped coat, she was sending challenging stares down onto the beach. The deep barks and fearsome growls from the other side of the wall indicated that her adversary was of some considerable size, a Great Dane or an Alsatian. G was playing a dangerous game.

As I flung open the back door, a black nose, large ears, and slavering jaws with sharp white teeth rose above the wall. The swipe of a giant paw knocked her off her feet before she could leap back out of range. One minute she was there, the next, gone.

Waaaaaghh GRRR GRRR GRRRR

I screamed. A man shouted. The frightening sounds from over the wall increased in volume.

Scree-e-ch waaaaaghh GRRR GRRR GRRRR scree-e-ch

No time to fill a bucket of water in the kitchen to throw over them, no time to go to cupboard for a broom. I ran, heart thudding, looking round in desperation for something, anything, to force them apart. I seized the garden hose lying under a shrub and twisted the nozzle. A powerful jet of water shot across the garden and arced over the wall.

' Hey! Watch it!' A man's face, hair plastered to scalp, poked over the wall.

GRRR GRRR GRRRR scree-e-ch scree-e-ch waaaaaghh

'Call off your dog. It's killing my cat!' I gasped.

Tugging the hose behind me and redirecting it off to his left, I rushed to look over the wall at the scene of battle below. Gorgonzola was leaping in the air, landing, twisting round, leaping again as an Alsatian, head lowered, lunged and snapped. Blood was streaming from a deep scratch on its muzzle, but miraculously G seemed as yet to have no obvious wounds. Another lunge and snap. I aimed the hose a second too late. The dog's teeth closed on her hind leg and with an almost human scream she fell on her side.

Splatt. The stream of water scored a direct hit between the Alsatian's eyes. Shaking its head, the brute staggered back onto its haunches with a yelp of surprise, giving Gorgonzola the chance she needed. Hind leg trailing, she limped towards the wooden steps that gave access to the gate in the wall and safety. The dog's owner, who had up till then been standing helplessly aside, fearful of putting his hand near the snapping jaws, seized the opportunity to grab hold of the dog's collar. It fell back choking, then wrenched itself free and bounded forward for the kill.

G had reached the bottom step. With my free hand I fumbled with the latch of the gate and pulled it open, directing the forceful jet at the dog's head while Gorgonzola slowly pulled herself up the steps. It seemed to take an age before she reached the top and dragged herself into the garden. I flung the hose aside and slammed the gate shut. An instant later, *thud*. 85lbs of dog crashed against the wood. *Thud Thud Thud*. The gate shuddered under the repeated onslaughts. I abandoned the hose, scooped G up, ran inside, and kicked the door shut.

I laid her on the table and with shaking hands stroked and caressed her. Beneath her ribcage I could feel her heart pounding as fast as mine.

'What were you *thinking* of, G? Promise me never, *ever* to do that again.'

She raised her head to lick feebly at my hand. She was suffering from shock, but apart from that how seriously was she hurt? Her most obvious injuries were the two bleeding puncture marks from the dog's fangs on her back leg. The grip of those powerful jaws could have torn muscles or snapped delicate bones.

'It'll have to be a visit to the vet for you, G,' I said.

And that meant I wouldn't be in time for the three o'clock rendezvous with Beaton.

I left G in the capable hands of a vet in St Andrews, reassured that G's injuries were not as serious as I'd feared. As I hurried towards the cathedral, I glanced at my watch again. Ten minutes past three. Would Beaton still be there? How long would she have waited beside the tower, looking nervously around her before she decided that the letter had been some kind of hoax? Or had she not come at all, just crumpled the letter into a ball and binned it?

The entrance to the cathedral grounds was by way of the arched doorway of the ruined West Gable. I'd chosen the rendezvous in the cathedral precincts, confident that I'd be in the company of a good number of tourists, but so far I hadn't seen anybody at all. The only indication of human presence was a thin skirl of bagpipes from the direction of the East Sands. If Mackay and his pals were lying in wait for me, there'd be no witnesses. Through an archway I looked over the intervening tombstones towards the doorway of the Tower. There was nobody standing there. Beaton had given up and gone. Despondently I turned away.

I'd almost reached the West Gable exit again when I realized that though I'd told her to meet me at St Rule's Tower, I hadn't actually specified that she was to wait at the entrance door. She could have gone inside, even climbed the stairs to the viewing platform at the top. I turned back.

A small group of people were standing towards the rear of the Tower listening to a guide in a tartan jacket. As I approached, the guide was saying, '... so I regret that the Tower and the area round it is closed to the public until further notice. Anybody who has bought an entrance token for the Tower will be refunded at the visitor centre.' He walked round to the front of the Tower and took up position at the door as if on guard.

So Beaton wasn't waiting for me inside. If she had turned up, I'd definitely missed her. Some of the group started to drift away in the direction of the visitor centre, but to my surprise most stayed where they were, staring up at the parapet.

'A dreadful business,' muttered the middle-aged man next to me, shaking his head. 'Dreadful business. Some poor woman's fallen from the top.'

I ran my tongue over suddenly dry lips. A terrible accident to a woman at the very time of our rendezvous. It was too much of a co-incidence. Spinks specialized in murder disguised as accident. If the woman *was* Beaton, she had been murdered, and I was responsible for her death.

I nerved myself to ask. 'She's *dead*, is she?'

'Looks like it, I'm afraid. She fell from the back of the Tower. Paramedics came half an hour ago, but she's not been taken away yet. Can't see anything from here, but the poor woman must be beyond help or they would have rushed her off on a stretcher before now, wouldn't they?' He sighed. 'Really brings it home to you, doesn't it? One minute you're here. The next, you're gone.'

A morbid fascination with being in the proximity of Death was keeping him and the other onlookers here waiting for the body to be carried away. I, too, stayed but for another reason. I wanted to know whether I had sent Nicola Beaton to her death. In my heart I already knew the answer.

CHAPTER TWENTY-EIGHT

I waited at St Rule's Tower till the body, covered by a blanket, had been carried away on a stretcher to the waiting ambulance. As it was lifted in, the blanket slipped a fraction giving a glimpse of a silver earring set with a red stone. That snuffed out any lingering hope: Nicola Beaton had indeed been the victim of an accident arranged by Hiram J Spinks.

Even the welcome from a much-restored Gorgonzola when I collected her from the vet didn't lighten my grim mood. As I drove back to Lower Largo, I cast a sideways glance at the cat carrier secured by the seat belt in the front passenger seat. 'You're to blame for this as much as me, G,' I sighed. 'Your dangerously silly antics made me late for the meeting with her.' If *only* I'd turned up on time … but if I *had*, Spinks might have engineered my death too. My little scheme had gone horribly wrong. Sunk in gloom, I drove on.

Something about Beaton's death was bothering me, something I'd missed. I pulled into a lay-by and sat, hands gripping the wheel, staring through the windscreen…. The paramedics came half an hour ago, the onlooker had said. That meant that her body had been discovered *before* three o'clock, so even if I had arrived on time that would have made no difference at all. I worked out what must have happened: Spinks had told her to arrive early for the rendezvous. Then he or a contract killer had lured her up the tower by telling her that it would be easy to deal with whoever climbed the stairs and identified himself as the writer of the anonymous note. Yes, that's how it must have been. As soon as he'd pushed Beaton over the parapet, the killer would have left the Tower. He might have watched from a distance to see who turned up at the appointed time, but once the body was discovered, he'd have melted away before I appeared at ten past three. Spinks would not be sure who was the writer of the note to Beaton, but as he'd recognized me at Pittenweem I'd be his prime suspect. He'd make it a priority to track me down.

Plaintive *miaowing* came from the cat carrier. Lost in thought, I made half-hearted soothing noises. How to get to Spinks before he got to me? The fact that I could recognize him and point him out to the police was useless because I didn't know where he was staying or what name he was using. The police files from the HMRC case I'd worked on two years ago were still open, but there was no accompanying photograph of the American I knew as Hiram J Spinks. If *only* there had been a photo of Spinks among those Terry had taken of golfers on the Old Course.

'The trail's gone cold, G,' I sighed. Now nothing could prevent me from being taken off the case.

But my low spirits didn't last long. That evening, just after I'd got back to Lower Largo, Terry phoned.

'I've found more photos on another memory card. Do you want to come over to see if you can spot that tax dodger of yours?'

Leaving the recuperating Gorgonzola well fed and comfortably settled on my duvet, I set off for the Lodge.

'That's him!' I said, in my excitement, stabbing my finger down on the glossy print of Spinks at the eighteenth hole of the Old Course. He had one foot on the parapet of the Swilken Bridge, golf club raised triumphantly in the air, in the background the imposing façade of the world-famous Royal and Ancient Golf Club.

Terry whipped out a lint-free cloth and reproachfully wiped off the all-too-visible whorls left by my index finger.

'Sorry,' I muttered.

'For future orders, I stamp a grid on the back and fill in date, name, address, and telephone number.'

Tracing Spinks was as easy as that, I thought jubilantly.

He turned over the photograph. The date was last week. The space for name and address was blank.

I sighed.

For a moment he looked as disappointed as I felt. Then, 'Nil desperandum, Vanessa.' He flipped the photo over. 'The caddie standing in the background with the golf bag is George MacFarlane. The golfer books the caddie and pays him on the completion of the round, so George will be sure to have the guy's name in his appointment book. You'll find him most evenings in the Road Hole Bar of the Old Course Hotel.'

When I left Terry, I drove straight to St Andrews. Once I'd got Spinks's alias from the caddie, I'd find out where he was staying and pass his photo to Attila with the information that this was the drug baron who had taken over Selkirk's organization. A request to the FBI would undoubtedly identify him as being among their 'most wanted'. Elated, I hummed a little tune. Now Attila would have to eat his words and reinstate me.

A small sturdy man holding a tweed cap emerged from the Old Course Hotel. He stood for a moment in the doorway and placed the cap on his head, carefully adjusting it to a precisely correct angle. I studied the photo in my hand. This was the caddie. I hurried forward.

'Tracked you down at last, George. Terry Warburton said I'd probably find you here.' I held up the photograph. 'Do you happen to remember who this is? Terry forgot to make a note of the guy's name and address.'

He took the photo and studied it for a moment.

'He's American,' I said. 'You caddied for him on Tuesday last week.'

'Aye, tight-fisted bastard. After all the help I'd given him to improve his game, didn't have the strength to bring his hand out of his pocket with a tip. But he didn't get away with it. I just stood there with a tight grip on his golf bag till he got the message. Then he fished in his pocket, sorted through his change – and handed me a £2 coin. "There you are, George," he said. "Treat yourself to a pint in the bar." I won't forget his face in a hurry, went by the name of ....'

I held my breath.

'Reid, was it? No ... Reedman? No, that's not it.' He clicked his tongue in frustration as the name eluded him. 'It'll be in my appointment book. I start my round at 8 a.m. sharp, so if you call tomorrow just before then at the caddies' hut, I'll look it up.'

He handed back the photo, touched his fingers to his cap in an old-fashioned gesture of courtesy and turned away. And with that I had to be content.

A pale early-morning sun was fighting its way through a bank of cloud when I parked in the public car park near the aquarium. From there it was only a short walk past the rather brutal architecture of the Golf Museum to the caddies' hut, the meeting place of golfers and caddies. Winners of the ballot to play the course at that time were already gathered outside in a small group. A few of the caddies were in close discussion with their clients, but George MacFarlane was not one of them, though he'd told me he'd start his round at eight sharp. At that moment he appeared in the doorway with an appointment book open in his hand and beckoned me forward.

'Saw you waiting out here. Last Tuesday, wasn't it?' He ran his finger down the page. 'Morton Rickmann's the name, staying at the Old Course Hotel, if you want to have a word with him.'

'That's great, George. Thanks a lot.' I scribbled down the name and address. 'Terry leaves it to the golfer to get in touch with him, and if Mr Rickmann phones to ask for one of himself on the Swilken Bridge it won't look good if he can't identify the print.'

I thanked George again and walked off. Spinks had taken good care to cover his tracks. To those on the St Andrews golfing scene, like caddie George MacFarlane, he was Morton Rickmann; to those involved in his shady cannabis enterprise, like Mackay and Beaton, he was Mr Martin.

At last I had a name for Spinks and knew where he had been staying a week ago. But criminals like Spinks keep one step ahead of the law by staying in one place for only a short time. So the chances were slim that he would still be at the Old Course Hotel. After yesterday's murder of Nicola Beaton, slimmer still.

And so it proved. The breakthrough had come too late, much too late. When I phoned the Old Course Hotel, I was told that Mr Rickmann had checked out early the previous day, some hours before Beaton's murder.

Disheartened, I slowly made my way back towards the car. I'd been so close to seeing the handcuffs snapped on. By now he'd have changed his name again, no longer be Morton Rickmann and could be anywhere in the U.K. or even have left the country. The hard fact had to be faced: I had no leads to follow up, nothing to persuade Attila to change his mind and reinstate me. A silver lining when everything looks black? There wasn't one.

But there *was*, of course there was. I had been so focussed on discovering Spinks's alias and whereabouts in St Andrews that I had overlooked the ace in my hand – a means of identifying him to the FBI. In my bag was the photo of Spinks on the Swilken Bridge, grinning as if he was taunting me in my disappointment and frustration.

I sat down on a bench near the Martyrs' Memorial. I'd send the photo to Attila on my mobile right now, and since I was officially off the case, I spent some time refining the wording of the accompanying message: *I have evidence that this man is running Selkirk's cannabis factories. American. Check FBI and Interpol. Preparing briefing report. Smith.*

I omitted an awkward couple of facts. Bert Mackay might be ready to pick Spinks out in an identification line-up in exchange for a shorter sentence, but I had no actual *proof* that Spinks was running the cannabis ring. Nor did I reveal that the photo I was sending was of Hiram J Spinks. At the very mention of that name, Attila would dismiss the text out of hand, convinced as he was that my recognition of Spinks on the Isle of May was mere delusion.

I put phone and photo back in my bag and continued on my way. I'd done all I could. For more than three weeks I had been intent on tracking Spinks down. Now it was up to Attila to close the net and round up those involved in the cannabis organization. Like a pensioner on the first day of retirement, I had a sense of freedom, but somehow too much freedom, too suddenly given. My day was without purpose and structure.

There being no need now to hurry anywhere, I paused outside the Golf Museum to look at the window display: two rows of pedestals, each with the name and picture of a famous golfer, and on top, a bronze cast of the golfer's hands demonstrating his grip on the club. Intrigued, I placed my hands round the shaft of an imaginary club in imitation of Nick Faldo. Was there a difference in the way Gary Player held *his* club? I studied the bronze casts and came to no conclusion. The backdrop was a photo wall of famous golfers depicted in a moment of ecstasy – or was it agony? I frowned at my reflection in the glass. What was it that Spinks and many, many others found so fascinating about hitting a little ball with a stick?

Behind me a voice said, 'Technology's changed the game out of all recognition. And I'm all for it. Who wants to go back to the Gutta-Percha ball and the hickory shaft? Nobody. I know *my* handicap would go sky high.'

'You're wrong about nobody wanting to play with the old-style ball and clubs,' another voice broke in. 'Especially Americans, like that chap Rickmann I partnered the other day. Bored me rigid going on and on about playing in the World Hickory Open Championship....'

Rickmann. I lost all interest in Gary Player and his grip. An American, name of Rickmann. It *had* to be Spinks. I edged closer to the speakers under the pretence of studying the Ernie Els grip on another pedestal.

'... had a bee in his bonnet about how only a wooden shaft lets you feel the shot as you play it. "No way is that a hickory shaft you're playing with," I said to him. "It's graphite." Rickmann slapped me on the back. "Got me there," he said. "Guess nobody would choose wood when up against steel or graphite shafts." '

A laugh. 'So he was talking through a hole in that fancy cap of his, eh?'

They moved away.

I stared after them. That American, Rickmann, who was fanatical about Hickory Golf and had spent the whole round talking about the World Hickory Open Championship ... it would be worth following up. When and where the Championship was held, that's what I needed to know. Was I too late? Had the Championship already taken place? The Golf Museum would be bound to know. Heart beating faster, I pushed open the door.

Five minutes later I came out with the information I needed. Knowing how passionate the Americans are about golf and anything historical, I'd assumed that the World Hickory Championship would be held somewhere in the States. To my surprise, it was due to be held in a few days' time here in Scotland, in East Lothian, on the oldest golf course in the world. I could be in nearby Edinburgh in less than two hours.

'We'll meet again, I know where, I know when,' I hummed as I inserted the key in the door of the cottage. *'Yes, I know we'll meet ag—'* The words died on my lips when I looked in the bedroom. There was no welcoming *miaow* from Gorgonzola. She didn't even raise her head. She was lying on her side, eyes closed, flanks rising and falling slowly. Laboured breathing! Blood on the duvet! The vet had assured me that there was no serious injury, but he'd been wrong, wrong, *wrong*. What *had* I been thinking of to leave her alone in the cottage? I should have taken her with me, left her in the car where I could keep an eye on her. Heart in mouth, I rushed over to the bed.

'G,' I whispered, 'what's wrong?'

She half-opened an eye. A loud *burp*. The eye closed again. It was then that I spotted the mouse tail and other unidentifiable bits of mouse on the floor beside the bed. Legs weak with relief, I leant against the wall, then taking a deep breath, rushed off to the kitchen for a bin liner. Lips tightly pressed together to quell rising nausea, I gathered up the grisly remains. How could I be angry with her? After yesterday's trauma this could be viewed as comfort food, in the same way as I might treat myself to a high-cholesterol cheeseburger to steady *my* nerves after I'd been attacked. Gently I wrapped G in a towel, and as a precaution against the possibility that her tasty morsel might prove highly indigestible, carried her off to the kitchen with its laminate floor.

I stuffed the duvet cover into the washing machine and to its background hum came to a decision as how best to inform Attila of yet another death, Beaton's this time. A phone call would expose me to awkward questions, loud recriminations and strict orders to report *immediately* to HQ. Texting would inform at one remove. A text message was the coward's way out and I was a coward when it came to facing Attila's wrath.

I put the best gloss I could on my report by saying that the fatal rendezvous at St Rule's Tower had been made before I had been taken off the mission (not strictly true, but it was only a *few* hours afterwards that I had left the anonymous note for Beaton); that the rendezvous once made had to be kept and couldn't be rescheduled for a week's time to suit my successor. I read the message over carefully. Satisfied, I sent it.

Umghh umghh hguugh. Mouth wide, Gorgonzola was standing back arched, retching … retching…. I rushed for another bin liner, managing to get it in place just as she spewed out the half-digested remains of mouse. I was still holding the plastic in position when the phone rang. I had enough to cope with at the moment. It could only be an irate Attila replying to my message and I didn't want to speak directly to him anyway. I let it switch to voicemail.

Bin liner consigned to bucket, kitchen mopped, I left G performing a personal clean-up and went off to buy a newspaper to read how the 'accident' at St Rule's Tower had been reported. Back in the cottage I thumbed through the paper and found what I had been looking for on page four:

WELL-KNOWN AUTHOR'S FATAL FALL FROM ST RULE'S TOWER

Alongside was a head-and-shoulders photo of someone who bore a resemblance to, but was definitely not, the woman I knew as Nicola Beaton. Only the bare facts of the 'accident' were given, there was no hint that foul play was suspected.

My heart sank. I hadn't composed that text message to Attila quite carefully enough. I'd omitted to tell Attila of my suspicion that Beaton was an impostor. The news that a well-known author had suffered a fatal accident so soon after the successful London launch of her latest novel would ensure coverage in newspapers south of the border, and when the authentic Beaton read about her own death....

Attila would demand an explanation of why the false identity hadn't been in my report. To reply, 'I didn't know' or 'I forgot to say' were both equally damning. Perhaps, if I hurriedly sent another text.... I reached for the phone, and saw the *'missed call '* in my voicemail. I sighed and selected it. I couldn't put off any longer finding out what Attila had to say. The number that came up wasn't Attila's. Or Terry's or Sapphire's. Who could it be? No one else knew my number.

With growing horror I listened to an American voice drawling, 'Guess you know who *I* am. I don't know where *you* are, but I'll sure as heck find out.'

Spinks. The phone dropped from my hand, landing on Gorgonzola at the paw-licking stage in her spruce-up. With a startled squeak she jumped up, only to collapse on her side as the injured leg gave way beneath her. I leapt to my feet, apologizing and fussing until she rewarded me with a forgiving *purr.*

While I caressed her, I tried to work out how Spinks had got hold of my mobile number. The link must be Sapphire McGurk. Beaton and Mackay would undoubtedly have told Spinks that I was sharing a venue with her. He, too, must have paid a visit to her studio, told her he needed to get in touch with me on some urgent matter. She had given him my mobile number, and though she didn't know where I was staying, I no longer felt safe in Lower Largo.

'Time to pack up and go, G,' I said.

CHAPTER TWENTY-NINE

After leaving Lower Largo I headed for Portobello, Edinburgh's seaside suburb, only a couple of miles from Musselburgh Links Old Course, this year the location of the Hickory Championship. I booked into the B&B where on two previous occasions Gorgonzola had been a favoured guest ridiculously spoiled by the owners.

Calculating correctly that this would gain her a *lot* of cosseting, G limped along the hallway ahead of me, overplaying her injury with all the dramatic embellishment of a footballer after an opponent's tackle.

Tom and Hilda Galbraith looked at each other in obvious consternation. 'Oh dear, the poor, poor thing. Er … you've got a new cat. Gorgonzola hasn't … has she?'

New cat? It took a moment for me to remember that the last time they had seen her, Gorgonzola had not yet undergone her crew cut make-over at Josie's Pet Parlour.

'Oh, no,' I laughed. 'This is Gorgonzola, all right.' I trotted out the same story I'd tried out so successfully on Josie. 'I had to leave her with a friend who couldn't be trusted to brush her every day. Best thing, I thought, was to give G a short back and sides. That way no nasty tangles. I'd just got her back and what does she do? She takes on an Alsatian and loses the argument.'

Gathering from my tone that G had not been badly hurt, the Galbraiths beamed: all was well. They loved Gorgonzola, but even more they loved the prestigious cat-painting with which G had ornamented the door of their fridge on a previous visit. Cats who paint are rare and their abstract-style paintings worth a fortune. Later, as I passed the open kitchen door, I saw Tom on his knees pinning up white paper in hopeful preparation. As G painted only when under stress, that unfortunate encounter with the dog might just prove inspirational.

She recuperated quickly with every whim catered for, and on the day of the Hickory Championship I drove to Musselburgh, taking her with me. I had intended to leave her with the Galbraiths, but when she'd seen me getting into the car outside the B&B, she'd rushed mewing down the path. After the Alsatian attack she had been somewhat insecure and reluctant to let me out of her sight, and I read her mind – she'd worked out that wherever I was going, it wasn't to the vet, since I hadn't advanced upon her, cat carrier behind my back, coaxing words on my lips. She'd leapt into the car, made straight for the carrier and, with no fuss at all, curled up inside it. That was preferable to being left behind.

An odd thing about Musselburgh Links Old Course is that it is enclosed by a modern racecourse track, so when I saw white rails and grass I turned off the main road, past a brick building with a clock tower surmounted by a galloping horse weathervane. Through an archway I could see the racecourse pavilion and the grandstand. Pinned to metal gates was a notice:

World Hickory Open Championship
Competitors.

In the courtyard it was as if a window had opened into the past: the competitors were dressed in the fashion of a hundred years ago: the men in knee-high woollen socks, plus-four trousers buttoned at the knee, long-sleeved shirt, pullover or tweed jacket and flat cloth cap; the women in a calf-length skirt, fitted jacket, and cloche-style hat.

There was space to park, but I couldn't risk an encounter with Spinks. I drove down the next side street and stopped the car at the far side of the racecourse near a brick-and-glass building where a tall black banner reading *Musselburgh Links The Old Golf Course* fluttered in the gentle breeze.

For a few moments I sat in the car, keyed up with anticipation, absolutely certain I was soon to come face-to-face with Spinks. Golf was his passion. He'd be drawn irresistibly to the unique golfing experience of playing with the type of club used a century ago, of walking the oldest surviving course in the world, the very links played four hundred years ago by Mary Queen of Scots and James VI. To an American an added attraction.

Yesterday I'd contacted Lothian and Borders Police, and when Chief Inspector Macleod had learned that the criminal who had outwitted him during my anti-heroin operation two years ago might turn up at the World Hickory Golf Championship, he had jumped at the chance of making an arrest. My plan was that if – no, *when* – I spotted Spinks, I'd slip away and phone Macleod, describe what Spinks was wearing and say exactly where he'd find him. On the signal from Macleod, plain-clothes police in radio contact would move in – and it would all be over.

Only *after* the arrest would I phone Attila with the news. If I let him in on my plan beforehand, I feared the conversation would be on the lines of: 'No, you will *not* call in Lothian and Borders Police. Are you *mad*, Smith? Disrupt an *international* event? Do you want to make HMRC (meaning himself, of course) a laughing stock, all because you have this obsession with the man Spinks? More to the point, your replacement tells me he has not received the report you were to submit. *Where* is that report? I want to see you in my office *tomorrow*. *Tomorrow*, do you hear?' I could imagine it all too clearly.

Once Spinks had been bundled into the back of a police car, surely Attila would have to acknowledge that the temporary disruption of a high-profile event was a small price to pay for the capture of an inter-national criminal. And since the cannabis ring centred on the East Neuk of Fife would be without its organizer and could easily be mopped up, there would now be no need for an *urgent* report, though Attila would still harp on about my failure to supply one when ordered to do so. I'd face that when I had to. Meanwhile I'd concentrate on more important things.

I studied the article I'd cut out of *The Scotsman* newspaper. I was going to find it more difficult than I'd thought to spot Hiram J Spinks. There were two Hickory competitions: the Pre-1900 and the Pre-1935. I thought back to the conversation I'd overheard outside the Golf Museum: Rickmann, it seemed, was fanatical about recapturing the feel of the golf shot and playing an old golf course in the way the players of the past had tackled it. There was a high chance, then, that Spinks would play with the pre-1900 golf club and the old-style Gutta-Percha ball rather than the pre-1935 club and the more efficient modern ball.

He would be on the lookout for me, just as I was for him, so for the moment I'd stay in the car. Once the competition was underway, when he'd be concentrating on his game, his guard lowered, that would be the moment for me to join the onlookers.

Out of the corner of my eye, I saw a ginger paw insert itself between the front seats. A moment later G thrust her head impatiently through the gap. Before I could react, she wriggled … squirmed … hooked her claws into the fabric of the upholstery and levered herself onto the passenger seat, where she curled up facing me, eyes narrowed, on the alert for any attempt to grab her and return her to the cat carrier on the back seat.

I pressed the button to open the driver's window and slumped down in approved surveillance position only to find my view of the racetrack and of the golf course beyond obscured by the beech hedge on the boundary of the car park.

I reached out a hand to stroke G. 'I know you're thinking that driving you here like this might be a trick, a new way of conning you into going to the vet. Relax. I'm going for a short stroll. You can lie under the car, as you like to do, till I come back.'

I held the door open for her and watched her disappear under the car. She'd be safe there, wouldn't go off on an exploratory hunt, the car was her assurance that I'd be back. I joined a thin line of spectators leaning on the white rail of the racetrack. In the distance, two golfers were preparing to tee off in front of the grandstand and the adjoining pavilion. One was standing, club raised to shoulder height, as he followed the line of the ball. They were too far away for me to make out if Spinks was one of them.

'Just starting off, are they?' I asked the man leaning next to me on the rail.

I wasn't prepared for his reaction. 'That's a good one!' He dug his companion in the ribs. 'Did you hear what the lassie said, Dougie? She asked if they were just starting off!' He turned back to me. 'No, no, they're going round for the second time.' He saw by my puzzled expression that more explanation was needed. 'The championship's over eighteen holes so they go round twice. The first players have already finished.'

'Finished? But it's just after eleven o'clock. How can any of them have *finished*?'

A burst of laughter. 'Easy seen you're no a golfer, lass. Since seven o'clock this morning they've been teeing off from the Graves. Got its name because dead soldiers were buried there – not recently, of course, five hundred years or so ago. The hole's a tricky one because the two bunkers you can't see from the tee catch out even those who know about them.'

We watched the three golfers shoulder their canvas golf bags and set off along the fairway to the next hole. It had all seemed so simple: arrive at the start, mingle discreetly with the crowd, make that phone call. But now the problems seemed insurmountable. By arriving late I'd missed the start, so Spinks could already have finished, or be anywhere on the course; I couldn't mingle with the crowd – there wasn't one, only sprinklings of spectators. As the fairway was only twenty-five yards away, I couldn't stay where I was to wait for golfers finishing the round – if I saw Spinks, he would be sure to see me.

With a faint *snick*, a golf ball soared into the air, a white dot against the blue sky, to land on the pitted and pockmarked turf of the racetrack a short distance from where we were standing. I contemplated the ball now nestling cosily in the depths of a deeply indented hoof print.

'Still in play,' Dougie murmured.

'What do the players do when they've finished their round?' I asked.

'They usually go off for a pint and a bite to Mrs Forman's. That's the white building beside the trees at the far end of the course.' He pointed off to the left. 'You can walk up alongside the race track or drive along the main road to the roundabout and turn left.'

Hope rose again. Now I knew where I could get a look at some of the players I had missed, I'd park beside Mrs Forman's on the off-chance that I might spot Spinks in the bar with a pint or, more likely, a dram. A quick glance through a window would tell me if Spinks was there. And if he wasn't, from the line of trees beside the pub I'd be able to keep an unobtrusive eye on those still playing.

Fifteen minutes later I was parked in the small cul-de-sac behind Mrs Forman's Inn. A row of substantial grey-stone Victorian houses lined the street on the right; on the left, a clump of low-growing pines and a tangle of prickly gorse bushes lay between the road and the golf course. As soon as I opened the car door, Gorgonzola leapt out, excited by the sight of rodent-populated undergrowth and the heady whiff of salt in the air, associated as that was with fish. Tail erect, whiskers quivering, she headed off into the long grass without a trace of a limp, and disappeared.

I stood for a moment beside the car. Golfers playing the hole beyond the line of trees were calling to each other. Shielded from their view by gorse bushes and low branches, I made my way along a narrow path winding among the trees until I could see the fairway. Halfway toward the hole, two golfers in old-fashioned plus-fours were standing beside one of the cluster of bunkers. I could see only the back of a third player's head and his shoulders as he prepared to loft the ball from the depths of a bunker.

'Heck of a difficult shot, this.' The accent was unmistakably American. My heart beat faster.

With a spurt of sand the ball arced into the air and rolled onto the green. I drew further back behind the screen of pine branches as the man scrambled from the bunker. Not Spinks. Disappointed, I turned away to investigate the clientele of Mrs Forman's Inn.

At the end of the stretch of pines and gorse, a mere hundred yards from where I stood, a six-foot wall enclosed the beer garden accessed from the golf course by a gate with the proud inscription *The Cradle of Golf*. Hidden by the wall from the view of those on the far side, I stood listening for some time to bursts of laughter and the babble of voices in the beer garden, golfers dissecting their game, reliving that amazing or disastrous shot. No American accents.

I'd try the bar. Conveniently for my purpose, two windows were set in the gable end a foot above the grass of the fairway. The windows were closed although it was August and quite warm, and all I could make out was the murmur of voices and an occasional phrase. I stood to one side of a window and peeped in. No luck once again. Reflections and the contrast with the brightness outside made it difficult to see clearly into the interior, but Spinks wasn't one of the men sitting at the tables in the visible part of the room, nor was he among those leaning on the bar counter, beer in hand.

I drew back from the window to decide what to do next. I could watch either the front entrance of the inn or the beer garden gate at the back, but not both, so if Spinks *was* here at Mrs Forman's, I couldn't be certain of being in the right place to spot him as he left. My best chance of finding him would be to look out for him again on the golf course.

I took cover once more amongst the pine trees. More than half the players were still making their way round. If *only* I had checked the start time of the competition. Perhaps I had already blown any chance of seeing him. I sat on the ground and made myself comfortable with my back against a trunk, well screened from the fairway by gorse bushes and the low sweep of the pine branches, but with a clear view of the tee.

Two golfers were taking turns to putt while one was holding the flag clear of the hole.

The minutes passed.... The golfers moved out of my line of sight. My attention wandered to something white, half-hidden amidst pine cones and dried grass under the low skirts of the nearest gorse bush. I leaned forward and reached for the small object, a lost golf ball. I was about to throw it onto the fairway, then slipped it into my pocket. G would have great fun patting it from paw to paw, rolling it, waiting at the ready, then pouncing for the kill.

As if conjured up by telepathy, a *rustle rustle* in the undergrowth gave warning of Gorgonzola's return from her hunting trip. With a proud *miaow* she deposited her trophy in my lap. It was small, brown and living. I stared down into the panic-stricken eyes of a trembling field mouse. I cupped a hand over its tiny body, pondering how to let it loose without its freedom being short-lived and bloody. Well aware that such gifts were not always appreciated, Gorgonzola was sitting back awaiting my reaction. If I could distract her for a moment.... With my free hand I felt in my jacket pocket for the golf ball, pulled it out and rolled it past her into the thicket of gorse bushes. She shot after it into the heart of the clump. I opened my cupped hand and watched the field mouse scurry off.

Without warning, I sensed a presence: someone was standing behind me, very close. I turned my head. A glimpse of a golf rake raised to strike. A blur of movement hurtling down towards my head. A fraction of a second too late I flung myself sideways out of its path. An agonizing pain in my head and shoulder beaded my forehead with sweat. Dazed and in shock, I lay unable to move, looking up into the cold eyes of Hiram J Spinks. He towered over me, golf rake poised to scythe down for the second time.

I had failed to find him, but he had certainly found me.

His thin lips stretched in a humourless smile. 'Any last words?'

CHAPTER THIRTY

With death an instant away, the Sword of Damocles hanging over my head by a single hair about to sever, I thought fast. Even the toughest can have exaggerated and illogical fears over harmless things like spiders, moths and snakes. Into my mind flashed a memory of Spinks's panic-stricken reaction to cats.

'Fish!' I gasped. '*Fish!*'

Not the words he expected. A flicker of astonishment crossed his face. Then he gripped the rake in both hands and raised it higher, preparatory to smashing it down on my head. Mesmerized, I was unable to wrench my eyes away from the murder weapon.

'*Fish!*' I gasped again.

Just as the rake began its descent, Gorgonzola bounded eagerly from the bushes, purring loudly, the amusing golf ball abandoned for something much more important – food.

Spinks registered the presence of a cat. The golf rake wavered, its momentum slowed as he recoiled in fear and revulsion at the prospect of the loathsome animal rubbing itself against his leg. All thought of disposing of me forgotten, he hurled the rake at Gorgonzola.

Taken by surprise, she managed to dodge, reacting instinctively to the threat by clawing her way up the trunk of the pine tree against which I'd been leaning. She crept along a high branch and crouched there hissing.

Driven by fear, and the compulsion to rid himself of the hated creature, Spinks became a man possessed. He snatched up the rake, reached up as high as he could, lashing out at trunk and branches. Under the onslaught, the whole tree shook. Twigs, pieces of bark, pine needles showered down on my upturned face while G clung determinedly on, claws hooked into the branch. I tried desperately to lever myself up, but fell back helpless to intervene, overcome by dizziness and pain.

Cr-e-eak cr-e-eak CRACK. Subjected to intolerable stress, the branch broke. G jumped free. Fur raised, legs outstretched, claws extended, she plummeted earthwards. I saw Spinks fling up an arm to ward her off as she landed spitting and yowling on his shoulders.

'*Aaah!*' He fell to the ground clawing at the back of his neck in a frantic attempt to dislodge her.

Despite all my efforts I could barely raise my head from the ground. G didn't need my help: she unhooked herself from his jacket and shot back up the tree. *Cr-e-eak cr-e-eak* CRACK. Too weak to bear her weight, the chosen branch broke. Once again she plunged earthwards, this time landing lightly on her feet. Panic-stricken, Spinks scrambled to his feet and ran off through the trees without a backward glance at me.

'Atta girl, G,' I gasped. And promptly blacked out.

The next thing I was aware of was G peering into my face and patting at my cheek with a tentative paw. I lay dazedly working out how best to summon help, fearful of the pain that might shoot through me if I moved. My mobile was pressing into me, hard under my hip, but to get to it would mean rolling onto my back, and even the thought of that.... I'd just have to wait until the next set of golfers came by – that wouldn't be long – and when I heard their voices on the fairway, I'd call out. Yes, that would be best....

Time passed, I had no idea how long, as my watch arm was pinned under me. Puzzled by my lack of movement and sensing that something was wrong, Gorgonzola sat, head on one side, staring at me and giving an occasional mew of disquiet. All at once she pricked up her ears and turned her head. Then I heard it too – the whisper of soft footfalls on the carpet of pine needles. Spinks had overcome his phobia and had returned to finish me off.

'Gotta be about here. *Goddamnit*, dog shit everywhere.'

An American. Spinks. In a moment he would find me. Heart thudding, I opened my mouth to scream, knowing it was hopeless: even if anybody was within earshot, they wouldn't be in time to save me. He'd deliver the fatal blow with the golf rake and be gone.

'He-e-elp!' It emerged as a pathetic squeak from a dry throat.

Lying as I was on my side and unable to turn my head, my line of sight was restricted to a tangle of pine branches that drooped to the ground. On the edge of vision over to my right their long silky needles shook violently, as a tweed-jacketed arm thrust them aside. Instinctively I tried to fling up my injured arm to ward off the coming blow. *Pa-i-n....* When it receded to almost bearable, I became aware of Spinks's legs in plus fours and woollen stockings standing over me. Why was he hesitating? He must be savouring the moment, making sure I was conscious before he killed me.

Then I remembered ... Gorgonzola had been sitting beside me, so Spinks wouldn't be standing here unless she had run off, or unless ... unless ... she was dead.

He summoned his thugs. 'Over here, guys. *Quick.*' As he bent over, his shadow fell across me.

I closed my eyes.

'Are you OK, ma'am?'

Startled, I squinted up at him. *Not* Spinks. Weak with relief, I whispered, 'Hit me ... my head ... my shoulder....'

'My *God*. I'm real sorry, ma'am. That was a terrible shot I played off the tee, terrible shot.' He raised his voice. 'Over here, *quick*. That sliced ball hit a woman. We'll need an ambulance.'

I heard the snap of small branches and the crackle of twigs as they forced a path through the bushes. Three concerned faces stared down at me.

'No, no,' I gasped. 'It wasn't your fault, wasn't an accident. Someone attacked me. Call the police, Chief Inspector Macleod. His number's on my mobile. I'm lying on it.'

They exchanged glances.

Mutters of, 'Mugged, I reckon.'

'No, must be a policewoman from what she said.'

They tried their best to be gentle as they extracted the phone from under me, but several times I cried out. One held the phone while I spoke to Macleod.

I chose my words, careful not to give too much away. 'I'm in the trees beside Mrs Forman's. He attacked me, but he's gone. I think my collarbone's broken.'

'Be right over. Don't go away,' he said, always one for a joke.

Macleod stayed with me till the ambulance arrived. He took care of Gorgonzola too. Spooked by the golfers crashing through the bushes, G had prudently gone to ground, but came out of hiding when I called her. While I was transported to Accident & Emergency at the Western General, she was whisked away in Macleod's car to the Portobello B&B; while I lay on a trolley awaiting attention, she was reclining on a sofa being fussed over by the Galbraiths.

I left the Western General clutching a packet of painkillers and with the instruction ringing in my ears that I was to 'avoid the potential for further trauma' for months to come. But what risk was there of coming to blows with anybody after this? Spinks wasn't going to attack me on Portobello promenade, or anywhere else, for I'd never see him or any of his thugs again. The make of his car was unknown and with a choice of roads going off in four directions from the roundabout in front of Mrs Forman's, he could by now be anywhere. Once again Hiram J Spinks had got clean away.

I was feeling sorry for myself, and it wasn't just that my broken collarbone was aching despite the support of the sling. The mission was out of my hands. Attila was now the one who'd decide how and when to intercept the final Spinks shipment and how best to close down the Fife cannabis ring. As a punishment he had put me on run-of-the-mill drug

surveillance duty, scanning the Forth from the B&B for any small fast
boat slipping away from a cargo ship during the hours of darkness.

The silence of the room was broken only by gentle snores and an
occasional purr from the bed where Gorgonzola was no doubt reliving
her role as saviour of DJ Smith on Musselburgh Old Links. But there'd
be no heroic role for DJ Smith in *my* dreams: falling victim to an
ambush by Spinks was nothing short of a disaster, an embarrassment I'd
take a long time to live down.

By 2 a.m. I was already bored, bored out of my skull. I stared out of the
window, counting the sodium lights that stretched in a line along the promenade and threw into sharp relief the footmarks trampled in the sand. The
streetlights were reflected in the wet sand at the water's edge, made distinct
by the glint of phosphorescence from a double line of breakers. Far off to
my left, the single white flash of the lighthouse on Inchkeith Island punctuated darkness black as my mood. Directly opposite my window was the
string of amber lights on the Fife coast, a gap marking the area of the Chain
Walk, Largo Law and the site of the cannabis factory. I sighed. Was Spinks
somewhere out there? I'd never know.

The sun was edging above the horizon. Another boring night's surveillance duty was over. I yawned and stretched. I'd lie down on the bed and
have a couple of hours' sleep before shower and breakfast. Ignoring her
protests, I shifted G off to the side of the bed, lay down on top of the
duvet and drifted into a troubled asleep.

It was not the alarm but my mobile that woke me. Still half-asleep, I
reached for it. *Damn* Attila! Two nights ago at three in the morning, in
the middle of my surveillance shift, he'd phoned with, 'Anything to
report, Smith?' Now here he was, checking up on me again.

But it wasn't Attila. 'Hi, Vanessa. Terry here, hope it's not too early,
but I thought you'd be interested. Yesterday I was on the west side of
Edinburgh taking some shots at a reception held by the Royal Burgess.'

'Oh yes? ' I yawned. I couldn't think why he thought I'd be interested,
especially at this time in the morning.

'Last night I was running through the images on the computer to send
the best ones to *Edinburgh Life* magazine. And you'll never guess....' A
dramatic pause.

'No, I don't suppose I will,' I said, trying to be civil. I wasn't in the
mood for party games. 'I've only had two hours' sleep and—'

'The Royal Burgess *Golf* Society, Vanessa, the oldest golf club in Scotland. The reception was for golfers from *overseas*.' He must have sensed that my sleep-deprived brain had not grasped the importance of his announcement, for he added, 'What I'm trying to tell you is that one of the guests was that tax-dodging golf-fanatic you were trying to track down in St Andrews.'

That got me wide-awake. Then after a moment of elation came the sombre realization that once again I was one step behind Spinks.

'But ... but that was yesterday, where is he...?' I trailed off.

'Where is he now? I don't know.'

'Oh well, at least I know that he *was* in town.' I couldn't keep the disappointment out of my voice.

Terry laughed. 'Just teasing, Vanessa. I don't know where he is *now*, but I know where he *will* be. You see, I chatted to the golfers while I was making a note of their names. The Lord Provost, it seems, is hosting an evening dinner for them in the Castle on Sunday, the night of the Firework Concert that marks the end of the Festival. Even though it's costing them £300 a ticket, I understand that all the overseas golfers will be there. So if you want to nab him, that's where he'll be.'

CHAPTER THIRTY-ONE

Chief Inspector Macleod didn't take much convincing that the Lord Provost's dinner in the Castle presented, in all probability, a final chance to arrest Hiram J Spinks.

'You'll want to be in at the kill,' he said. 'I'll make arrangements. Anyway, I'll need you to be there to make a positive identification. Wouldn't do, would it, if we were to arrest the wrong chap?'

At 7.30 on Sunday evening, an hour after Edinburgh Castle had closed to the public, I presented the police pass at the barrier. With four tonnes of explosives for the nine o'clock Fireworks Concert laid out on the ramparts of the Argyle Battery, security was especially tight, and it was only after a phone call to Macleod that I was allowed through onto the parade area known as the Esplanade. Tiered stands, set up as seating for the Military Tattoo, reared up on either side, shutting out half the sky and narrowing the view to the semi-circle of cannons that peeped out of the Half-Moon Battery, the guardian of the drawbridge and entrance to the Castle.

I crossed the drawbridge and hurried up a narrow cobbled way between the four-hundred-year-old walls of the Inner Barrier defences. I was on edge, all too aware that I was risking more than a reprimand if Spinks once again slipped from HMRC's grasp and it all ended in humiliating failure. I tried, not very successfully, to convince myself that, as an American, Spinks would have been unable to resist the welcome by a piper and a viewing of the Scottish Crown Jewels, followed by the Lord Provost's candlelit dinner in the romantic setting of the Jacobite Room.

Ahead of me lay the short tunnel formed by the Portcullis Gate. A figure detached itself from the shadows beneath the long iron teeth. It was Macleod.

'Has he come?' I asked, voice sharp with anxiety.

He nodded. 'They're all in the Jacobite Room. Dinner started half an hour ago.'

Together we walked up the incline to the paved area in front of the Argyle Battery. By day it was an area crowded with tourists admiring the view across to Fife over Princes Street Gardens and the grey slate roofs of the New Town. Tonight a wire-mesh fence barricaded off the cannons and the parapet. On the other side of the fence a small group of specialist technicians moved purposefully, stepping carefully over the spaghetti lines of wiring, moving into position clusters of gigantic rockets, checking the long row of waterfall mines and removing the protective plastic sheeting from neat rows of black boxes.

'The Jacobite Room's in that low building just over there. Everything's in place for the arrest.' Macleod sounded confident. 'When dinner finishes, we'll move in on him.'

'Why not now?' I said, dismayed. The longer we waited, the more chance there was that something might go wrong.

'We're walking on eggshells as it is. If we burst in to make an arrest, chances are he won't come quietly, and since this is a prestigious event and the tickets cost a hell of a lot....' He fell silent.

Both of us envisaged a scene of overturned tables, spilt wine, broken glass and smashed crockery.

'And then, there's the candles ... fire ...' I murmured.

He nodded. 'Too big a risk. So the plan is that when the guests come out to board the bus taking them down to Princes Street Gardens for a view of the fireworks, a plainclothes squad will grab him out in the open. That way nobody's expensive dinner gets trampled underfoot. There'll be a bit of a commotion, but with the bus on the point of leaving, the chief thing on everyone's mind will be getting down to the Gardens in time for the fireworks.'

Time dragged. As twilight faded, the lights of the Victorian-style lamp posts glowed into life. Behind the mesh fence, a huge ground-mounted flood lamp cast a powerful white light on the dark-clothed technicians preparing the serried ranks of fireworks.

At 8.15, ten minutes before the dinner guests were due to emerge, we heard the sound of a vehicle approaching the Portcullis Gate.

'That'll be the bus. Not long now.' Macleod took out his phone, spoke quietly into it, then turned to me. 'We'll get a grandstand view of the proceedings from up there beside Mons Meg.' He pointed up at the ramparts where the huge siege cannon squatted, black and menacing.

It took only a few minutes to walk up the steep slope to the vantage point fifty feet above. There was still some light in the sky, though at ground level it was dark. A spillage of light from the technicians' flood lamp on the Argyle Battery dimly illuminated the cobbled road below and the forecourt in front of the Jacobite Room. Five guides in tweed jackets, kilts and sporrans were waiting beside the stationary bus, ready to shepherd their charges on board. Of Macleod's plainclothes snatch squad there was no sign at all.

As if reading my thoughts, Macleod said, 'The guides down there are my men. One of them will delay the boarding of the bus by reading out the arrangements for the reserved seating in the Gardens. The others will organize the diners into an orderly queue, giving my chaps a pretext for moving up and down the line. Thanks to that photo identification you provided, it'll be easy for them to pick our man out from the other guests, but they're under strict instructions not to make a move until he's about to board. That way he'll be trapped against the side of the bus. He'll have nowhere to run when they grab him. If he does make a run for it, there are more men waiting to cut him off at the Portcullis Gate and the Governor's House.'

The outer doors to the Jacobite Room opened, spilling a path of yellow light across the cobbles. From inside came the rising drone of bagpipes tuning up. Cheeks puffed, a piper marched out to send the stirring notes of *Scotland the Brave* drifting over the battlements. I barely noticed. All my attention was on the burly 'guides' in their Royal Stewart tartan kilts, to all appearances genuine, unthreatening, as they moved towards the emerging guests.

'I suppose the handcuffs are hidden in their sporrans,' I murmured.

Macleod merely smiled.

Everything was going according to plan: one guide stood on the steps of the bus reading out the seating arrangements for the fireworks; the other four coaxed the guests into forming a queue, then moved along the line in pairs, making a show of counting heads. They reached the end of the queue and came back. One by one the guests boarded the bus. No one was pounced on and hustled away.

'He's not there.' My voice flat, stomach a tight knot of tension.

One of the guides spoke into his radio.

Without taking his eyes off what was going on below, Macleod said, 'He's reporting that there are five people missing. It's not a concern. There will always be a few who hold things up with a last-minute dash to the toilet. They'll be out very shortly. You'll see.'

We waited. Four figures came hurrying through the doorway ... were intercepted ... then, to my dismay, were allowed to board the bus.

'Something's gone *wrong*.' I gripped the railing, knuckles white.

'There's no need to worry,' Macleod soothed. It'll be all to the good if our man stays lurking in the toilets so that the arrest takes place inside.'

I watched his men enter the building and disappear from sight. I didn't share his confidence.

He spoke into the radio. 'Now that the last one's boarded, get the bus away, John.' He turned to me. 'We don't want them around if bullets start flying.'

The sound of the bus engine died away. Off to the right, behind the mesh fence, the technicians were running last-minute checks. Silence flooded back. Nothing moved on the cobbled area in front of the Jacobite building....

As seconds dragged into minutes I couldn't rid myself of the sinking feeling, the awful *certainty*, that Spinks had somehow outwitted us once again.

Macleod thumped his fist on the iron muzzle of Mons Meg. 'They're telling me that there's a fire door open at the foot of the stairs beside the toilets. Don't know how he's done it, but the bastard's slipped through our fingers. Something must have alerted him.' His discomfiture was plain.

He spoke rapidly into his radio. Dark figures materialized from the shadows beside the Governor's House: one group raced along the side of the Jacobite building towards its rear; others formed a cordon across the slope leading to the upper section of the Castle. Simultaneously headlights blazed out from a vehicle stationed in the dark tunnel of the Portcullis Gate.

'That's him cornered.' He spoke with quiet satisfaction. 'The fire exit door gives onto a lower-level rampart. If he turned left when he slipped out, he'll come face-to-face with my men; if he's making his way round the side of the building, he'll come out over there, and be trapped behind the technicians' fence.'

It wouldn't be as easy as that, I was sure. 'What if he goes over the rampart wall?'

A grim smile from Macleod. 'If he climbs down the Castle Rock in the dark he'll be stuck there like a fly on flypaper till daylight. Either that, or he'll fall to his death. All ways, we've got him.'

I leaned over the railing, eyes searching for furtive movement in shadows rendered black and impenetrable in the glare from the technicians' flood lamp and the car's headlights.

The radio crackled. Macleod tapped me on the shoulder. 'The fireworks begin in a few minutes. For safety reasons my men will have to withdraw from the ramparts. They'll wait near the Governor's House. Wherever he's holed up, he'll have to stay there. In forty-five minutes, when the fireworks finish, we'll flush him out. Meanwhile, might as well enjoy the spectacle.'

The technicians' floodlight dimmed to a faint glow, the headlights at the Portcullis Gate were switched off. We stood in silence, lost in our thoughts, looking down at Princes Street and the New Town. In the Ross Bandstand in the Gardens, the public address system boomed into life. 'Good evening, ladies and gentlemen. As the International Edinburgh Festival draws to a close, we welcome you to the celebrated Fireworks Concert.' Applause drifted up.

Swooosh Swoosh Swoosh. To the rhythmic beat of a Brahms *Hungarian Dance*, rocket after rocket soared up, criss-crossing in giant white Ws. *Pop. Crackle.* Fireworks rose lazily in the air in chrysanthemum bursts cleverly choreographed to the varying tempo of the music. Dense grey smoke, colour-washed green ... blue ... red by powerful floodlights, engulfed the ramparts, catching the throat, blotting out Jacobite building, technicians, the cordon of men stationed across the roadway, everything. Though he was standing only feet away, Macleod was a grey, shrouded figure. I pulled the collar of my jacket over nose and mouth and thought about Spinks trapped on the lower rampart, assaulted by choking smoke and ear-splitting noise. He'd make a break for it as soon as the last firework died in the sky, and then we'd get him....

To the lingering notes of Barber's *Adagio for Strings*, floodlights turned the stones of the castle buildings a warm gold; a line of white flares flickered like flaming torches along the ramparts. Music and flames died slowly away.... The dark surged in. The dim glow from the screens of computers controlling the fireworks was the only source of light in the forecourt below.

Macleod's voice broke the silence. 'That was the build-up to the next set piece: the Waterfall. A pity we won't be able to see it from here, it's quite spectacular. The water effect stretches all the way across the ramparts and pours down the Rock. Picture the Victoria Falls and you've—'

'*Hey!*' A startled shout from amongst the technicians. 'What the hell do you think you're doing? Get back! Get *back*!'

Dark shapes crouched over the equipment behind the wire fence sprang to their feet waving their arms wildly. They were looking in the direction of the rampart wall. Through the darkness and haze of the dispersing smoke, I detected a movement on the parapet.

Sizzle … *hissss*. A long line of flares blossomed along the span of the ramparts, sparkled, coalesced as if into a foaming white torrent of raging water. The intense, blinding light threw into sharp relief a dark figure running along the top of the wall.

'He's making a break for it,' I gasped.

All at once the figure stumbled, arms flailing in a desperate attempt to keep its balance. Then, as if swept off its feet by the force of a current, it toppled over the lip of the waterfall and was lost to sight.

I heard no long-drawn-out scream. Only the *fizzzz* … *sppputter* of fireworks….

The black speck falling down the face of the Waterfall went unnoticed by the cheering crowds applauding the white streams pouring over the ramparts … splashing off the Castle Rock … outlining projecting spurs with light. Smoke hung above the flow like fine mist thrown up by the thundering force of a mighty cataract.

The Waterfall faded … died. The Castle and its Rock were plunged into darkness, every light extinguished. At that moment of total blackout, a lighting tour de force stained the clouds of smoke drifting above the silhouetted Castle a deep, fiery red.

CHAPTER THIRTY-TWO

I crossed to the window in the B&B. Through my binoculars, just visible breaking the line of the horizon, was the faint grey shape of the Isle of May where I'd first spotted Spinks stride away, job done, having sent Selkirk tumbling to his death at Pilgrims Haven.

I put down the binoculars and picked up *The Scotsman*. On the front page was a striking photograph: the Waterfall cascading down the Castle Rock beneath the silhouette of the Castle. In the write-up of last night's Festival Fireworks Concert was a brief reference to the fatal fall from the Castle Rock of a foolhardy spectator. The sole obituary for Spinks, the man who had for so long outwitted me and the forces of law and order.

Mission accomplished. There'd be no more boring surveillance work when I sent in my report. I yawned and stretched and folded up the newspaper, ready for the Galbraiths' full Scottish breakfast. G yawned and stretched too. For her, breakfast was always something to look forward to.

I had opened the bedroom door to go downstairs, when a text from Attila came in on my mobile. *Location of statues? Phone NOW.* I stopped short, hand glued to the door handle. Not surprisingly, it had completely slipped my mind that Attila had been arranging for the statues to be picked up from Sapphire's studio. Where, of course, they no longer were. In the few days following the end of the Pittenweem Festival, so much had happened: Beaton's murder, Spinks's phone call that had spooked me into leaving Lower Largo, his attack on me at the Hickory Championship, and not least, the events leading to the death of Spinks.

An appetising aroma of coffee and bacon wafted up from the kitchen. G and I quickened our pace down the stairs. I would put off phoning Attila till fortified by the Galbraiths' excellent breakfast. By then I'd have worked out how best to account for the statues not being at Venue 102 for collection, something along the lines of, 'They're no longer at the studio. I had to put them in storage because I had to leave Pittenweem so suddenly.' *In* storage was, perhaps, not *quite* a completely accurate description of their outside location in the grounds of the King James Lodge.

Not unexpectedly, the 'storage' explanation generated a five-minute harangue from Attila: the subject being the unnecessary expense incurred by HMRC and the British Taxpayer due to my failure to inform him that the statues had been moved. 'And what is more, Smith, I sent the van to the address in School Wynd, only for the men to be told that the statues were no longer there. That made it appear to be *my* slip-up, *my* slip-up, do you hear?'

'But, Mr Tyler, surely the men who delivered the statues to storage knew where they were?' I said in the aggrieved tone of the unjustly accused. 'I thought they'd have told you that the statues had had to be moved.' And in a masterly stroke designed to mislead, 'You see, they couldn't remain at the venue because the Festival had ended.' That interweave of truth, half-truth, and untruth succeeded in its aim of fogging the issue, and he contented himself with another long-winded lecture on the folly of my *assuming* that the same men who had delivered the statues would also be making the pick-up and would know where the statues had been left.

'I should have thought of that, Mr Tyler,' I said, feigning contrition. 'Where they're stored now is a difficult place to find, but if you tell the van to meet me down at the harbour in Pittenweem, I can guide the driver straight to where they are.'

'Tomorrow, at eleven o'clock,' he snapped. 'I'll text you the registration number of the van. See to it that nothing goes wrong *this* time, Smith.'

I punched in Sapphire's number. When the van men had called at the studio, why had she not handed over the White Lady, the one statue I'd kept at the venue?

'Natural-Dyed Wools. Sapphire McGurk speaking.'

'Hello, Sapphire. About the White Lady statue—'

'Ah, Mrs Dinwoodie, I was just about to phone you. Your £500 came into my bank account yesterday. You can collect the statue any time after 11.15 tomorrow. I'll have to pop out to post some wools, but I'll be back by then.'

She'd sold my White Lady. For a moment I stared at the phone, outraged, unable to utter a word.

'Hello, Mrs Dinwoodie, are you still there?'

'No, she is *not*, ' I ground out. 'This is Kirsty, Kirsty Gordon the sculptor. That statue belongs to *me*. And, as the owner, may I remind you that I *certainly* did not give you permission to sell it.'

'*Ex*-owner. Belonged,' she said smoothly. 'Let me remind *you*, Kirsty, that on the last day of the Festival you took off, vanished, upped and left town as far as I knew. And with my *many* voicemails to you unanswered, what else was I to think but that you had abandoned the statue?'

The angry retort I was about to deliver died in my throat. I had indeed left Pittenweem without telling her; she had indeed left many messages on my voicemail when she'd stridently demanded my help at her studio on the night of the fireworks. But since then there had been no phone call asking what I wanted done about the statue, no phone call at all. Had I myself not been guilty, only a few minutes ago on the phone to Attila, of a similar artful stratagem of truth, half-truth, and untruth? I held out a spindly olive branch.

'I can see why you thought I had no more use for the statue, Sapphire, but now that you do know—'

The olive branch was snapped in two and brusquely tossed aside. 'Sorry, dear.' Her tone was uncompromising, betraying not the slightest trace of sympathy. 'On eBay, once it's gone it's gone. You could have bid for it yourself, if you had called *yesterday*.' The line went dead.

That was it. The gloves were off. It was *war*. There was only one way I'd be able to rescue my White Lady from being sold to Mrs Dinwoodie and that was to snatch her while Sapphire was away from the studio. I plotted my moves as carefully as a general his front-line strategy. Assuming that she would leave for the post office just before eleven o'clock and be back within a quarter of an hour, the window of opportunity was very narrow, even narrower from my having to meet the van at the bottom of the wynd at eleven. If the timing was wrong, a violent confrontation with Sapphire was a distinct possibility, but that was a risk I'd have to take. Success depended on my getting help to carry the statue down the wynd. With my arm in a sling, I couldn't manage it myself. After a moment's thought I phoned Terry Warburton.

Eleven o'clock. One minute … two … three minutes past eleven.… I bit my lip, mouth dry. If the furniture van didn't arrive in the next couple of minutes, there wouldn't be time for us to dash up the wynd to the studio, pick the lock and spirit the statue away.

Terry was feeling the strain too. He looked at his watch. 'Guess it'll have to be plan B, Vanessa.'

The trouble was, there wasn't a plan B. By quarter past eleven Sapphire would be at her window on the lookout for Mrs Dinwoodie, see me coming up the wynd and refuse to open the door. I knew exactly how it would go: there'd be no reasoning with her, she'd make it quite plain there was no way she'd give back the £500 to Mrs Dinwoodie and suffer the embarrassment of explaining that she'd sold the statue by mistake.

I had just resigned myself to the loss of the White Lady when the furniture van came into sight. Impatiently I watched it manoeuvre into a parking place on Mid Shore.

I rushed over. 'Have you come to pick up Mr Tyler's statues?'

A bearded face looked down on me from the cab. It nodded. 'Aye, and we've a schedule to keep, so where are they?'

'Only a little way out of town, except for one in a studio up there.' A vague gesture in that direction. 'It'll save time if we bring it down to you.' Without giving him time to object, Terry and I disappeared up the wynd.

'Seven minutes past,' Terry panted as we turned the corner and the entrance to what had been Venue 102 came into sight.

No plump, henna-haired figure was hurrying towards us down the upper stretch of the wynd; no face was looking expectantly out of her window. Perhaps we still had a chance. Hope surged, and faded again at the thought that if Sapphire's errand had taken her less time than anticipated, she might already have returned to the studio but not necessarily be at the window.

'Let me know if she's coming.'

I turned into the narrow passageway, its walls bearing the scars of Danny and Harry's determined efforts to ram the crated statue through a space too narrow to receive it. A piece of paper was pinned to the studio door. Scrawled on it was *Back in a few minutes!* We weren't too late. I felt in my pocket for my picklocks. A moment later the door swung open.

'OK, Terry.' I called. 'We're in.'

The White Lady was reclining on the table, *Mrs Dinwoodie* written in large black letters on a label tied round her neck by a loop of green wool. I tugged at the wool, tugged again, then seizing a pair of scissors, snipped. I tossed aside the offending label and stood back.

'She's quite heavy.'

With an effort he lifted the statue from the table. 'It's OK,' he grunted. 'Think I'll manage.'

I locked the door and followed his silhouetted figure along the short passageway. If Sapphire were to appear now.... I braced myself for an angry shout as we came out onto the wynd, but there was only the plaintive cry of a seagull swooping overhead and an impatient *toot toot toot* from the direction of the harbour. I cast an anxious glance up the wynd. Once round the corner we'd be safely out of sight. By the time Sapphire had worked out what had happened, the van would be hightailing it out of Pittenweem.

Just as we reached the corner, our luck ran out.

'Sto-o-p! *Stop!*' It was the cry I had been dreading. 'How *dare* you, Kirsty! That statue's *mine*! Put it back!'

There was only a short flight of steps to negotiate, then we'd be out at the harbour and the waiting van.

'Sorry, can't go any faster,' Terry panted, feeling with his foot for each step.

'One more step and you're on the level,' I cried.

I glanced back. Behind us, Sapphire was rounding the corner, face fiery, fists bunched. Without pausing, she charged down the steps.

'Gotcha!' she gasped, a plump hand grabbing for my shoulder.

I dodged. She stumbled, recovered her balance, and gave a howl of pain.

'Bloody hell ... my *ankle!*' She came to an abrupt halt, hopping on one foot.

Pursued by some very unladylike cursing, Terry staggered across the road with his burden. This time our luck was in. Eager to be on their way and keep to schedule, the ramp was down, a man in overalls standing ready to raise it and close the doors. Terry stumbled up the ramp. I thumped on the cab door and was hauled up beside the driver.

The rear doors slammed shut, the driver's mate climbed in, the engine revved and the van moved off.

Framed in the wing mirror, the receding figure of Sapphire McGurk waved its fists in furious but impotent rage.